# The Diamond Dragon

## By G. H. Teed

Illustrated by H. M. Lewis

First published in the Union Jack magazine,
New series, No. 493, 22 March 1913.

## Stillwoods Edition

*Stillwoods.Blogspot.Ca*

**Catalogue Information:**
Title: The Diamond Dragon
Author: G. H. Teed (1886-1938)
Illustrated by H. M. Lewis
First published anonymously in the Union Jack magazine, New series,
    No. 493, 22 March 1913.
Second published anonymously in The Sexton Blake Library No. 233.
This Edition by: Stillwoods, 2023
ISBN Canada: 978-1-998819-15-7
Blog: Stillwoods.Blogspot.Ca
Author Blog: http://ghteed.blogspot.com/
Storefront: http://www.lulu.com/spotlight/lulubook22

https://tinyurl.com/ve25d42s This link should go to a spreadsheet of all known Teed stories. The list is annotated with various information on the stories and my progress with recapturing the work. The library of Teed's stories increases almost weekly. Check at the Lulu.Com for the latest arrivals. Search for Teed. /drf

**Keywords:** Sexton Blake, Dr. Huxton Rymer, Australia and London.

**Cautionary Note**: This series of books by Stillwoods are intended to make the stories of G. H. Teed, born in New Brunswick, Canada, available to collectors and researchers. The editor, or rather digitizer has not altered the original publication.

This story may contain language and racial terms that are not appropriate to today. I apologize for them; I know that the author was using his voice to excite and entertain an adventurous English audience. These works were published from 82 to 110 years ago. Most every work has characters of redeeming ethnicity within.

I hope you enjoy and share these stories; I have.

Doug Frizzle

*Contains offensive racial language.*

*Contains offensive racial language.*

Grand Easter Double Number.
Dr. Huxton Rymer V. Sexton Blake.
A Tale of Chinese Peril, in London and Abroad.
Easter 1913 Double Issue
Specially Written for Readers of All Ages.

EVERY THURSDAY.    (March 22nd, 1913.)    No. 493. New Series.

THE DIAMOND DRAGON.

WITH A MOCKING LAUGH HE SAW HIS TWO VICTIMS SWEPT ALONG.

A TALE OF CHINESE PERIL IN LONDON & ABROAD.

WITH HIS FREE HAND HE PULLED THE WINDOW DOWN ON PEDRO'S HEAD.

Dr. HUXTON RYMER v. SEXTON BLAKE.

# Grand Easter Double Number.

DR HUXTON RYMER EASTER 1913 V. SEXTON BLAKE.

# The Union Jack 2D

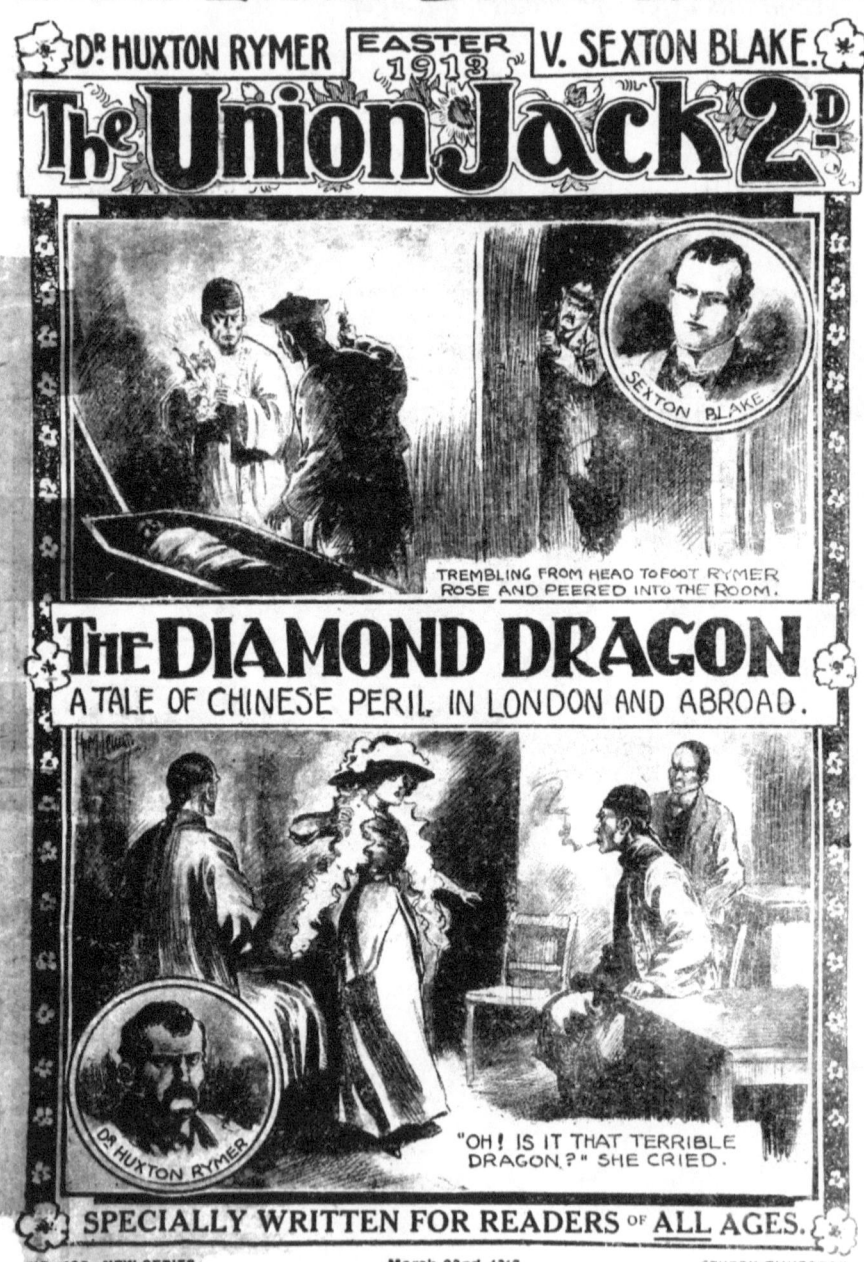

TREMBLING FROM HEAD TO FOOT RYMER ROSE AND PEERED INTO THE ROOM.

# THE DIAMOND DRAGON
## A TALE OF CHINESE PERIL IN LONDON AND ABROAD.

SEXTON BLAKE

DR HUXTON RYMER

"OH! IS IT THAT TERRIBLE DRAGON?" SHE CRIED.

## SPECIALLY WRITTEN FOR READERS OF ALL AGES.

NO. 493, NEW SERIES. March 22nd, 1913. [EVERY THURSDAY.

### THE FIRST CHAPTER.   Dr. Huxton Rymer Down on His Luck —A Bid for Wealth.

THE Chinese quarter of Melbourne may not be as populous or as flourishing as was the burrowed Chinatown of San Francisco before the earthquake which shook it so completely a few years ago; but it is quite large enough, dark enough, and odoured enough for the Queen City's desires.

Bordering on this quarter are innumerable bars, their staring fronts as yet hardly lessened by the purging labours of the Licensing Commissions.

In these numerous saloons, presided over by the inevitable barmaid of ready tongue and amazingly puffed hair, foregather the "heads" and "touts" of the race-track after the day's toil (?). All grades are there, from the dandified "Pride of the Push," to the young novitiate.

While these gentlemen regale themselves on "pony stouts" and "shandies," their conversation waxes eloquent of the pints of wine which they consumed after the third race, when so-and-so's mare got home at twenty to one.

Then, according to their tale, they had cashed into the tune of a hundred and fifty pounds —a mere trifle to them —but, unfortunately, whether on account of the wine or not, they had backed the favourite on the next race, putting up the whole lot at evens, and, of course, lost by a nose.

Many and wondrous are these fairy tales, and the remarkable thing is that the listening touts, from the youngest to the oldest, who had passed through the paddock, and degenerated again to the silver ring, quaff their drinks and listen as though they really believed it.

The glib-tongued "heads" are prepared to work in with each other to any extent. Should one of them have a man with them with a well-lined pocket, but a desire to meet the owner of a horse before backing it, one of the "push" poses as the owner, and his companions wander in carelessly, and ask in loud whispers what are the prospects of "his horse."

The victim begins to finger his money with growing excitement, and, in order that he may keep the inside information for himself, hustles the "owner" away, and the deed is done.

Such is the method of the "heads" and "touts", of the Queen City; and, although New York has the reputation for its ability to make a rapid exchange from one man's pocket to another's, Melbourne, young as it is, could give New York instruction in a few points of the game.

On a certain night the usual crowd of "touts" and "heads" were gathered in a certain bar in Bourke Street. The girl behind the bar served the "usual" with barely concealed boredom at the tiresome repetition of their tales.

But one among them drank his beer in gloomy silence, accepting all that was offered, but buying none in return. Through his blotchy, dissipated features could be seen the shattered remnants of past refinement, and the very manner in which he raised his glass told of a past when his companions had been far different.

His brown hair was still guiltless of silver, and his drooping, brown moustache hid a jaw which spelled power. And Dr. Huxton Rymer had power, but drink had been more powerful. Once a polished, suave, successful practitioner, he had for a time followed a moderately successful criminal career.

But Sexton Blake, the great British detective, had taken a hand, and Rymer's last exploit had been ruined by the astute Blake.

With plenty of money still in his pocket, Rymer had journeyed by quiet routes to Melbourne. There, as Dr. Rigby, he had lived at Scott's Hotel, and before a month had passed had become a well-known figure on the racetracks.

For a time he had won, and his wagers, being large, his winnings had been of an equally generous size. But, as is often the case, success made him careless. He spent too much time in the bars and too little watching the trials of the horses, and ere long his money had gone.

From that Dr. Huxton Rymer's fall had been rapid. Such was his unenviable position on the night of the Derby.

As the boasting crowd scattered to pursue their own individual game, Rymer set his glass on the bar, and, with the unfailing courtesy which was a part of him, bowed to the barmaid and shuffled out.

His thoughts were very bitter as he turned into Swanston Street and headed towards the friendly darkness of Little Bourke Street. For Rymer knew of a little place in that street, which was given over to the Chinese, where a man could have a little game, and, if he were lucky, might turn half-a-crown into a pound, or, with great luck, even more.

That he had never yet succeeded in corralling this luck did not deter him from the hope that he might yet do so, and he grasped his solitary piece of silver with anxious clasp as he shuffled along past the dark, shuttered buildings inside which teemed the silent life of Melbourne's Celestials.

He stopped before a low, dingy door, and ticked the latch lightly. The signal was evidently known and understood, for the door swung noiselessly open a few inches, and the face of a Chinaman peered out.

Satisfied with his scrutiny, he reached out a bony hand and drew Rymer inside, closing the door as noiselessly as he had opened it.

Rymer silently followed his guide down an evil-smelling passage to a back room, which was fitted up as a rough shop. A rough counter stretched along each side, and on the shelves behind were piled a few small caddies of tea and some dried herbs. Truly, a harmless-looking interior.

A smoky oil-lamp dangled from the ceiling, and the Chinaman stopped, swinging round to inspect once more the visitor, for they had need to be careful who they admitted in those dark retreats in Little Bourke Street.

Satisfied with his second scrutiny, he turned with a grunt to a harmless-looking empty barrel which stood behind the rough counter. Reaching inside, he fumbled about for a moment until his hand reached a tiny button secreted in a bare half-inch of rubbish at the bottom. A click followed, and the whole floor silently sank, stopping when it had dropped three feet.

Turning again, the Chinaman turned another button in the part of the wall which had just appeared. A small panel slid open, and through its narrow aperture crept Rymer. It closed after him, the floor rose, and the Chinaman retired behind the innocent-looking counter until another should relieve him.

Rymer found himself in familiar surroundings, and their strangeness now excited no curiosity in his mind.

A long table stretched almost the full length of the apartment, at the head of which sat a Chinaman, whose wrinkled, withered face and thin, bony hands with the marvellously long nails were those of great age. The deep-set eyes, inscrutable as the Sphinx, seemed to possess all knowledge in their piercing depths.

Before him was a roulette-wheel, which he spun with one hand the while he incessantly rolled thin, yellow cigarettes with the other. His dress was rich, with the richness of Old China and the loose, silken sleeves swished softly as the ball clicked and he raked in the bets.

All around the table sat men of all nationalities and creeds, drawn into temporary fraternity by the lure of the gambling-table. Chinamen of all classes predominated, but throughout was a generous sprinkling of white men with the pasty complexion of the opium and drug fiend, while here there sat a German and an occasional Swede.

A richly-chased brass lamp threw its light over the black-topped table, its rays enriching with a shadowy beauty the heavy silken hangings which covered the walls. The feet sank noiselessly into a thick carpet.

Rymer was evidently well known to the patrons of this luxurious hidden gambling retreat, for no attention was paid to his entry, and he shuffled silently into a seat.

A man had to be very "safe" before he was admitted to this select retreat, and a thorough investigation was made before Hang Lee, the proprietor, admitted him. And so rigid was the examination that the place flourished under the very noses of the police, and none suspected its existence.

But once admitted, whether you came with sixpence or a fortune, you could make your bets, the only condition being that cash only was used and no money was loaned.

Rymer drew out his solitary half-crown and pushed it across to a Chinaman who sat on the right of Hang Lee, holding up five fingers as he did so. Five sixpences were thrust silently over to him, and one of these modest pieces he placed beside a neighbour's stack of sovereigns.

Others followed, the individual bets ranging from Rymer's sixpence to a thousand pounds. The wheel turned, the ball clicked, the call was made; and while Hang Lee raked in the tots the Chinaman on his right paid out the winnings.

Rymer collected his modest pile, now doubled. He placed all his winnings on the same number. Again the wheel swung round, and the game went on.

From time to time a player rose and moved silently past the head of the table and stood behind Hang Lee. Without flicking an eyelash or stopping the occupation of his hands, the old Chinaman pressed on the floor with his foot. A panel behind him opened, the waiting man passed through, and the panel closed.

Luck seemed to have decided to smile more kindly on Rymer this evening, for he had been playing a bare hour, and already his silver piles had several times been changed to gold. A neat pile of twenty sovereigns was placed before him, and one of these he risked. He lost, and for once having the wisdom to stop, he rose and passed up to the head of the table.

The panel opened, and he found himself in a room, the hangings of which were almost a duplicate of the one he had just left. It had no table nor chairs, but along the whole length were ranged small mattresses covered with large, soft cushions. Most of them were occupied by devotees of the pipe, two silent Celestials being kept busy by the demands of the smokers, who were in all stages of the drug's effect.

Some were just beginning, some were in the most exotic moment of the dream —babbling on meaninglessly, and not expecting or desiring an answer —and others were in the last stage of the heavy, restless sleep.

Rymer had not entered the opium-room with any desire to smoke, but more as an excuse to depart with the winnings which, for once, he had gained; but as a silent Chinaman led him to a pile of cushions, he dropped down and waited while the attendant prepared his pipe.

Several times the attendant fixed the tiny pill and lit it; but Rymer, beyond smoking the first, had faked the others, and as yet barely felt the effects.

Another hour went by, and the babbling was gradually ceasing as the drug-saturated creatures sank into silence and Rymer, who had been feigning sleep, was debating whether to leave or not, when the panel slid back, admitting no less a person than Hang Lee himself.

He glanced sharply around with his all-seeing eyes; but Rymer who lay on the very further mattress, looked out beneath lowered lids without being seen. The gambling-table was empty. The players had departed, only the Chinaman who had sat at Hang Lee's right remaining.

Hang Lee softly closed the panel and walked slowly down between the mattresses, looking closely at the sleepers.

Rymer lay back as the old Celestial drew near and breathed heavily, babbling meaninglessly.

He had seen innumerable stages of the drug, and his old power of adaption did not desert him in that moment, for, after pausing and looking at him closely, Hang Lee passed on.

Rymer was astonished at the early break up of the game, and that, with Hang Lee's careful scrutiny of the sleepers, something of more than ordinary moment was afoot. That Hang Lee was the originating source of many far-reaching plots, Rymer was well aware, but so carefully were they organised and carried out that no hint ever leaked out. He knew that Hang Lee was the head of a circle to which none but a chosen few were admitted, but even he, in his wildest imaginings, never realised the full extent of the power wielded by that ancient, wrinkled Celestial called Hang Lee.

Rymer risked peering forth again as Hang Lee passed and stopped at the silken-hung wall barely two feet away from the supposed sleeper. His hand disappeared in the heavy folds, and Rymer barely suppressed a gasp as a soft click followed and Hang Lee disappeared through a parting in the silk. Another click, and the heavy breathing of the sleepers reigned once more.

As the smokers had gradually succumbed to the effects of the drug one of the attendants had left, leaving his companion in sole charge of the opium-room. That silent individual moved noiselessly to and fro, watching for any move which would require his attention.

Rymer's mind was working quickly. The strain of his present circumstances had brought him face to face that night with the depths to which he had sunk.

The pile of sovereigns which he had won had thrilled him once more with the old lust for wealth and ease, and a disgusted revulsion at his present drunken existence.

As the wheel had turned his luck, so had his resolve turned during the evening, and when he had risen from the table it was with a reasserting of the old power and a firm resolution to give up the drink which had ruined him. He would apply his fertile brain once more to wresting from others the wealth which he desired, and live again the life which appealed to him.

And now luck seemed to still further favour him, for Hang Lee must have business afoot, and if Rymer could discover its nature it might be just the opening he desired. But there was risk in the venture, more risk than he had probably ever taken.

For he would have short shrift indeed were he discovered poking into matters in that retreat. More than one man had disappeared inside its silken-hung walls, never to return, and Rymer knew of the thoroughness and artistic agony of the action of the long crooked-bladed Chinese knife.

Once, in Thursday Island he had seen its effect, and he had no desire to experience it. But in his new resolve death seemed better than his present existence, and he at least had his revolver, which through all he had stuck to.

As the attendant approached Rymer stirred and half sat up, groping feebly for the pipe. The Chinaman moved silently over and bent to assist him, when, throwing all his force into a spring, Rymer leaped, his fingers closing with a desperate strength on the Chinaman's throat.

The astonished attendant stumbled back to his knees, his emotionless face for once mirroring his surprise. Rymer lost no time in following up his lead, and bore down heavily on the Chinaman.

Silently the struggle waged about in the narrow space between the mattresses. The Chinaman reached persistently for Rymer's throat, and, failing in that, worked desperately to break the choking hold on his own throat, but the force of desperation was behind his assailant, and his head gradually relaxed, until with a choking gurgle he dropped unconscious.

Rymer knew any moment might bring discovery, but there was nothing for it now but to go ahead. With strips torn from the cushion-covers he bound and gagged the Chinaman. Then, still panting from the unusual exertion, and with his revolver in his hand, he moved silently to the silken hangings where he had seen Hang Lee disappear.

He thrust his hand in and felt about, pressing gently as he did so. Up and down stole his fingers, until a click and a faint current of air told him the panel had opened. Parting the hanging, he slipped through, almost, but not quite, closing the panel behind him, for he might have need to make a rapid exit.

He found himself at the foot of a very narrow staircase, which apparently ascended in the space between two walls. At the top shone forth a feeble flicker from the square of an open door, and as he peered up, the soft, guttural murmur of voices floated down to him.

Hang Lee's great thoroughness was in that critical moment Rymer's friend, for the steps were sound and well-built, and as he crept up one by one he breathed easier as no warning creak resounded.

As he gained the top the murmur of voices sounded more plainly, and he found, by dropping to the floor and squirming along as near the door as he dared, he could hear what was being said.

The conversation was being carried on in the guttural tongue of Southern China, and Rymer, a linguist of no mean order, held his breath in tense silence as he listened.

The purring voice of Hang Lee was speaking, and Rymer bent close to catch what he said.

"Your news is good, Wang Ho, better than I dared to hope. That matters were going ahead well I knew, but was not aware that things are so well stirred up in Mongolia, that troops will be sent in large numbers, and that then the prince will move."

The Chinaman addressed as Wang Ho muttered a guttural assent, and Hang Lee continued:

"Your passport is correct, and I will deliver the Dragon to you, but many things are working by night and scheming by day to locate it. It cost much money and much time to secure it, and I who know tell you no effort will be spared to get it back. And you know as well as any that the possession of it carries the power. All the faithful will rise at the sight of the sacred emblem, blessed by Confucius himself. But I have formed a plan, Wang Ho, which will baffle those sons of a thousand dogs."

"What is it?" grunted Wang Ho, for the first time speaking audibly.

"Watch, and I will show you," replied Hang Lee.

The rustle of his flowing silk jacket followed, and the watching Rymer, risking the danger of discovery, crept ahead a few inches, and peered cautiously into the dimly-lit room.

Standing with his back to the door was Hang Lee, while sitting on the further side of a rough table was Wang Ho. The room had no other occupants, and for the moment neither Chinaman was aware of the watching face at the door.

On a rough stand against the wall was a plain coffin, and beyond the table and two chairs the room was bare and empty. As Rymer watched, Hang Lee picked up the candle, whose feeble flame lighted the room, and, beckoning to Wong Ho, walked over to the coffin. He passed the candle to Wong Ho, and, bending down, felt at the bottom of the coffin. His hand released a spring which released the lid, and after pushing it aside he bent down.

Rymer's eyes opened wide; he saw that the coffin contained a perfect wax reproduction of a human figure.

Hang Lee put his hand under the body and pressed a spring, which caused a part of the bottom of the coffin to slide back, revealing a cavity about six inches deep, under which was the real bottom of the coffin. Hang Lee put his hand into the cavity and drew from it a magnificent gold dragon, literally covered with diamonds. The body was cleverly reproduced in diamond-set scales, and the eyes were formed of two huge blazing solitaires, set off by a circle of glittering emeralds. It was over a foot in length, and Rymer was judge enough to know that the blazing masterpiece at which he looked was the famous Diamond Dragon supposed to have been blessed by Confucius himself.

Its age was unknown, and its value untold. His surprise was almost his undoing, for in his eagerness and excitement he leaned forward until his head and shoulders were plainly in view of the two Celestials, and he had barely time to draw back as they turned.

"You see my plan, my friend? This coffin goes back to China with the wax body in it. It is a good reproduction, and will pass. Inside will be the dragon, and after you arrive you will need care to get it safely to the prince. All hangs on its production, as you know."

"I have my orders, and have taken the oath," grunted Wong Ho.

"True, but you will listen to my words, which are words of wisdom," returned Hang Lee; and Rymer could almost feel the force of the deep, unfathomable look which he knew accompanied the words.

"But see, I will return the dragon. It will leave tomorrow for the steamer, and will be there when you arrive."

In that moment Rymer made up his mind to make one desperate attempt to secure the glittering dragon. The sight of the blazing gems had made him drunk with the old lust. There at his hand was untold wealth, and only two Chinamen stood between him and possession.

He knew from what he had heard, that its theft would put thousands of Chinese secret societies on the track, and almost anything would be pleasanter to anticipate than the punishment and torture which would be meted out to its possessor. But in the force of his desire he could see only one thing —the beckoning lure of those blazing gems.

Trembling from head to foot he rose, and again peered into the room. The two Chinamen had returned to the coffin, and Hang Lee was instructing his companion in the secret of the spring.

For a moment their backs were towards him, and Rymer, taking his life in his hands, grasped his revolver around the barrel and tiptoed noiselessly into the room.

Two —three —four steps. One more would bring him in reach of Wong Ho, and they had not yet heard him, so absorbed were they. He stealthily raised his arm and lifted his foot for the step. Two seconds more, up —up went his arm, and then down with unerring force on the back of Wong Ho's head. The Chinaman dropped without a word, and as the candle clattered to the floor and was extinguished Rymer leaped for Hang Lee.

But before the candle went out he had seen the look in Hang Lee's eyes, and so silently and, mysteriously deadly was it that Rymer shook with nervousness as he grappled with the old Celestial. The awful menace of those inscrutable eyes seemed to threaten him with a fate of horror, and in his nervous state a panic seized him.

He dropped all caution, and strained with all his strength to overcome Hang Lee, who, though old, had a remarkable fund of strength. But Rymer's life had left some shreds of his once powerful muscles, and the old Chinaman dropped unconscious, still clutching the Diamond Dragon.

Rymer, satisfied that his two victims were unconscious, grasped the coveted prize with trembling fingers, and started for the door. But half way there he stopped and returned. The thought had occurred to him that he would need money, and Hang Lee was almost sure to have some.

He felt rapidly in the loose pockets of the unconscious man, and was rewarded by a packet of notes and a handful of sovereigns. Thrusting them in his pocket, he made again for the door, and began stealthily to descend the stairs.

He had been some time, and hardly dared hope his attack on the Chinese attendant had not been discovered.

But he drew his revolver again, and held it ready, for now that he had gone so far his only way was to shoot his way out, and he shivered again as he thought of the deadly menace which Hang Lee's eyes had flashed at him before the candle went out. He knew that the old man had recognised him, and he knew what it meant, "but," he muttered "they would have a chase before they caught him."

He reached the bottom of the stairs in safety, and softly pushed back the panel. Parting the silk hangings he peered cautiously out, and could hardly believe his eyes when he saw that the opium-room was exactly as he had left it. The sleepers still tossed restlessly, and the attendant still lay bound where he had fallen.

Certainly Fate was smiling kindly this night on Dr Huxton Rymer.

He stepped into the room and snapped the panel after him. Without stopping he passed up between the rows cushioned mattresses and pressed the button which released the panel leading to the gambling-room. It was still lighted, but empty, and he breathed easier as he crept through and shut off the opium-room.

Quickly now he hastened to the other end and pressed the button which notified the man on watch in the harmless-looking outer shop. An almost imperceptible noise came to him, followed by the opening of the panel. He stepped out on to the floor of the shop, the panel closed, and the floor rose again.

Without speaking, the Chinaman on watch led him along the passage and opened the door, and five minutes later Dr. Huxton Rymer stood free in the narrow confines of Little Bourke Street with the sacred dragon of a hundred million bloodthirsty Chinamen in his pocket.

Had he realised fully just what that dragon meant to those hundred million Celestials he would have been appalled at his own daring, and would have done well to seek the remotest ends of the earth where he might have found at least a temporary retreat.

## THE SECOND CHAPTER.  *Harry Graham's Luck —Dr. Hutton —Foul Play.*

HARRY GRAHAM was not an extraordinary young man. Rather, he was an average healthy, optimistic specimen of the English Public-School boy, and when his hopes of going to the bar had collapsed with the death of his father he had not moped and grumbled, although it was a keen disappointment.

After winding up his father's affairs he had gone back to the now lonely apartments where the two had lived, and faced the future squarely.

To stay on in the rooms was impossible, and besides, in any case, he would not care to do so, for father and son had been close pals, and the vacant chair on the other side of the fire looked strangely lonely now.

He counted up his small store of cash, and grimly decided to tackle the Colonies, about which he had no illusions. He carefully weighed the pros and cons of Canada and Australia, and finally decided on Australia, for no other reason than that it was most remote.

He knew settlers were going to those far-off lands, drawn there by alluring tales of wondrous opportunities, but he knew such tales were to be discounted and that although chances might be more plentiful than in the older home country, he would not get anything without buckling to and probably doing work which he would never dream of doing at home.

With this decision he put on his hat and went round at once to see Grace Lansing and tell her of his decision. Grace and Harry had known each other from babyhood, and the childhood chums had developed later into young lovers, and only a bare month before the death of Harry's father had Grace said the word which made Harry desire more than ever to get along.

Grace took his decision hard, a fact which Harry had anticipated and prepared for. But calm consideration of the matter from every point caused her to acknowledge that, hard as it was, it was the only thing to do.

Consequently, a week later, with only the necessary luggage with him, with Grace's photograph inside his waist-coat and her kisses still warm on his lips, Harry had departed on a crowded, littered emigrant boat by way of the Cape.

If it is expected that Harry landed in Australia and immediately did wondrous things and amassed great wealth, it is wrong to do so.

On the contrary, he landed in Melbourne with five sovereigns in his pocket, and any amount of hope in his heart. But harvest was over, farmers were getting rid of men, and Melbourne was filling up with others as anxious for a job as Harry Graham.

The chief drawback to the more rapid development of Australia is the anxiety the majority of residents have to cling to the cities and neglect the country. Very many new arrivals seem to catch this fever, and after a week in the silent bush, or a spell on the hot plains where the thistles along the irrigation channels are the nearest approach to shade trees, they drift back to the city and write fervid letters home of the lack of opportunity in Australia.

But Harry Graham was a single-minded young man, and although he enjoyed a horse race as well as the next man, he realised that horse-racing and promenading Bourke and Collins Streets were not the roads to building the future he had in view.

Consequently, he seized on the chance to go across the Victorian border into New South Wales as jackeroo on a decent-sized sheep station at a salary which took longer to spell than it did to spend. However, he hoped for better things, and kept an eye open for the main chance.

It is a regrettable fact, but true, that most of Harry's pay went in the purchase of lottery tickets, which, regardless of the stern eye of the postal authorities, find their way to the remotest part from Tasmania.

And it was one of these tickets which nearly a year after Harry's arrival, nearly caused his jaw to dislocate with gaping surprise when he read that he had drawn the capital prize —a trifle over ten thousand pounds.

Tommy, the fat, smiling, competent Chinese gardener on the station, was also a devotee of the lottery, and happened to be the only other one at hand when Harry startled the grazing sheep by his warhoop.

Tommy took the lucky ticket and turned it in order to bring him luck, and grinned cheerfully at the excited Harry.

"Me velly glad, Mistal Hally. Tommy get one, too, some day. You buy station you'self now?" he asked naively.

"Not much, Tommy, my boy! I'll make tracks for England as fast as I can get there. I'm going to be a lawyer, Tommy. Do you understand —a lawyer?"

"Oh, yes," smiled Tommy. "Me undelstand what lial is. You going to be one —eh, Mistal Hally?"

"No, you heathen rascal! Not a liar —a lawyer, barrister, advocate, solicitor."

"Allee samee," replied Tommy. "Me undelstand."

And Harry gave up in despair.

That night he was busy packing, and the next morning, with the new dignity of a capitalist, he climbed into the jinker, and Tommy, who was to drive him to the village, clicked cheerfully with his expansive smile.

It was thirty miles to the railway, but Harry didn't mind. He glanced with eyes of affection at the grazing sheep, and gazed in farewell at the well-known track through the paddocks which he had ridden so religiously for the past year.

They pulled up at the primitive bush pub., which was the chief excuse and existence of the railway-station, and while Tommy drove over to the store which was also the post-office, Harry entered the pub.

"Hallo, Jack!" he greeted the proprietor, who sat in shirtsleeves studying the lithographed sheet of an "Off Shears" sheep sale.

"Hallo, Graham!" responded that worthy. "What's happened to bring you in at this time, and —Good heavens, man, you're all rigged out. Not going to be married, are you?"

"Not yet," laughed Harry; "but what do you think, Jack? I've won the capital prize in Tats."

"Great jumping kangaroo and hopping wallaby!" gasped the publican, too amazed to say more. But he soon recovered his senses, and moved with alacrity to the door.

A resounding "coo-ee!" brought several tousled heads into view, and a moment before where hardly a man could be seen, there emerged from all sorts of odd corners a crowd which rapidly filled the bar.

Harry grinned good-naturedly, and did the necessary. He was a teetotaler himself, but knew the capacity of the bullockys and drovers who had assembled.

After he had supplied the wherewithal for several rounds and had accepted the grip of many horny hands he broke away, and made for the dining-room, calling back to the publican to look after Tommy and the horses when the Chinaman returned.

On his way along the passage to the dining-room, he pulled up in surprise as a tall, lean, bearded man emerged from an adjoining room.

"Why, hallo, Dr. Hutton! I thought you had left for Melbourne."

The man turned sharply with a sudden frown, but his features relaxed as he saw who it was.

"Oh, it's you, is it, Graham?" he smiled, holding out his hand. "Glad to see you! Are you in for long? I intended leaving last week, but don't feel too strong yet, and thought I'd put in another week or two."

Dr. Hutton, so called, had come to the little bush township some two months before, presumably for his health. He had plenty of money, was a good rider, and generous, and before he had been there long, was on intimate terms with the surrounding station owners. He had been invited regularly, and had not been niggardly in returning the hospitality.

He and Harry Graham had met several times, and though Harry was not too keen on the agreeable doctor, still he had seen no reason for his feeling, and had swallowed it under the doctor's persistent friendliness to all.

Besides, he felt rather indebted to the doctor ever since the latter had assisted him to save a mob of ewes and lambs from being cut to pieces by the train, and had suppressed his feelings in a show of cordiality.

No one knew that Dr. Hutton's real name was Dr. Huxton Rymer, alias Dr. Rigby, and that the ailing doctor had sought the bush with a deeper purpose than the regaining of his health. He looked pretty healthy for an invalid, but being a doctor, no one had questioned what his malady might be.

On the night he had succeeded in obtaining possession of the diamond dragon, Rymer had lost no time in getting away. Straight to a garage he went, and inside half an hour had made full arrangements to be motored through to Sydney.

On the way he had formed his plans for the future.

He knew that every Chinaman in the Commonwealth who had any connection with the far-reaching Hang Lee would be on the look-out for him. Moreover, he knew that every out-going ship from Fremantle to Port Darwin would be watched, and that no temporary disguise would avail under the scrutiny of those Celestial bloodhounds —past-masters themselves in the art.

Hang Lee knew positively that it was Rymer, and the doctor still shuddered when he remembered the Chinaman's last look before the candle went out.

Hang Lee, with his thousand and one underground and mysterious methods, would make a far more thorough inspection of departing travellers from Australia than the police could dream of doing.

No, he decided, it would be too risky yet to leave the Commonwealth.

He would leave Sydney and travel out to a remote bush township where he would live an open-air life and grow a natural beard. A couple of months would eradicate his dissipated slouchy appearance, and good food and plenty of riding and not a drop of drink would make a radical change.

He purchased a long leather case in Sydney, in which he carefully placed the glittering diamond dragon. He then had a special belt, which he strapped next his skin, the leather case being pushed around to the small of his back. When he garbed, so well did it fit, no sign showed, and after these precautions and changing his notes to a draft and gold, he took the train to Ginging, the remote bush township, where he posed as Dr. Hutton, the ailing medico.

His two months had made a very radical change. The old slouch had disappeared as the pure air braced him; the old blotchy, dissipated look faded away under a vigorous regime of abstemious and outdoor life, the eyes grew clear, the slack flabby jaw stiffened and grew clean cut again, and the fast-growing beard added dignity and a distinguished look.

Beyond the fact that his boarder had plenty of money, spent freely, and paid his bills, the publican knew nothing and cared nothing.

The others round about followed his example, and accepted the new-comer for what he was worth.

And this was the explanation of Harry's cheery greeting made cheerier under the buoyancy of his feelings.

After shaking hands with the doctor, they passed along together to the dining-room, the door of which was dignified by the painted name "Commercial."

They were the only occupants of the table, and across the net-covered dishes, and between the vicious attacks on the swarming flies, Harry told the congratulating doctor of his luck.

"And I'm going to boat it for Old England as fast as a P. and O. will get me there," he wound up.

"Ah, that is so!" smiled Dr. Hutton. "Then perhaps I will have the pleasure of seeing you there, for I myself am going on shortly."

"Why, yes," agreed Harry, trying to make his tone cordial. "Look me up when you come."

"By the way, do I understand that you are leaving by the next steamer?" went on the doctor.

"Yes —first one I can get."

"I wonder if you would mind doing a slight favour for me Graham?" continued the doctor. "It's a trifle, but I would feel greatly obliged if you would. It is only a matter of taking a small package to England for me and holding it against my orders. I don't mind telling you that it extremely valuable, and that for reasons that I can't explain I desire to send it on now."

"Well, I wouldn't mind doing the favour if it were not valuable," demurred Harry. "But —"

"Oh, that is just the reason I ask you!" smiled Hutton. "You see, I am not very strong yet, and it will be safer with you than with me, and I don't care to trust it to the post."

Harry remembered about the sheep, and when the doctor put the request on the basis of his ill-health, he could only yield gracefully. And besides, he thought it would be pretty raw to refuse to do it.

The doctor smiled as Harry assented, and the busily-eating young man did not see the look of relief in the doctor's eyes.

"If you will come along to my room now," said the doctor, as they rose, "I will give you the packet before the train arrives."

Harry nodded, and they started along the passage. As they went past the general dining-room Harry nodded to Tommy, but did not notice a radical change in the cheerful Celestial's manner.

When Harry descended from the jinker, Tommy had driven over to the store to get some supplies and the mail.

In the bundle of letters had been one for himself, and though not unusual in itself the envelope had borne a small peculiar mark in one corner, which had caused Tommy to seek a more secluded spot behind the railway-station.

There he opened it, and as he read, the round, cheerful countenance changed magically, and the eyes, which before had beamed pleasantly, contracted to two slits of blazing anger, fading away to the inscrutable expression which long generations had taught him to assume.

For Tommy's letter had been one of Hang Lee's far-reaching missives, and in the minute description given with Chinese attention to detail, Tommy had seen float before him the beard-masked countenance of Dr. Hutton, the visitor at the pub.

Reading the communication again, Tommy, with a stealthy look around, struck a match and watched the paper and envelope change to ashes. Then adopting his previous cheerful expression, he had betaken himself to the pub.

While Dr. Hutton washed for dinner, he was unaware that Tommy was watching him through the window from the shelter of a jinker in the yard, his Oriental mind going over every particle of Hang Lee's description, and making the comparison with the thoroughness of the Bertillon system.

And when Harry had sauntered along to the doctor's room to receive the packet, Tommy stole silently out to the yard, and while tinkering at the jinker watched the two men in the doctor's room.

The doctor threw off his coat and waistcoat as Harry closed the door, and to the young man's amazement unbuckled the special belt to which was attached the leather case.

"Here it is. Graham!" laughed Hutton. "It looks imposing, doesn't it? But if you put it on as I had it you'll find it won't bother you a particle. I sealed it some time ago, and I see the seals are still there, so I won't bother about doing so again."

"How about a receipt for it!" asked Harry, as he struggled with the buckles.

"I've thought of that," replied the doctor. "I prefer no writing, and so I've decided on this. It's better than any receipt, and it can't be forged."

As he spoke he took from his pocket a common lead pencil and broke it in half.

"There you are, Graham!" he said, handing Harry one of the pieces. "Whoever hands you the half which fits the broken end of your half, no matter who it is or when it is give him the packet."

"That's ingenious, anyway," replied the wondering Harry. "There seems to be a lot of mystery about this. I'm half inclined to withdraw my consent."

"Oh, you'll find it won't be a bother to you, Graham! Don't refuse now, there's a good chap!"

He turned as he spoke, and his gaze travelled out of the window where Tommy was working at the jinker.

"Good heavens, the blind!" he gasped. "That China-man—"

"What's the matter, doctor?" asked the surprised Harry, jumping forward. "That's only Tommy the gardener at the homestead, and as harmless as a fly."

"I'm sorry if I startled you!" answered Hutton, pulling himself together with an attempt to pass it off. "One of my sudden seizures, and the Chinaman looked like a man I treated some time ago, and who afterwards died."

"He's lying." thought Harry. "Why has the sight of Tommy upset him, so? Is it because it is Tommy, or just because he is a Chinaman?"

But the whistle of the train cut short his thoughts, and after carefully tucking away the broken half of the pencil, and hastily giving Hutton his English address, he hurried out.

Every stockman and drover who had partaken of Harry's generosity an hour before went over to the train to see him off and in the noise of their good-natured send-off he did not see the peculiar look in Tommy's eyes as the Chinaman saw to the luggage.

He marvelled exceedingly, however that Tommy did not say good-bye to him, not knowing that the Chinaman had suffered on the same account.

But Tommy had seen that small leather packet which nestled in the small of Harry's back, and he suspected what it contained. That being so, the thing was defiled by alien hands, and Tommy would court the eternal wrath of Confucius and the present wrath of Hang Lee did he shake the hands of the possessor.

He was fond of the cheery young Englishman, and it hurt him, but the message which he sent on to Hang Lee as the train pulled out hurt him still more, for he knew what awaited the unsuspecting Harry on his arrival in Melbourne.

Now, Harry Graham, with the true instinct of a coming barrister, was a careful soul in business matters, and on the long journey to Melbourne he had time to think at length, and repent at leisure, of his hasty assent to Dr. Hutton's request.

"It certainly must be valuable to make the doctor take such precautions," he muttered. "and then, why all the mystery attached to it. If everything were straight and above-board, why was that necessary? No, I don't like it," he muttered; "but now there's nothing else for it but to see the thing through. But I've got enough to do to look after my own ten thousand, and I'll be jolly glad when he presents his silly little piece of pencil and claims it."

But the thought of his prize sent his thoughts castle building in the rosy future, and at the entrance to each castle was Grace waiting for his return.

But the upshot of his cogitations on the train was that on his arrival in Melbourne Harry changed his plans regarding the doctor's mysterious packet.

When he elbowed his way through an early-morning crowd at Spencer Street Station, he was too absorbed in his thoughts to notice that two Chinamen in European clothes had watched him descend from the train, and pattered along behind him.

Harry caught one of the ancient, out-of-date trains which are Melbourne's relic of other days, and rode up Collins Street until he came to the bank with whom the sheep-station on which he had been jackeroo did its business.

Hopping off, he discovered the doors had just opened, and five minutes later was closeted with the manager.

That gentleman made no difficulty about arranging for the transfer of Harry's ticket into a draft on London, Harry only retaining two hundred in cash for current expenses.

Then, with his draft safely tucked in his pocket, he went up to Scott's Hotel, where he engaged a room, and deposited most of his two hundred with the clerk. And fortunate was it that his new-found prosperity led him to such a hostel, for through those exclusive portals the two Celestials, who still followed, were not admitted.

After a refreshing wash he rang, and sent a boy out for a sheet of strong, heavy paper and twine, and on the lad's return he set to work.

"Never can tell," he muttered. "Something might happen to me. Anyway, I'll be on the safe side."

As he spoke, he undid his garments and took off the belt which fastened the doctor's packet. Folding these up in a neat pile, he laid them down, placing on top his draft. Then, writing a short note, he added it to the pile, and, with the paper and twine, made a strong package of the whole lot.

After this had been done, he reached for the pen, and addressed the package to Miss Grace Lansing in bold printed characters.

Then he muttered as he finished:

"I'll just toddle along and post this by registered post to Grace. His Majesty will carry this safely enough, and I won't risk losing them by any accident."

He suited the action to the words, and took his way down Collins Street to Elizabeth, and along to Bourke, on the corner of which stood the G.P.O.

He registered the package to Grace, and thrust his receipt carelessly in his pocket, but as he turned away he collided a Chinaman clad in European clothes.

"Sorry, sir!" apologised the latter.

"Oh, that's all right!" replied Harry, pulling out a cigar, and sauntering out to put in his time sight-seeing, now that his mind was relieved of the responsibility of his wealth.

But the polite Celestial had stood at Harry's elbow as he registered the package, and the narrow almond eyes had read in one swift glance the name and address.

He followed Harry out, only stopping long enough to jot down an exact copy of the address which his eyes had photographed, and then, joining his companion across the street, the pair continued their unobtrusive shadowing of the unsuspicious Englishman.

After returning to Scott's for lunch, Harry lit a cigar, and strolled along Collins Street and around the block until he reached Bourke Street again. There the gilded, gingerbread front of a picture palace, with its attendant's shrieking tout and monotonous electric piano, attracted him, for his year in the bush had been one in which entertainment of any kind had not entered.

He bought a ticket and went in, his faithful Chinese shadows doing the same. From the picture palace Harry wandered about, stopping at the P. and O. office to book his berth, after which he returned to the hotel.

At dinner he decided to take in a theatre that evening, and spent a lazy half-hour of enjoyment in choosing which one.

His enjoyment of the piece was fresh and whole-hearted, and aroused sympathetic smiles from his neighbours.

"Guess I'll have a bite to eat," he thought, as he emerged from the theatre and joined the jostling crowd. "By Jove, I wonder if I can find that Chinese restaurant where I had chop-suey the night I first landed? Let me see, was it Bourke or Little Bourke Street? Ah, I remember now —Little Bourke Street! Might as well walk; it's not far, and the air is good after the theatre."

With this reflection, he strode along until he reached the narrow confines of Little Bourke Street.

Entering a bar at the corner, he inquired the way to the Chinese restaurant, and was directed by a loud-voiced girl, who called after him, that she'd "Be glad to go along if he wanted anyone to help him eat it." But he disregarded her words and slammed the door.

A few minutes later he located the restaurant, and as he ascended the steps never dreamed that the two studious-looking Chinamen who followed him had been almost as close to him the whole day. Nor did he see the momentary glance which passed between them and the Chinaman who approached to show him to the table.

All around, at small tables, were seated people who had just come from the theatre, and although there seemed to be plenty of vacant tables the man apologised, saying they were all engaged. But he had a small private room! Would the gentleman be served there?

Harry indicated that he didn't care two buttons where he was served, and the obsequious Celestial led him to the room.

It was a small cupboard affair, and, with the exception of two large mirrors against the further wall, was devoid of decorations. The attendant drew out a chair for Harry, which brought him facing the door and with his back to the mirrors, one of them being directly behind his chair.

The waiter got his order, and returned with it almost at once, and Harry, who was hungry, fell to with a will.

But he was destined never to eat that chop-suey, for barely had he begun when the mirror behind him swung open noiselessly. Two yellow, wrinkled, bony hands protruded, from which dangled a thin silken cord.

With unerring aim the hands threw the cord at the head of the unsuspecting Harry, and as his fork clattered to the table the cord was drawn tight, cutting off his startled exclamation.

One of the Chinamen who had followed him all day leaped softly into the room, followed by his companion, and as Harry's bursting lungs gave out, and he sank into unconsciousness, they lifted him, and, as noiselessly as they had come, retreated with their burden through the hole. The mirror swung back, and a moment later the waiter entered the now empty room, and calmly cleared the table, as though nothing out of the ordinary had occurred.

The two Chinamen carried their burden down, down until the narrow steps, hidden between two partitions of the building, ended on a mud floor. A narrow, tunnel-like passage ran ahead for some distance, and along this they went until they came to another staircase. They ascended several steps until they reached a blank wall.

Pressing a hidden panel, they passed through and closed it, and where they now stood was where Rymer had stood after following Hang Lee through the secret panel from the opium-room.

The way Harry's captors had brought him was another secret exit which the careful Hang Lee had provided, and which had formed Wong Ho's mode of entry on the night Rymer got the diamond dragon.

Up the steps which Rymer had ascended in such trepidation they carried the unconscious Harry.

A light flickered in the bare, upstairs room, and beside the rough table sat Hang Lee, in unchanging inscrutable, brooding thought.

Laying their captive down, the two Chinamen bowed low, murmuring:

"It is he, Excellency."

"You have done well," replied Hang Lee, in guttural accents. "Loosen the cord. Is the son of a pig dead?"

One of the men bent down and cut the cord, after which he placed his hand on Harry's pulse.

"No, Excellency; he lives yet," he answered, rising.

"That is well —for now, I will decide his fate later. What else have you to report?"

Rapidly the spokesman of the pair related in minute detail what they had been able to discover of Harry's movements during the day.

"This packet?" broke in Hang Lee. "You have the address?"

"Yes, Excellency," replied the man, handing over the slip on which he had copied Grace's name and address.

"Do you know if the packet contains it?" went on the old Chinaman.

"No, Excellency."

"Strip him and search him," ordered Hang Lee, and it was done with perfect thoroughness.

But nothing rewarded their search excepting the receipt for the registered packet, and this went to join the paper which contained Grace's address.

"You, Chan, are about the same build as this fellow," went on Hang Lee slowly. "Put on his clothes, take his keys, and go to his hotel. This tag on his room key gives the number. Open his luggage and search every inch. You, Won, go also and wait outside."

So perfect was the discipline of Hang Lee's organisation, and so much in fear was he held, that neither Chinamen dreamed of questioning his orders.

They obeyed silently, and departed the way they had come.

For two hours the old Chinaman sat at the table, smoking his eternal yellow cigarettes; but beyond that, immovable. Not once did he glance at the unconscious figure on the floor, and if the captive was the subject of his thoughts, he gave no indication.

He stirred slightly as a soft, shuffling noise came from the stairs outside, and a moment later his two emissaries appeared, one of them in Harry's clothes.

"Well?" jerked Hang Lee shortly.

"It must have been in the packet, Excellency," replied the Chinaman in Harry's clothes. "I searched thoroughly, and found nothing but this." He drew out a broken piece of lead pencil as he spoke and passed it over. "It is the piece of pencil. Excellency, which Sing So —Tommy's Chinese name —said in his message had been passed over in the room as a token. Perhaps, Excellency, you will know for what purpose."

"I will keep it," returned Hang Lee briefly. "This son of a dog is the other's tool. Put his clothes on and take him out, blindfolded, through the opium-room. All the smokers are asleep, and there is no game to-night. Give him a drink before you take him out, to revive him, and then lead him, blindfolded, down the street. Let him go there."

They proceeded at once to obey. Deftly Harry's clothes were replaced, and as they finished they picked him up and carried him out. Down the stairs and through the panel into the opium-room they went. Then a draught of some heavy liquid was forced between his lips, and as the still form stirred to life again, Chan deftly knotted the handkerchief about his eyes.

Still hazy, and at a complete loss to gather what was happening, he was jerked to his feet and passed through the panel into the gambling-room, and from there out to the innocent-looking shop.

Silently his guides led him along the passage and out through the door into the darkness of Little Bourke Street, stopping a short distance down and releasing him. Before the fast recovering Harry could tear the bandage from his eyes, they had melted away in the darkness; and when he at last tore the handkerchief off, he could not, if his life had depended on it, have formed the faintest idea from which of those dark, silent doorways he had been thrust.

With bursting head and aching throat, his mind hardly yet clear, the puzzled Harry made haste to get out of the dark, narrow street into a more lighted thoroughfare.

There he hailed a taxi, and lost no time in getting back to Scott's. Hastening up to his room, he went rapidly through his pockets, and his look of puzzlement deepened as he found not even a halfpenny missing. His luggage had been rearranged with perfect exactness by Chan, and gave not the slightest sign of the overhauling it had received a little earlier.

More puzzled than ever, Harry disrobed and crept into bed.

"Who ever it was, must have taken me for someone else," he muttered, "and, when they discovered their mistake, let me go. I was lucky to get away as I did, but that's enough of Little Bourke Street for me. I'll keep a weather eye open for any more such tricks until the boat goes the day after to-morrow."

And with this reflection, he fell asleep, ignorant of the fact that the broken half of a lead pencil was missing from the hiding-place under a pile of clothes in his cabin-trunk, where he had carefully secreted it earlier in the day.

## THE THIRD CHAPTER. In London —Enter Sexton Blake —The "Murder."

SOME two months after the mysterious and puzzling attack on Harry Graham, two Chinamen sat in a back room at the Chinese Embassy in London.

Both were dressed in orthodox European fashion, and, beyond the undeniable cast of features, looked no different from the usual diplomat. But it was also evident that both were of the upper caste, for the pure Manchu complexion told of no taint of Tartar blood.

Although, garbed in the Occidental fashion, the close observer would have recognised in one of them the Oriental-clad visitor who had made a secret call on Hang Lee in Little Bourke Street on the night Rymer —or, Hutton, as he chose afterwards to be called —got possession of the Diamond Dragon. And his recognition would have been correct, for it was none other than Wang Ho, who had been dropped so suddenly by the butt-end of Rymer's revolver.

The other had a similar cast of countenance, a few more lines, perhaps, creasing his yellow skin, forming the only visible sign of greater age than his companion.

Li Hong, the individual in question, had travelled from Canton by rapid stages on receipt of a cable from Wang Ho, and the latter, having departed from Australia immediately after Rymer's successful attack, had been awaiting the other's arrival for nearly a month.

Although neither had any official connection with the Chinese Embassy, it was evident they represented influential quarters. On their arrival, the ambassador of that teeming new republic had greeted them with many flowery phrases.

He would be for ever honoured if they would accept of his miserable hospitality, and deign to use the most unworthy back room for the transaction of the business which they had together —which, by the way, must have been fairly weighty to bring them half round the world to discuss it.

Wang Ho was speaking in low, guttural tones, and the closeness with which Li Hong listened indicated that the tale was of intense interest.

"This cursed son of a pig who knocked me down and stole the dragon," he said, "has, as you see, Excellency, upset all our plans. Hang Lee, as clever and as powerful as he is, did not suspect for a

26

moment that I represented the republic and not the prince. With all his strings of information, not he, nor any, suspected the truth. Like a babe in swaddling clothes, he showed me where he had secreted the dragon, Excellency.

"Oh, it was very clever, I tell you! He had had a waxen image made, Excellency, and none could tell it from a real body. Underneath was the dragon, and I held it in my very hands, Excellency! And then to have this thieving son of a pig get it!"

"And what did you do then?" grunted Li Hong, stroking his seamed face.

"I said nothing to Hang Lee, Excellency; and after discussing the thief's probable movements with him, I came on here, pretending to Hang Lee that I would search for the thief here, but in reality to see you. I dared not return to China —Hang Lee would have suspected.

"He has sent out a general alarm and description to all his agents, he says he knows the thief, and will get him; but on my arrival here, Excellency, I found a cable waiting from Hang Lee, who says he has got no trace yet. Half our countrymen in Australia are on the watch, and Hang Lee has notified America."

"He must be found," remarked Li Hong, "and you, Wang Ho, must find him before Hang Lee does so. If the old man gets the dragon again he will not risk another loss, and will take it himself to the prince. And you know what that means. Every Tartar in China will follow the prince, and the republic will die before it has been born.

"Don't be too sure Hang Lee doesn't suspect you. He may have been playing with you. I will do what I can to help you, and will instruct the ambassador here to countenance any of your actions in London; but let them be secret.

"There is a great detective here in London —one Sexton Blake. I met him years ago in Canton, and his brain is as subtle as the finest in the Orient. He knows Europe and America as you know Canton. Go to him and seek his aid. Tell him as little as necessary. Between your knowledge of your own country and his brains, you ought to succeed.

"But remember, the Diamond Dragon must be recovered, or the republic will fall. I give you one month. If you fail you know the penalty. Go!"

"Yes, Excellency," murmured Wang Ho, rising. I will do as you say, and I will recover the Dragon. If I fail I will not be slow to pay the penalty."

Wang Ho bowed as he spoke, for although powerful and influential himself, he was a mere cipher compared to the inscrutable, seamed man who called himself Li Hong.

China had no higher, no more powerful man than the quiet Chinaman who had thought it worth while to leave his country at a critical time and journey secretly to London to himself direct the search for the lost Diamond Dragon.

Wang Ho lost no time in following Li Hong's suggestion.

Ho hastened through the Embassy to the street, and hailing a taxi, headed at once for Baker Street.

Sexton Blake, with discarded coat, and sleeves rolled up, was spending a day of what he termed relaxation, although it must be confessed he had peculiar ideas on the matter, for the relaxation consisted of a myriad of technical experiments in his laboratory.

But to Blake this was indeed relaxation, for he loved a long day with his "stinks," as Tinker called it, and many a baffling case had owed its clue to the results of his many experiments.

He glanced up with a frown as Mrs. Bardell, the landlady, knocked on the door of the laboratory.

"I thought I gave orders that I was on no account to be disturbed to-day?" he snapped testily.

"Well, I told 'im so," she broke in, bridling, "but it ain't a pretty sight to have a Chinaman a-settin' on the front step all day."

"On the front step?" asked Blake irritably, raising his brows. "Explain yourself."

"Well, I've told him you were out, ill, dead, and wouldn't see him anyway, but he just smiles and chatters 'Velly well! Velly well! I must see him, and will wait.' I wouldn't let him come in, so he's settin' on the step, and refuses to move. Now if I've done wrong I'd like to know it."

"You've done right," answered Blake, smiling slightly, and sighing as he surveyed a half-filled crucible. "Show him in. I'll see what it is."

The landlady bustled away, and Blake, putting on his coat, entered the consulting-room.

Wang Ho, who was the persistent caller, entered a moment later, and although Blake made no sign his interest quickened, for although he had among his other clients several high-caste Chinese, he knew from experience that the Celestial did not seek the help of the European without the matter being one of the greatest urgency and importance.

Consequently he prepared himself to listen to an interesting tale, and was not disappointed in his expectations.

"You are Mr. Blake?" inquired Wang Ho, depositing his silk hat on the floor and looking at Blake.

Blake nodded.

"I am."

"My name is Wang Ho," went on the Chinaman, "and I come to seek your assistance, Mr. Blake. They tell me you never fail," he added, with a few flowery Oriental expressions.

Blake shrugged his shoulders.

"Kindly be seated, and tell me the details of the matter you mention," he answered, seating himself. "You have not come to me, Mr. Wang Ho, without good reason, and I might tell you at the outset that, unless you are prepared to tell me everything, it is useless to go further."

"I will tell you all," replied Wang Ho, with a mental addition: "All but what I wish to conceal." But, all the same, he looked at the great detective with added respect, for he had anticipated eager acquiescence in his desires, and where he had intended simply making known his wants and securing the use of Blake's knowledge, his sensitive Oriental mind told him the cold-faced Englishman was not that type. It was for him to dictate and make use of others, and Wang Ho, in that second of hesitation, changed his plan of campaign.

"As I said, Mr. Blake," he went on in almost perfect English, although he had deliberately spoken "pidgin" talk to Mrs. Bardell, "I will tell you all. It is a matter of the greatest importance —in fact, none would be of more importance to the great nation to which I have the honour to belong."

"Do you mean the monarchy or the republic?" inquired Blake carelessly as he lit a cigar.

A gleam flashed through Wang Ho's eyes, to pass again as quickly as it had come, but his face was expressionless. "The republic, Mr. Blake. Shall I proceed?"

Blake nodded

"Belonging to the government of my country," went on Wang Ho, watching his listener closely, "is a —how do you call it in

English? Ah, yes! —a mascot. It is of untold value, Mr. Blake, not from its material worth alone, which is enormous, but of its great age, and the fact that it received the personal blessing of the great Confucius himself."

Blake barely suppressed a start, but made no comment.

"This sacred and valuable article, Mr. Blake, was stolen in China, and, after many adventurous travels, came to rest in the care of one Hang Lee, an ancient Manchu in the city of Melbourne. Hang Lee is great and powerful, and desires the return to power of the monarchy.

"With this purpose he made arrangements to return it secretly to Prince Fong, who is at the head of the monarchist movement. It would mean the success of the prince, Mr. Blake, if he received it, for by entering a place of worship and holding it aloft every Chinaman who is faithful to the law of Confucius would follow the commands of its possessor.

"That, Mr. Blake, is what has been stolen, and which was the reason of the success of the republican movement. But in Melbourne, Mr. Blake, on the eve of its departure for China, it was stolen, and not by a Chinaman."

"Ah!" breathed Blake. "Who by?"

"A European," replied Wang Ho, "and I can say almost positively by an Englishman."

"So the position is that the monarchists, in the form of Hang Lee, stole it from the republicans, and in turn it was stolen by a complete outsider."

"That is so," agreed Wang Ho.

"And I suppose Hang Lee is straining every nerve to recover it, as well as you?"

"That is correct."

"How do you know it was an Englishman who took it in Melbourne?" asked Blake quickly.

"I have it on good authority. Mr. Blake," he replied.

Blake rose.

"That is not the truth," he said coldly. "We may as well bring matters to a close."

"No no!" cried Wang Ho, for the first time showing emotion. "It was an untruth, but I will tell you the truth. I swear it. Don't refuse your help, Mr. Blake, I beseech you!"

"If you are prepared to tell me the whole truth I will listen, but only on that condition."

"I will promise you," almost wailed the anxious Wang Ho.

"Very well. Answer my question. How do you know it was an Englishman who took it?"

"Because," answered Wang Ho, dragging the words out slowly. "I —was —there —with —Hang —Lee —when —it —happened."

"Ah, that is better!" snapped Blake. "And what were you, a republican, doing with Hang Lee, the power of the monarchists?"

"I was posing as a monarchist, and was to be the messenger who took the Dragon back to China."

"And instead of passing it over to the prince you were to hand it over to your own party?"

Wang Ho nodded.

"And you think this Englishman who stole it has come on to London?" asked Blake.

"Yes, Mr. Blake." And Wang Ho rapidly related the details of Rymer's successful attack on him and Hang Lee.

"Hang Lee," he continued, "has warned all his agents, both here and in America, but he thinks the thief is bound to try and work through to Europe."

"Doubtless," answered Blake shortly. "Have you the Chinese Embassy here behind you?" he asked.

"Yes, Mr. Blake; but I came to you at the suggestion of another —one whom you knew in China."

"Ah!" remarked Blake, raising his eyebrows. "Who?"

Wang he leaned over, and, after a sharp look around, whispered a name in Blake's ears.

"He —is he here?" asked Blake, starting up.

"Yes."

"Where is he?"

"At the Embassy."

"If what you tell me is the truth —and I am disposed to believe you —I will take the case, if only in return for the favours he showed me in China. Will he be in London long?"

"His Excellency is here under the name of Li Hong," answered Wang Ho, "and will be here until the Dragon is recovered."

"I will call on him at the Embassy," replied Blake. "The case must indeed be urgent to bring him to London."

"Then, Mr. Blake, will you help me?" eagerly asked Wang Ho.

"I will take the case," replied Blake, smiling, "and you can help me, Wang Ho."

"His Excellency has only given me a month. And there are a hundred million Chinamen, with the most cunning of all at their head —the old and wise Hang Lee —ready to die in the recovery of the Dragon. If I fail —" And he touched his throat expressively.

"Hang Lee and a hundred million Chinamen," mused Blake thoughtfully. "Truly a formidable array, and I know something of their methods. It will be unpleasant if I fall into their hands, but I think it will have to be risked."

"Now Wang Ho, listen," he went on, speaking aloud. "Don't come here again. No one must know I am on this matter, and no one must see us together, at any cost! I will call to-night at the Embassy to see his Excellency. No one will see me arrive, and no one will see me leave. I will be there at ten o'clock sharp, and we can discuss further details."

Wang Ho rose.

"Very well, Mr. Blake. I will give His Excellency your message."

Two minutes later the Manchu departed, and Blake was alone.

He waited until the noise of Wang Ho's taxi died away, when he rose, and, walking to his desk, drew out his private index. Turning to the letter D, he turned over several pages until his eyes rested on what he was seeking for

"Dragon" he muttered to himself, "Diamond Dragon, sacred and secret emblem of power of Manchu rulers. All powerful with Chinese on account of supposed blessing of it by Confucius. Influence extends as far as Thibet, whose religion is really an evolved form of Buddhism.

"Mysteriously stolen in 1890, and was held for huge ransom. To pay this ransom, and personally recover the diamond Dragon, was the real purpose of Li Hung Chang's journey to Europe some years ago. Again stolen two years ago by the revolutionary party and taken to San Francisco.

"Brought back from there, and secretly used in influencing the troops to desert the Emperor and join the rebels. Chinese Republic really owes its existence to its power on the minds of the soldiers and lower classes. Believed to have originally been made by a goldsmith of ancient Egypt, when China traded with that country in its palmy days over two thousand years ago."

Blake closed the index with a snap.

"To think that the fate of a nation containing over four hundred million souls rests on the recovery of that!" he muttered, pacing up and down. "For if it gets known that it is lost for good China will be submerged in the throes of the worst war mankind has ever seen. And if a European thief has secured it, he will naturally remove the diamonds and melt down the gold.

"The proposition is difficult enough, without the added antagonism of Hang Lee. I know that gentleman only too well. He is the deepest, subtlest, shrewdest Celestial living, and Wang Ho did not exaggerate when he said a hundred million Chinamen would die at the snap of Hang Lee's fingers. But I got the better of him once, and know, at least, a few of his tricks."

Blake again turned and approached the desk. Picking up his old black pipe, he stuffed it and dropped into a chair. As the smoke ascended in heavy clouds, he hunched himself up, and his eyes closed as he began to concentrate with that brilliant deductive brain on the few shadowy details of which he was at present in possession.

Once during the afternoon, Mrs. Bardell tapped and entered, but scuttled hastily away on reading the signs.

Not till after eight did he rouse himself, and when he did his eyes were still clouded with puzzlement.

He entered his dressing-room, and slipped into evening clothes, dressing with punctilious care, for Li Hong was indeed a great personage —a personage whom, if he came publicly to London, would be shown Royal honours. Blake knew him for a man of power, despite his nationality, and more than once had he smoothed Blake's path when the detective was in China.

Consequently, Blake desired to show him the courtesy of proper formality in the matter of his dress, and while he struggled with his tie, evolved a plan for getting to the Embassy unseen. No one realised more plainly than did Blake that if Wang Ho's duplicity were suspected by Hang Lee the latter's agents would already be on the track.

If that were so they would be aware of Wang Ho's visit to the detective, and from that moment Blake knew they would have him under surveillance. To guard against this possibility and shake them off if there were any followers, great care was necessary if he were to see the so-called Li Hong secretly.

As he slipped into his overcoat and picked up an opera-hat, he made his decision.

He slipped along the passage, and, hailing a passing taxi, gave, in a distinct voice the order, His Majesty's Theatre. The driver nodded and started, and although Blake glanced sharply through the windows, he did not see the speeding figure which leaped out and tore after the taxi until it had grasped the back and pulled itself up.

In the back of the taxi was a small look-out glass about nine inches long and six inches wide.

The noise of the taxi made it impossible for Blake to hear the soft, swishing noise as the silent, sinister figure, clinging to the back drew a knife, and cut rapidly around the glass.

As it loosened and dropped, the figure grasped it and stowed it away with the knife. Then a long, skinny arm crept noiselessly through, guided by a pair of piercing, menacing eyes set in the yellow, parchment-like face of a Chinaman.

With lightning-like rapidity and unerring aim, the Chinaman threw a silken noose at Blake's head. It circled and dropped to his collar, and before the startled Blake could throw it off and leap up, the Chinaman had dropped off still holding the cord, which drew together with unyielding force as it felt the weight of the Chinaman at the other end.

Giving an extra pull, the Celestial released the cord and faded away just as the cab rolled into Oxford Street. The taxi-driver, all unconscious of the extraordinary attack on his fare, who was lying back unconscious, kept on through the traffic down Regent Street until he crossed Piccadilly and rolled down Haymarket.

He pulled up in front of the theatre, and sat waiting while the liveried attendant hastened to the door of the cab. But no gentleman in evening clothes descended, and with a slightly-puzzled brow, the man stuck his head in the cab.

His look changed to one of amazement as he saw the fare apparently asleep in the corner, but he gave an ejaculation of horror as he saw the opened mouth and bulging eyes. A policeman standing near hastened over as the attendant gave his ejaculation and peered in at the relaxed figure.

"Here, you," he said roughly, leaning over to shake him, "you'd better wake up and go —Bless my soul," he cried, "it's Mr. Sexton Blake! Quick —he's fainted or something! Help me get him out and carry him into the office of the theatre!"

Together they dragged the detective out and carried him through the rapidly-gathering crowd.

Someone had heard the constable mention the famous detective's name, and so rapidly does the rumour grow and enlarge, that barely had the constable and attendant disappeared into the theatre with their burden when every tongue on the street had it that Sexton Blake had died in a taxi.

As the policeman bent to make an examination of the recumbent form of Blake on the office floor, he saw, for the first time, the trailing end of a thin, powerful, silken cord.

With a surprised exclamation, he bent Blake's head, and his face grew grave as the tight cord buried in the soft part of Blake's neck told him the reason of the detective's unconsciousness, or, as the policeman thought, death.

He jerked out a knife, and rapidly cut the cord, and began feverishly giving the detective first aid. The attendant had gone for the manager, who came in at that moment, and a doctor was immediately sent for. As the last tinkle of the telephone died away, an enterprising reporter forced his way in and approached the little group in the centre of the office.

"I came as a critic for the play," he whispered, "but I heard Sexton Blake had died in a cab on his way here. Is that, right?"

"More like murder!" growled the policeman, who could bring no signs of life into the still form of the detective.

That was enough for the enterprising reporter. Without waiting for more, he tore out to get to his paper with one of the biggest "scoops" of the year, and later that evening, when the crowds were emerging from the theatre, their ears were greeted on all sides by the cry: "Extry Speshil! Murder in a taxi of the great detective, Sexton Blake!" And, needless to say, the newsboys did a rushing trade, for all and sundry were anxious to read the details of the murder of the man whose name was a household word wherever English was spoken, and many places where it wasn't.

But had the enterprising young reporter not been so precipitate, and had he waited half an hour until the doctor's arrival, he would have seen a faint stirring of that lifeless form follow a stiff injection of strychnine. Many things had been tried first, but all had failed, and, as a last resort, the doctor tried the powerful poisonous stimulant.

As Blake's eyes opened, the anxious watchers heaved a sigh of relief; but at that moment the detective's ears were greeted by the cries of his own murder. Even there, on the borderland of death, and reeling under the shock of its sudden suspension, he called upon his wonderful brain to serve him, and at the moment he made such demands upon it it did not fail him.

A daring plan had flashed into his mind, and barely had his eyes opened, when they closed, and he sank back again into apparent unconsciousness.

"By Jove!" cried the doctor, wiping the sweat from his brow. "The injection has been too strong! His pulse is going weakly, but if he remains unconscious the heart may stop at any moment! This is too much responsibility for me alone! Can't we get him out of here quietly and take him to a hospital?" he asked the manager anxiously.

"Yes —yes!" replied the worried man. "Out, through this side door into the street. Run and get a taxi," he said, turning to the attendant, "and tell him to pull along the street!"

The man did so, and the three remaining men again picked up Blake and carried him out by the side door into the dark street.

"Will you come with me?" asked the doctor, turning to the constable.

"Well, you see, doctor," he said, hesitating, "I couldn't without a relief; but I'll write my notes and be a witness at the inquest that you did everything in your power."

"All right. Tell him to drive to the Central Hospital," replied the doctor, closing the door and supporting the lifeless figure beside him.

"I'll be obliged if you will countermand that order," said a quiet voice, and the doctor nearly collapsed as the supposed dead man sat up and drew a cigar from his pocket.

"W-what the dickens!" gasped the doctor.

"I don't wonder you are a little startled," smiled Blake; "but, really, I have been conscious ever since you gave me the strychnine which you thought finished me off. But I am beginning to think I have more lives than a cat."

He explained as much as he thought necessary to the doctor, and then said:

"By the way, doctor, I wonder if you will oblige me by neither confirming nor denying my death? I have a particular reason for asking this, and can only say that it will be of great assistance to me if you will. I trust I will not trespass on your goodness for more than a week. Will you do this for me, doctor?"

Blake turned his head around, with his rare smile, and the doctor, who had begun to demur, capitulated.

"I ought not," he said. "It's strictly against the principles of my profession to do it. But your case is exceptional, Mr. Blake, and if, as you say, big things may hang on it, why. I'll do it."

"Thank you!" replied Blake quietly, putting out his hand. "Believe me, doctor, you won't regret it. There are very big things in the air, and your assistance in this matter may mean the saving of my life, which I so nearly lost to-night. And I am not anxious to lose it," he smiled, "until I have finished one or two things I have to do. Now, doctor, if you will tell the driver to turn and drive to your house, I will play 'possum' again, and between you you can carry me in. Then our probably loquacious driver won't know anything."

The driver did as Blake suggested, and twenty minutes later they pulled up in front of a quiet house in Chelsea.

The doctor explained matters to the driver, and that worthy was only too pleased to have the opportunity of assisting. How he helped to carry in the dead body of the great detective would form conversational ammunition for many a night amongst his pals.

With many grunts they managed to get the body into the house, and the driver would have been a very astonished young man had he known that the dead man had shown sudden signs of life, and was watching him through the coloured glass of the door with amused eyes as he drove off.

"Now, doctor," smiled Blake, turning around, "I won't take up any more of your time. Thank you for your attention. I will send you a more tangible acknowledgment later. Is there a lane at the back of your house?"

"Yes," nodded the doctor. "Do you wish to go out that way, Mr. Blake?"

"Yes; I think it would be safer. But before doing so I will make a little change in my appearance."

The astonished doctor watched in amazement as Blake folded up his opera-hat and thrust it in his overcoat-pocket, then taking off the well-cut garment, he turned it inside-out, revealing a very shabby affair.

"It never does for a man in my business to be unprepared,

doctor," he rattled on as he put the coat on again. "A soiled neckerchief to cover up this collar and tie, this very shabby cap" — and he drew an old cap from his pocket— "my coat buttoned up, this slight twist to my face, a cigarette stuck at a 'tough' angle in my mouth, and there you are!"

"Well, by thunder!" gasped the medico. If I hadn't seen you actually do it I wouldn't believe you were the same man! And it's so simple, too!"

"Oh very simple!" said Blake, with a smile; but the smile was at the thought of the result the uninitiated doctor would achieve if he attempted the "very simple" change.

Without further delay Blake followed the doctor through the garden at the rear, and a few moments later stood in the dark, quiet lane.

Then, with the cigarette stuck at an angle in his mouth, he started off at a brisk pace, and, as Big Ben struck ten, was standing in the back room at the Chinese Embassy greeting the seamed Celestial who called himself Li Hong, and explaining, with a smile, to that individual why his suit was so immaculate and his overcoat so dilapidated.

THE FACE OF A CHINAMAN PEERED OUT.

IN HANG LEE'S GAMBLING-DEN.

A PANEL SLID OPEN AND THROUGH ITS NARROW APERTURE CREPT RYMER.

RYMER LAY BACK AS THE OLD CELESTIAL DREW NEAR.

## THE FOURTH CHAPTER.  Dr. Huxton Rymer Up Against It.

WHEN Dr. Hutton —or, Rymer, to call him by his real name — saw Harry Graham off at the little station, he walked back to the pub., smiling with satisfaction at the absurd ease with which he was getting the Diamond Dragon safely out of the country.

"He's as honest and as safe as a bank!" he muttered as he sipped a whisky-and-soda. "Now that I've got that safely disposed of I'll shake the dust of this place off my feet, and make tracks for London as fast as I can get there. My best plan will be to go on to Sydney from here and go by way of America."

He finished his drink, and, after getting a day old copy of the "Argus," he betook himself to his room to look up the date of the next steamer from Sydney to 'Frisco.

His search was rewarded by finding that two left within a week —one by way of New Zealand, and the other direct.

He decided to take the latter, and two days later saw Dr. Huxton Rymer on his way to Sydney.

As the train pulled out, he congratulated himself again on his astuteness.

"Graham sails to-day," he reflected, "and we will both reach London about the same time."

It was true Harry Graham was sailing that day, but he was still unconscious of the disappearance of the broken piece of pencil from his luggage.

A conversation which took place the same evening in the secret upstairs room of Hang Lee's den in Little Bourke Street would have considerably startled Rymer had he known its tenor. But he did not know, nor did Harry Graham have the faintest notion of the complications which were weaving themselves about his unsuspicious head.

Hang Lee sat in his usual attitude —rolling cigarettes and smoking them with his usual impassive demeanour. At the other side of the table sat the same two Chinamen —Chan and Won —who had made the mysterious attack on Harry Graham in the Chinese restaurant.

They were dressed as before, in European garments, and were listening closely to the words which dropped slowly from Hang Lee's lips.

The room was lit with a flickering candle, as though it were night, although outside it was still early afternoon. But for obvious reasons, Hang Lee's retreat was free from any invasion of daylight.

The feeble flame threw its wavering light over the shrivelled features of the old man, but his eyes were in the shadow, and the deep, fathomless power of those intense orbs was felt by his listeners rather than seen.

Before him was a cypher telegram, which he kept tapping from time to time, and which had evidently been his reason for sending for his two agents.

"Now listen," he said, in guttural tones, "and mark well! Wang Ho, who was here with me the night the Diamond Dragon was stolen, was a traitor. I knew it before he reached Melbourne, and the son of a pig thought to play with me —me, Hang Lee! I intended using him to convey the Dragon to China, for it would go safely in that way; but on his arrival my agents there would have secured it and taken it to his Illustrious Excellency, our Prince.

"However, that thousand times cursed Englishman, who got it, upset my plans. But look you, Wang Ho left for England afterwards, and is even now in London. But my suspicions that the Dragon was still in Australia proved correct. Sing So —Tommy, the gardener at the station —has done well. That the young fool you caught, and whose luggage you searched, has not the Dragon, we now know. It was in the package he sent to England. You, Chan, will leave by the Adelaide Express to-night and join the Martah there. This young fool, Graham, is aboard. Watch him closely, and when you get to London, don't lose sight of him.

"I have had papers prepared for you, which gives you a diplomatic standing, and will avoid all trouble for you. This latest word from Sing So —Tommy —says the other man —that man who stole the Dragon," and Hang Lee's eyes blazed, "is leaving for Sydney by the train to-day. You, Won, will leave for Sydney to-night. Find him and follow him. He will go to England at once now that he has got the Dragon off his hands, but will probably go by way of America. As the laws relating to our illustrious race are hard in America, I have had full diplomatic papers made out for you as well. Follow him night and day. He has not the Dragon —no —but he has the other part of this." Hang Lee drew out the small piece of pencil which had been stolen from Harry Graham's luggage, and held it up

"It will be on his person," he went on, "not in his luggage. Between here and London, Won, get that piece of pencil."

"And then, Excellency?" inquired Won.

"Then bring it to me in London."

"But, Excellency, in London?" exclaimed both Chan and Won in surprise.

"Yes," snapped Hang Lee, "in London! I am leaving for there also, so see that you both do your work well, or—" And he touched his throat. "It is best that you know all," he went on. "Wang Ho, as I said, is already there, and is searching for the Dragon. I have a hundred agents there on his heels already, and if he gets it before I arrive he won't keep it long. But he won't get it, for we will be in London almost as soon as the Dragon.

"Now away with you! If you need help in New York or San Francisco, Won, you know where to get it. Kill your man, if necessary, but get that piece of pencil. Now go!"

The two Chinamen rose and bowed respectfully, and, after receiving their papers from the old Celestial, took their departure on their different errands —one to sail with Harry Graham on the Martah, for London, and one to follow Rymer by night and day.

For the time being, at least, Chan's duty was the easier. His instructions were simply not to lose sight of Harry Graham. But Won's, although brief, were explicit, and he knew the penalty he must pay did he fail in carrying out Hang Lee's instructions.

With the fatalism of the Celestial he laid his plans as well as possible, and left the rest to Fate. Consequently, when the self-satisfied Rymer arrived in Sydney he was under surveillance constantly. His suspicions, however, were not aroused, and when the steamer for 'Frisco departed two days later, Rymer chuckled with satisfaction at the last sight of Sydney.

"That's the last of you!" he said, half aloud, as he leaned over the rail. "A month will see me in London, and then to get the Diamond Dragon turned into coin of the realm. Rymer, my boy, your trip to old Hang Lee's that night was a stroke of luck for you!"

He turned to pace along the deck, when he came face to face with a distinguished-looking Chinaman. Rymer started visibly, and for a moment an awful fear seized him, but as the Celestial passed on without noticing him he shrugged his shoulders.

"I'm nervous over nothing," he muttered. "This fellow can't have any connection with the matter, and, besides, Hang Lee isn't powerful enough to put that class of Chinaman on my track. He's probably going to relieve at the Embassy in the United States."

How little Rymer really knew about the far-reaching power of that old Chinaman who sits and smokes in the dingy upstairs room in Little Bourke Street!

He laughed off his fears, and a few days later, when he got into casual conversation with the Chinaman, that individual lulled his suspicions entirely.

"Yes," said Won, "I go to Washington to relieve at the Embassy there. And you, sir —do you remain in the United States?"

"Oh, no!" laughed the relieved Rymer. "I'm going through to London."

"I may go on there," remarked Won, watching his man closely. "I will know when I reach America."

Rymer rose, with a nod, and strode aft to the smoking-saloon.

"I knew I was right," he muttered. "He's not the type of Chink to be after the Dragon. Probably doesn't know yet that it's gone."

With this reflection Rymer gave himself up to the lazy enjoyment of the South Pacific. Not for many months had his funds permitted him to bask in the lap of luxury as at present, and his affected nature sipped it greedily.

The long days on deck, with nothing to do but read and smoke; the lazy rolling of the blue Pacific, which seemed for once to really deserve its name; the occasional stops at the palm-fringed islands, where the short stay was coloured by the diving of the black boys and the grinning invasion of the natives.

Then across the line, with no further stop until Honolulu was reached. From there the short last lap of the journey was a period of preparation, and before the luxurious holiday had time to grow stale the Golden Gate was sighted, and at last 'Frisco.

As they slipped through the gateway of the Pacific, Rymer leaned against the rail, smoking, building hugely of the future. The solitary Chinese passenger had long since passed from his mind, and his every energy was bent toward reaching London, and once more holding in his hands that magnificent blazing mass of jewels, which to him represented only its intrinsic value, but to hordes of Celestials represented all that was sacred and blessed.

His musings would perhaps have been of a less pleasant nature had he known that the Chinaman whom he deemed so harmless had, by dint of patience and cunning, managed to go through every particle of his luggage. With the wonderful patience of the Oriental, Won had seized every opportunity that offered.

While Rymer was ashore at Samoa, Won had managed to go through his bags. At Honolulu he had seized the opportunity to complete his work; and now, as he stood not far away, also leaning over the rail and staring unemotionally at the near city and the distant hills, he had in his pocket a detailed inventory of every article which Rymer possessed except one —the piece of broken pencil.

He had hardly dared hope to find it in the luggage, but his search had told him for a certainty that Rymer carried it on his person. And while Rymer was building his golden castles on the foundation of the Diamond Dragon, Won was scheming, with Oriental cunning, how he could gain possession of that little piece of pencil.

Rymer lost all sight of Won in the Customs, and with the final disappearance of the Celestial went Rymer's last flickering thought of him.

But Won did not lose sight of Rymer, and on the express for the east, which Rymer lost no time in catching he had as fellow-passenger an aged-looking Chinaman. Won had disguised himself in simple fashion.

His papers, showing him to be of diplomatic rank, had passed him through the Customs without trouble, and, after the necessary formalities had been completed, he had set about changing his appearance. It was a simple matter to seam and line his face and hands, giving them the appearance of age, and when he had changed his European garments for those of the common laundryman, it would have taken Blake to discern in the old man the same individual who had crossed on the steamer from Sydney.

Rymer breathed a sigh of satisfaction as he stepped into a taxi at the Grand Central Station in New York and ordered the man to drive to the Breslin Hotel.

"By heavens," he muttered, as the cab swung into the Broadway, which was crowded with the early evening theatre crush, and which from Twenty-Third Street to Forty-Ninth Street blazed like day with a myriad of lights and electric signs— "by heavens. I had about given up hope of ever hitting this town again. If it wasn't for my business in London, I'd stay here for a bit and paint the old town red before going on to England! But I'll have two days here, anyway, and you can bet I'll make good use of them. Let me see. I'll have dinner first, and then a stroll, after which —well, maybe a theatre, a cafe, or a music-hall. I'll decide that later." His thoughts broke off as the cab pulled up with a jerk at the entrance to the Breslin, and, after giving instructions about his luggage, he strolled into that quiet but luxurious hotel.

After dinner, Rymer put on his coat and hat and strolled up Broadway. The crowds were still as thick, despite the fact that the theatre-goers were all within the brilliantly-lighted playhouses. He strolled aimlessly along, trying to decide what to do, when he suddenly remembered a little Bohemian cafe down on the East Side.

"By Jove," he chuckled, "it's years since I was there! This is Friday night, too. I'll pop into a taxi and see if there are many changes there."

Suiting the action to the word, he hailed a cab and gave the order. Then, lighting a cigar, he leaned back and gave himself up to pleasant reverie, all unconscious of another taxi which kept close behind.

Leaving Broadway, they swung across Fourteenth Street and down Avenue A, past the first dark buildings which heralded the entrance to the prevailing gloom of the East Side.

Just as Rymer's cab was swinging into Houston Street he started up as he heard a shout, and saw his driver turn in alarm. The man threw the wheel round sharply, but before he could do anything else another cab crashed into them, the wheels of both taxis interlocking.

With a muttered curse Rymer started up and opened the door on the off-side. He was half way out, but turned he heard the other door open.

"What do you want?" he began angrily; but at that moment the dark figure who had entered leaped forward.

Half in and half out, Rymer was in an awkward position, but a powerful man at any time, his recent abstemious life had hardened up his muscles.

His first thought as he turned was that his assailant was only one of the numerous East Side "toughs," who, taking advantage of the absence of any policeman, was risking an assault on the well-dressed man in the taxi.

But as the dark figure sprang for him he saw the features of a Chinaman, and a sudden cold fear gripped him. His arm went up, and without any attempt to confine himself to Marquis of Queensberry rules he lashed out with his foot.

His assailant grunted from the kick, but did not stop in his advance, and a moment later Rymer's arm crashed through a pane of glass as they grappled and struggled for the mastery in the confined space of the cab.

Clever as he was, Rymer's assailant was rapidly being overcome by the more powerful European, when another man left the second taxi and leaped in on top of the struggling pair, joining his strength to that of his companion. Rymer's driver had jumped down when the crash came, and had begun making a rapid examination to ascertain what damage had been done to his car, at the same time passing several uncomplimentary remarks to the other driver.

"What in blazes are yuh tryin' to do?" he growled. "You ought tu be wheelin' a baby carriage. Couldn't yu hold yer sixty-horse power racer?" he sneered as he ran his eye over the dilapidated taxi which had locked with his.

"Aw, gwan! Wotcher givin' us?" replied the other. "Next time don't take up all the road."

It was at that moment that the Chinaman had leaped into Rymer's cab, and the driver turned with a curse as he saw the collision had been premeditated.

"That's yer game, is it?" he growled, springing at the other driver. "I'll fix yer fer that, my beauty! Git down off yer perch, or I'll knock yer down!"

"Gwan, yer old cab ain't hurt!" growled the other. "I seen to that. I harely touched yer! Let those coves fight it out. 'Tain't no business of ourn, and we'll git paid."

Rymer's driver hesitated, probably weighing his chances of being paid for any damage to his cab, or the result if a policeman should be attracted by the racket.

It was then that Rymer's arm crashed through the window, and that decided him. Had he used strategy he would have gone to the assistance of his passenger, but the broken window made him see red for a moment, and he sprang for the author of all his troubles.

Catching the other driver by the arm, he dragged him to the road, and that individual nothing loth, they were soon going for each other hammer and tongs.

Rymer inside the cab was fighting hard, but the confined space made it difficult to swing. The coming of the second man turned the scales against him, and, as he felt a pair of bony hands gripping his throat, he tried to call for help, wondering why his driver hadn't come to his assistance.

Making a supreme effort, he raised himself and gave a quick cry, but the hands renewed their grip too quickly, and it broke off into a croak as he sank back. His struggles became weaker and weaker as the awful pressure on his throat made his lungs almost burst. He realised now how foolish he had been to stir into such a neighbourhood, and cursed himself for allowing his old love of amusement to cause such a false move.

As the thought of the glittering dragon flashed through his mind, he gathered his fast-fading senses together for one more effort, but it was too late, and before he could move his tortured lungs gave out, and he dropped into a bottomless black pit.

The whole struggle had not lasted more than a few moments, and the two taxi-drivers were still fighting outside when Won and his companion, whom he had recruited from New York's Chinatown, lifted Rymer's insensible body, and like a blurred shadow passed across the narrow space between the interlocked taxis and deposited him in the bottom of their own cab.

"Quick!" grunted Won, as he straightened up. Those fools will have a policeman here in a minute. Lend a hand and drive off the other while I secure this one."

The other Chinaman jumped out to obey, and rushed towards the struggling men. A quick grip, and Rymer's driver doubled up with excruciating pain as his arm was twisted around. He dropped his hold on the other driver, and twisted himself to ease the pain, but the Chinaman held him tight while he spoke quickly to the other driver.

"Back away and get ready, and be quick! There is a policeman coming up the street!"

The man looked along, and the sight of the blue coat spurred him to lose no time. With a bound he gained the seat, and began slowly backing away from the other cab, twisting and turning to unlock the wheels.

The bluecoat, seeing something was wrong, quickened his pace, but he was still a hundred yards down the street, and every moment was seeing the taxi backing farther away.

As the wheels finally cleared the Chinaman released his hold on Rymer's driver, and sent him to the ground with a crash. Leaping into the moving taxi, he slammed the door to, just as the policeman started to run.

The driver needed no instructions, knowing his position would be more complicated were he caught. The insensible man in the cab would be hard to explain away, even to a constable on the East Side of New York, and the fact that his passengers were Celestials would not make things any easier.

Consequently, he became conveniently deaf to the policeman's shouts, and he threw in the clutch, swinging along into Houston Street.

Houston Street, on the East Side of New York, is a narrow street at any time, but when lined with fruit-barrows, as it usually is, it becomes a labyrinth of danger. On Friday evenings half the Hebrew population of the district promenade up and down, and on such occasions the middle of the road is equally in favour for pedestrians as the footpath.

Consequently, Won's driver had his work cut out to get through. With one hand on the wheel, and the other continually pressing the horn, he tore through at a reckless pace, sending the pedestrians scattering amongst the loaded fruit-barrows accompanied by a pandemonium of curses in almost every tongue.

Barrows went crashing to the ground as the scurrying crowds crashed into them, bringing down upon their heads the frenzied wrath of the luckless owners of the barrows. Apples, oranges, bananas, and vegetables went rolling about, causing a still worse mix-up, as, to add insult to injury, the rolling fruit tripped up those who managed to gain their feet.

Still, the taxi kept on its reckless course, and if it got the barest fraction of the wrath that was called down upon it by those angry Hebrews, it would have disappeared on the spot. At that moment the bluecoat came plunging along in chase.

Not until he was right into the pandemonium did he see what had really happened. Before he could save himself he had stepped on a particularly juicy orange with one foot, and a crushed banana with the other. His hat flew off as his feet shot from under him, and the juice from the orange, shooting up into his eye with terrific force under the pressure of his heavy foot, he dropped his stick and applied his attention to his smarting eye.

It would be as well to draw a veil over the subsequent events of that impromptu fruit salad. Those of the crowd who were wise, swallowed their anger on seeing the plight of the policeman and faded quickly away while there was yet time; but the luckless owners of the barrows had perforce to remain, and on their innocent heads the raging policeman vented his anger.

In the meantime, the escaping taxi had cleared the last of the barrows, and was swinging along at a rapid pace. It had gained the wider road in front of the brilliantly-lit Little Hungary Cafe, and, swinging around to the right, took several turnings, until a quarter of an hour brought it back into Chinatown. It pulled up in a dark, silent blind alley, and the driver opened the door and stepped out.

Won stepped across the narrow pavement to a dark, silent, battered door, and swung it silently open, revealing a black, impenetrable interior.

Returning to the cab, the two Celestials lifted the still unconscious Rymer and carried him through the doorway, disappearing with their burden into the sinister blackness within.

A moment later Won returned, and silently handed a banknote to the driver of the taxi. With a grunt, the latter took it, and after carefully examining it by the light of a side-lamp, stuffed it carefully in his pocket. Then descending from his seat, he walked around to the rear of the cab, where he busied himself for a moment. When he straightened up his number had been changed, and with another grunt of acknowledgment he backed slowly out of the alley.

Won watched him until he had turned out of the alley. He then turned softly back through the dark doorway, which he silently closed, and once more silence reigned in the shadowy alley.

Won passed along the dark passage, and up a rickety flight of stairs. At the top he turned and lifted a heavy curtain, revealing a room lighted by two candles, and occupied by tall Chinamen and the inanimate body of Rymer. Like himself, Won's companion was dressed in European fashion, but the other Celestial, almost as ancient-looking as the powerful Hang Lee, wore the flowing jacket of the mandarin class.

He looked up as Won entered, and spoke in a voice of exceptionally deep tone:

"Foo Ling tells me you were pursued, Won. Is there any danger?"

"No, no, Excellency," answered Won quickly, with the ghost of a smile flickering for an instant in his eyes. "The policeman pursued us, but I looked back, and saw that he was forced to stop. The driver of the cab is safe. He named his price and has got it."

"That is well, Won! Yonder son of a pig is stirring," went on the old man. "What will you do with him now?"

"Search him for what his Excellency commanded me to get." answered Won, dropping to his knees beside Rymer. "It is small, and may be well hidden, but I will find it. It must be on him, for I went through all his luggage."

The old Chinaman and Foo Ling watched impassively as Won began his search. Through every pocket he went first, but as he had not expected to find it in such a place, he was hardly disappointed when his search revealed nothing.

"He is no fool," he remarked gutturally; "but I'll find it even if he has swallowed it."

Beginning systematically, he began a thorough search of every particle of Rymer's clothing. Every inch was felt carefully in an endeavour to locate the small, hard piece of pencil, but nowhere was it to be found, and Won sat back on his heels with a puzzled frown.

He thought in silence for some time, not asking and not receiving any assistance from the other two. Finally, he bent over and untied Rymer's shoes. Tearing them off, he reached a coarse file from the table and began prying the heels off. The first revealed nothing, but as he got the other off, even his impassive face worked with satisfaction, as there before him, laid in a carefully-made groove of the heel, was the broken piece of pencil.

Barely glancing at it, he picked it up and thrust it in his pocket then, replacing the now heelless shoes on Rymer, he stood up.

"I have succeeded," he said simply. "His Excellency will be pleased."

The old Chinaman nodded slowly.

"Yes, he will be pleased," he said, in his deep tones. "But what of him?" And again he nodded at Rymer's body. Won turned and surveyed the unconscious man.

"It is unwise to have too many disappearances," he said slowly; "but if we turn him loose, he might yet cause complications. I think the best plan will be to drop him as he is into the river."

"That is wise," nodded the old man. "The English pigs have a saying, 'Dead men tell no tales.' If he goes free he may yet cause trouble."

"True," replied Won, and, signing to Foo Ling, he seized Rymer's feet. Foo Ling lifted his shoulders, and as they straightened up the old man rose, and lifting a candle, led the way down the rickety staircase. He turned at the bottom, and passed along until he came to a small door.

Pulling it open, he again turned and descended another flight of stairs, the dripping stone walls indicating that it was a riverside cellar. He then crossed the hard mud floor until he reached a scattered number of empty barrels, which were thrown carelessly in one corner. He was compelled to set the candle down on one of these until he had thrown several aside, and then, picking up the light again, he approached the stone wall.

A moment's fumbling in the corner, followed by a slight click, and a large foundation-stone swung back, admitting a cool, damp draught of air, which threatened to extinguish the feeble flame of the candle.

Signing to the others to follow, he crept through, standing on the other side in such a way that the candle illuminated the cellar he had just left. Foo Ling supported Rymer's unconscious body, while Won crept through after the old man. Then, lifting the body up to the hole, he passed it through, and followed after.

Again picking up their burden, they followed the old man with ghostly, dancing light along a mud-walled passage, whose sides were even more moist than the walls of the cellar. A couple of turnings brought to their ears the sound of lapping water, and a moment later the old man brought them up before another stone wall.

Won and Foo Ling stood and held the body, while the old man placed his finger on a certain spot on the stone, and then extinguished the candle. A moment later the noise of the lapping water grew more distinct, telling them that the stone had swung back.

"Now," whispered the old man, and the other two moved forward with their burden. Through the square opening they thrust it slowly, until all but the shoulders was through. Then Won, releasing it gently, listened until he heard it drop with a splash into the water beneath.

## THE FIFTH CHAPTER. Graham's Luck —In London —Tinker Has Bad News.

IF a number of men, each from a different part of the world were to gather together in a London hotel, and compare dates as to what each was doing at a certain hour on the certain day, the result would undoubtedly prove amazingly interesting.

How little does a man in, say, London, dream that while he may be going through the throes of a civilised danger, another penetrating Briton may be at the very same moment fighting drought in the back blocks of Australia, toiling across the blinding snow wastes of Northern Canada, or raving with fever in the tropics.

But it is a fact, and by the same ruling of Fate, the chief actors in the rapidly unfolding drama of the Diamond Dragon were almost at the same time experiencing the first results of the Celestial web.

While Sexton Blake was standing in the back room of the Chinese Embassy in London discussing the details of the lost Dragon, Hang Lee's agent Won was making his report to Hang Lee himself in the back room of a certain opium den in London's Chinatown, Hang Lee had travelled by Suez, and after reaching Marseilles had come overland to London, arriving there in time to direct the attack which so nearly proved fatal to Sexton Blake.

Won had arrived that day with the piece of pencil which he had got from Rymer in New York, and it was now reposing in Hang Lee's pocket with its other half. But away on the other side of the globe, Harry Graham was going through experiences which were quite sufficient to drive from his mind, for the time being, all thought of his mysterious adventure in Little Bourke Street.

He had boarded the Martah at Melbourne without any further misadventure, and before they had reached Adelaide had chummed up with another young fellow about his own age, the son of a station owner going "home" for a trip. Harry and his new friend, Dick Roberts, had many things in common, and in the discussion of the matters appertaining to sheep and cattle, neither paid any attention to a certain high caste Chinaman who joined the Martah at Adelaide.

"By Jove," remarked Dick, as the Celestial came aboard, "the Chinese are certainly coming along, Graham! Look at this fellow coming aboard. He's dressed like a Cabinet Minister."

"He is that!" laughed Harry. "He's probably in the Chinese

diplomatic service, or else a merchant. By the way, which method of 'marking' lambs do you prefer —cutting or burning?"

And the conversation branched off again to the eternal sheep.

Little did Harry dream that the well-dressed Chinaman gloried in the name of Chan, and that less than forty-eight hours previously he had not only assisted in the mysterious assault on Harry, but had even entered Scott's Hotel in the very suit that young man now wore.

The Martah was going by way of the Cape, and after leaving Adelaide, the chronic disturbance of the treacherous "Bight"[1] kept a large number of the passengers below, including Chan. But after the last point of Australia was left astern, and the steady boat started on the straight run across the Indian Ocean to Durban, the passengers began to gradually make their appearance, looking pale and sheepish.

Harry and Dick were both good sailors, and in the tearing gale which hit them half-way across to Durban, they were among the very few who kept the deck, the majority once more forced to keep their cabins.

For two days the gale raged as though determined to sweep before it any ships who dared to brave its might. The lack of wireless made it impossible for them to know how other ships might be faring, and, indeed, the captain of the Martah had his hands full to look after his own ship.

About midnight of the second day the gale seemed to gather itself together for one final, terrific blast. After a momentary lull, it came on with redoubled force, and the staunch steamer reeled under the shock of its attack. Overhead an occasional cold star could be seen, only to be blotted out almost immediately by the scudding clouds. All around, the sea boiled and tossed and churned, each terrific wave throwing the ship into the air like a cork.

For a bare second she rested on the crest, her propeller racing madly before she took the plunge down the watery elope. Down, down, down she went, and it seemed certain that she must plunge straight down through these boiling, white-fringed waters into the black, cold depths beneath. But, true to her nature, the bow took the next slope, and the mountainous wave which threatened to be her pall broke in crushing thunder over her bow.

---

[1] The Great Australian Bight is a large oceanic bight, or open bay, off the central and western portions of the southern coastline of mainland Australia.    /drf

Harry and his friend stood in the shelter of the promenade deck, braving the driving rain, and shouting to each other in the teeth of the howling wind, watching in fascination the boat's brave fight against the raging elements.

They stood, balancing unconsciously as the ship rested on the crest of the wave, and then swayed back as she took the plunge.

"By Jove, Graham," shouted Roberts, "she seems to be going straight down when she takes that plunge!"

"Yes," shouted back Dick. "But she's game. Besides, she's head on, and —"

They were at that moment on the crest of another monstrous roller, and the racing of the propellers reached their ears as they whirled in the air several feet out of the water. Dick's remark broke off as the noise of the racing changed to a peculiar whistling noise, accompanied by a crash, and as the ship took the plunge and started up again, she veered suddenly, and for a breathless moment heeled over on her side as though she had finally given up the struggle.

"Something wrong!" cried Harry. "It was aft. Let's make our way back and see what it is."

Dick nodded, reserving his strength for the struggle of the trip.

As they made their way slowly along, several seamen in oilskins staggered past them towards the poop, and when the two friends arrived there they saw a circle of anxious faces.

"As near as I can make out," a seaman was shouting to the drenched mate, "one propeller has gone, and has smashed the rudder. She don't answer to the wheel at all, sir!"

The mate nodded, and began rapping out a shower of orders. The Martah was now side on to the seas, and each time they sank into the trough, Harry expected it to be the last.

All hands had been ordered up, and a spar dragged aft. By the light of several lanterns they started to work to fit up a temporary rudder, apparently oblivious of the fact that they stood a good chance of being swamped before they succeeded.

Of the succeeding work and racking anxiety which followed, it is not necessary to speak in detail. The temporary rudder, after several attempts, had been fixed, and all that it was possible to do was to keep her head to the gale and watch out for a passing steamer to give them help.

It was a week later that the look-out sighted a steamer wallowing along with the tail end of the gale. She was battered, but sound, and was bound for Adelaide.

It galled the captain to seek her assistance and return to Australia, but he had passengers to consider, and decided the sacrifice must be made. Consequently, when Harry Graham ought to have been reaching Durban, he was on his way back to Australia, chafing at the delay in his plans, but thankful at their escape.

And that day was the same date on which Sexton Blake took up the case of the Diamond Dragon, and the attack on Rymer.

Once again that curious ruling was playing with the puppets called men, and yet another was swept within the web.

That other was Tinker, Sexton Blake's assistant. Tinker had taken the day off in order to attend a programme of sports, and, consequently, was not at Baker Street when Wang Ho called on Sexton Blake and persuaded him to take on the search for the Diamond Dragon.

Tinker got back to Baker Street just after Blake had departed for the theatre, and, being tired from his long day, not to mention hoarse from incessant cheering, he curled up in the armchair, with Pedro at his feet in order to await his master's return. In less than five minutes he was fast asleep, and Pedro, following Tinker's lead, blinked a bloodshot eye around the consulting-room, and slumbered also.

It was several hours later when Pedro bounded to his feet with a growl, and Tinker awoke suddenly as the bell from the street door rang furiously. Still dazed from sleep, Tinker stumbled yawning along the passage, and opened the door.

On the step stood three alert-looking young men with reporter stamped all over them, and each held in his hands an evening paper still odorous and damp from the press.

One of them knew Tinker, and addressed him by name. His grave tones filled the lad with a vague fear of impending trouble, and he bade them enter.

When they had entered the consulting-room he saw by the light that their faces were as grave as their tones, and he turned sharply.

"What is it, Mr. Wallace?" he said quickly, addressing the reporter whom he knew. "Do you wish to see Mr. Blake?"

"Don't you know the report, Tinker?" asked the reporter, in surprised tones.

"The report! What report." exclaimed Tinker, taking a step

forward. "What do you mean, Mr. Wallace?"

"Steady, my lad," replied the young man. "I'm afraid you don't know. You must prepare yourself for a shock. We thought you would know long ago, and we came here for confirmation."

"Came here for confirmation; thought I'd know long ago," echoed Tinker. "My heavens, Mr. Wallace, it isn't anything about the guv'nor, is it?" he cried.

The young reporter was a little older than Tinker, and never before had he been in such a position. Like every journalist in London, he knew what Tinker was to Sexton Blake, and how much the lad thought of his master and friend.

But he had not dreamt that the news of Blake's murder was unknown to the lad, and he hardly knew how to break it to him. His two companions were similarly embarrassed, and each moment that passed increased Tinker's fears.

"What is it, Mr. Wallace?" he cried, seeing the reporter's hesitation. "Tell me please. If the guv'nor has had an accident I will go to him at once."

"Prepare yourself for a great shock, my poor lad!" said the reporter, in husky tones. "It is about your master, and he has met with an accident —a very great accident, my lad. But here is the paper. Read for yourself, and bear up, Tinker. It may not be correct, you know."

But his words did not carry conviction, and even if they had Tinker would not have heard them. He had snatched the paper, and, with heaving chest and blurred vision, was reading the sensational report of Blake's "murder" in a taxi. He was still trying to grasp the details of the awful report, when the telephone began ringing, and one of the reporters took upon himself to answer it.

"Yes —yes," he said, "this is Sexton Blake's! Yes! Oh, I don't know! There are three of us up here now trying to confirm the report. Yes, this is Willis, of the 'Gazette.' Oh, you can come along if you wish, but Tinker knew nothing of it until we told him, and we haven't been able to confirm it yet. Right-ho! Good-bye!" And he rang off.

"It was Hanson, of the 'Telegraph,'" he said, turning around. "He wanted to know if the report were true, but —"

He broke off, and leapt to his feet, as Tinker, with a choking gurgle, dropped to the floor in a dead faint, the paper with the fatal news clutched tightly in his hand. For the next few moments those three pushing reporters, trained to harden themselves to emotion, and only to get news, put aside their notebooks, and worked valiantly over Tinker, while Pedro stood puzzled, not knowing whether to treat them as friends or foes.

It was some minutes before Tinker revived, and looked up with eyes of horror.

"Tell me, Mr. Wallace," he whispered hoarsely— "tell me, did I read that awful report about the guv'nor, or did I dream it? Oh, it can't be true —it can't. The guv'nor, strong and well and good, to be murdered in a cab. I won't believe it. It's a lie!"

He lurched to his feet and sank heavily into a chair at the desk. Another peal came at the bell, and Wallace opened it to admit two more reporters.

"It's no use coming up," he said, as he admitted them. "Tinker knows nothing. Do any of you know the address of the doctor who looked after him?"

"No; we just came from the theatre. They say he was taken to the Central Hospital."

"Well, can't you find out anything there?" asked Wallace.

"No," replied the new arrival. "He never arrived there, and there seems to be a confusion of names in the doctor's address. However, we've sent a man to look that up."

While he was speaking the telephone rang again, and at a nod from Tinker, the reporter answered it.

It was another inquiry for confirmation of the report; this time from Scotland Yard, but like the previous inquirer, they were disappointed. Barely had the reporter hung up the receiver when another ring came at the street door.

Wallace went to answer it, and hesitated for a moment before admitting a tall, elderly, well-dressed gentleman who stood there. His flowing silver beard and immaculate silk hat impressed the reporter, who scented the possibility of news, and the old gentleman's first words on entering the consulting-room strengthened that anticipation. Turning to Tinker, the new arrival addressed the lad in grave tones:

"Are you Master Tinker, Sexton Blake's assistant?" he asked, in pleasant, mellow tones.

"Yes, sir," replied Tinker, rising, his voice shaky, and his eyes bloodshot.

"And those gentlemen?" inquired the old gentleman, waving his hands at the attentive reporters.

"They are reporters, sir," answered Tinker, "but if you came to see Mr. Blake, sir," blurted out the lad brokenly, "I'm afraid —you can't!"

"I didn't," replied the old man, and not one of those sharp reporters saw his eyes soften at Tinker's emotion. "I came to see you, Master Tinker, and wish to speak to you privately. If you will excuse us for a few moments, gentlemen," he added, turning to the reporters, "I will on my return give you some news of interest."

"About Sexton Blake;" they cried, in a chorus, and Tinker looked up startled.

"I will say nothing yet," replied the old man, smiling faintly at their eagerness. "I have business first with the lad. Be patient!"

Wonderingly, Tinker turned and led the way into the adjoining room, and the old gentleman closed the door carefully after them.

"It's all right, my lad," he said, in a low tone, putting his hand on Tinker's shoulder. "They didn't get me this time, but almost. I didn't want my reporter friends outside to know, however, that I am uninjured, and would have made my announcement before only for your very evident suffering."

"You, guv'nor?" gasped Tinker, as he recognised Blake's voice. "Oh, I can tell now. I didn't recognise you through that disguise. Oh, guv'nor, it gave me such a shock!" he said, in trembling tones. "I thought it might be true."

Blake's eyes were wet as well as the lad's, but he only smiled and patted Tinker's shoulder.

"There, lad, forget it; I'm still safe and sound, and hope they won't get me yet, anyrate. But come, we must return to the consulting-room. Say nothing, and leave the reporters to me."

He turned and led the way back to the consulting-room, and stood facing the impatient reporters, who stood with notebooks ready, eager to dash back to their papers with an account of the affair.

"Gentlemen," said Blake, returning to his assumed tones, "I have read the report of Sexton Blake's murder, and, in fact, have been with Mr. Blake all the evening. It is true an attempt was made to murder Mr. Blake, but happily it failed, and for the time being he still lives."

"Then he is in danger?" they cried.

"I think I may say he is in danger," answered the kind old man, which was strictly true, for hardly a minute of the day or night went by that Sexton Blake's life was not in danger of some kind. "However," he went on, "if he grows worse bulletins will be issued, but if he grows better that will not be done. He is not in a hospital, and his whereabouts, at his own request, will be kept secret. That is all I can say, gentlemen, but what I have told you comes direct from Sexton Blake himself."

He waved aside with a smile their shower of questions, and seeing nothing more was to be elicited, they one and all condoled with Tinker, and left at top speed to get the latest authentic report in their paper.

"Thank Heaven!" sighed Blake, wearily sinking into the big chair and removing his disguise. "I'm fagged out, but I knew the place would be invaded with reporters, and prepared for them at the Embassy."

"But, guv'nor, is this report of the attack on you true?" asked Tinker.

Blake nodded

"Yes, all too true," he said grimly. "It was a new dodge to me, and a minute longer would have achieved their purpose."

"But who was it, guv'nor?"

Blake leaned back and lit a cigar before replying. Then he drew from his pocket the thin silken cord which had almost succeeded in accomplishing its purpose. He held it up, and Tinker's eyes opened.

"That, my lad," said Blake, slowly puffing his cigar— "that was what they used. The nationality of the man who used that is stamped all over the attempt. Can't you guess, Tinker?"

"Oh, I think so, guv'nor!" replied Tinker, holding out his hand for the cord. "It would be a Chinaman, wouldn't it?"

Blake nodded.

"But, guv'nor," went on Tinker wonderingly. "What Chinaman has such a grudge against you? We aren't working on any Chinese case at present."

"Aren't we?" smiled Blake.

"Are we, guv'nor?" asked Tinker, in surprise.

"My lad," said Blake, "while you were shouting yourself hoarse at the sports to-day many things have happened."

"I should think so!" muttered Tinker, thinking of the attempted murder.

"This afternoon," went on Blake, not heeding his remark, "I took on a Chinese case, and the attempt to murder me is a direct outcome of that. It bids fair to be one of the most important and at the same time most dangerous cases we have had for some time. That is why I wish to let the general public believe that I am lying at the point of death. If the people who made the attempt on me believe that, I can work with less danger, but on the other hand, if not, it will be a continual risk. And you, Tinker, will from this minute be running a great risk as well, so let me warn you now to keep your eyes open.

"Now, lad, sit down here and I'll review the case aloud as far as I know it myself. That will serve the double purpose of posting you on matters and refresh the details in my mind. Firstly, though, get the 'Index D.' Find 'Diamond Dragon,' and read what it says, then you'll understand better."

Tinker did as he was bid, and rapidly ran his eye over the same particulars which Blake bad read earlier in the day.

"All right, guv'nor," he said, after a few minutes, as he closed the "Index" and returned it. "I'm ready now."

Blake briefly sketched the main points of the case which he had gathered from Wang Ho. Then he ran over his movements from the time he had left for the theatre, when the attempt on his life had been made.

"So you see, my lad," he said as he finished, "as far as I can tell now there are two equally strong forces of Chinamen straining every nerve to secure the Diamond Dragon. That Hang Lee's agents know of Wang Ho's duplicity and are hot on the trail, is proved by the attack on me in the taxi. At present I haven't the faintest idea as to the identity of the English criminal who now possesses the Dragon, and Hang Lee, the powerful head of the monarchists, has the advantage of us, for he knows who the man is.

"That the thief is either on his way to London, or in London, is certain, for the activity of Hang Lee's agents prove that. That means we must look for the Dragon here. I wouldn't be surprised if the matter is important enough to bring Hang Lee himself to London, for it has proved urgent enough to bring Li Hong here, and, if anything, he is more powerful, and certainly a more important personage, than Li Hong.

"If it were a simple case between European and Chinese, it would present fewer complications; but it is war to the death between the Chinese themselves, with the added complications of an European, and I think —Yes, I really think, my lad, every resource and every cunning of the deepest, shrewdest minds will be brought to bear on this matter. Any who are caught in the toils will meet a swift fate, and I shudder to think of the fate of him who is caught with the sacred Diamond Dragon in his possession.

"But now for my plans. In order to prosecute the investigation, it will be necessary for me to assume my old Chinese disguise and live their life with them in Chinatown. Tonight I will assume it, and leave by the back-way, late. It will be necessary for you, my lad, to keep on watch every moment, for you may get a message of instructions from me at any hour of the night or day."

"But, guv'nor, it will be mighty risky living with them there. Your accent and disguise is perfect, but how about when you are asleep? An accident might give you away, and their move to-night shows they won't stop at much."

Blake laughed.

"That is just the reason why I am going to beard them in their den. It will be a chase worth while if old Hang Lee should come to London, and their attack to-night bears the earmarks of Hang Lee's decision and promptness. The old man knows me, and he will do all he can to beat me. But while I change, Tinker, jot down the notes of what I have given you, and get everything fixed in your mind. You must have every detail perfect, for in this case we are pitted against the very source of cunning."

Blake tossed away his cigar as he finished giving Tinker his directions, and rose to go and adopt the famous Chinese disguise which many times before had served him well in the Chinese quarter of almost every large town, not to mention China itself.

He opened the dressing-room door, and took a few steps, feeling along the wall for the electric-switch. His hand felt the button, and was just about to turn it, when an almost imperceptible rustle sounded to his left. He turned sharply and reached again for the button, but out of the darkness descended the heavy butt-end of a Colt revolver, and for the second time that night Blake dropped unconscious.

His assailant intended taking no chance this time, and from the loose folds of a Chinese jacket he drew a long, crooked kriss one of those terribly deadly knives so favoured among the Malay pirates. Stooping, he felt the unconscious Blake, in order to locate his heart, when the door, which had not been fully closed, burst open, and, with a fierce, low growl, Pedro sprang straight for the throat of Blake's assailant.

Tinker had begun jotting down his notes as Blake left the consulting-room, and so silently had the Chinaman worked, that he had not heard anything suspicious in the adjoining room. But as Pedro lifted his head and sniffed suspiciously, and then had dashed at the door of the dressing-room, Tinker leaped to his feet.

"Here, I say, Pedro, what's the matter?" he exclaimed, following the dog. "It's only the guv'nor, and —"

But by that time Pedro was through the door, and, by the light which shone in from the consulting-room, Tinker saw, with a gasp of horror, what had happened.

The Chinaman had leaped back as Pedro sprang, and his alacrity barely saved him. As Pedro's teeth grazed his throat, he lunged with all his strength at the great body as it flashed past him; but Tinker had followed Pedro closely, and before the knife reached its mark he knocked up the Chinaman's hand, and, weaponless as he was, grappled for the possession of that deadly blade with his naked hands.

Pedro had stopped his rush and turned as Tinker and the Chinaman grappled. The powerful beast renewed the attack. He leaped again for the Chinaman, and this time, when the jaws came together they met on the Chinaman's arm which held the knife.

He gave a yell of pain as Pedro's teeth sank in, and the knife dropped with a clatter from the nerveless hand. Tinker released his hold and stooped for the knife; but his antagonist, mad with pain, and burdened with Pedro's weight as he was, made for the window, whose open condition told how he had entered.

With Pedro still clinging to his arm, he partly fell, partly-crawled over the sill, and before Tinker could grapple again, he had reached up with his free hand and pulled the heavy window down with a jerk on Pedro's head, which was right underneath.

The shock forced Pedro to drop his hold, and the Chinaman, seizing his opportunity leaped to the ground and dashed away.

Pedro, nothing daunted, tried to follow; but the panting Tinker, seeing a chase would be almost hopeless, and not knowing the extent of Blake's injuries, called the brave fellow back.

Tinker hastened to the switch and turned on the light.

Blake lay as he had fallen, one arm bent under him and the other still stretched out in the direction of the switch.

With feverish haste Tinker procured some brandy and water. Forcing a stiff dose of the raw spirit between Blake's lips; he then bathed the detective's temples with the cold water. He heaved a sigh of relief as the unconscious man stirred and muttered brokenly.

"He's not dead, anyway!" muttered Tinker, renewing his efforts. "But if it hadn't been for you, old chap," he added, looking affectionately at Pedro, "he would have had that knife in his heart now."

Blake stirred again and opened his eyes.

"Why, what's the matter, Tinker?" he asked, in puzzlement. "Ah! Yes, I remember! Somebody was in here in the dark and tried to get me."

"They nearly succeeded, too!" replied Tinker grimly. "How's that for an attempt?" And he picked up the long, crooked-bladed knife.

"Ah! A kriss!" said Blake, sitting up. "So it was our Chinese friends again —eh? And they know already that their attack in earlier in the evening failed. By thunder, things are getting a bit too hot!" he snapped, his eyes flashing. "They seem to be playing all the cards, and I think it's about time we dealt a hand, or we won't get a chance. How did you stop him, Tinker, and what became of him?"

"I didn't stop him, guv'nor. I never heard a sound. It was Pedro, dear old chap. He was through the door and at the fellow's throat before I heard a sound."

Blake stretched out a hand and placed it on Pedro's head.

"Go on!" he said briefly. "What happened then?"

Tinker told him what had occurred, and how the Chinaman had got away.

"But it shows you haven't over-estimated them, guv'nor," he concluded.

"No; of course not!" said Blake, a trifle testily, for the repeated attempts on his life were rousing his anger and his fighting blood. "But Diamond Dragon or no Diamond Dragon," he muttered savagely as he got stiffly to his feet, "I'll stick to this thing now until I pay out my mysterious assailants for their attentions to me."

At that moment the street-bell rang, and Tinker looked inquiringly at Blake.

"Answer it," he said grimly, reading the look, "but have your revolver handy, Tinker, in case it is any more of our Celestial friends. Be on your guard."

Tinker secured his revolver, and with Pedro at his heels, hurried along the passage and threw open the door. But instead of further enemies, it was a messenger-boy with a telegram for Blake, and he thrust his revolver back in his pocket as he took it and closed the door.

"Telegram, guv'nor!" he announced on reaching the consulting-room.

Blake reached out for it and tore it open. He read the words over twice, and then tossed it over to Tinker.

"Read it, and file it away!" he said rising. "I'll not leave to-night. I'll get some sleep instead. You'd better turn in as well."

"All right, guv'nor! I will as soon as I finish my notes. Is this important?" he asked, referring to the telegram.

"I don't know," sighed Blake, as he departed. "I'll let you see her first when she calls."

As the door closed. Tinker read the telegram again.

"Must see you, please, on very urgent matter. Will be grateful if you will be in tomorrow-morning at nine."

"GRACE LANSING."

"H'm!" he muttered as he filed it away. "I wonder what she wants? I think, from the pace at which things are moving, we've got about all we can handle!"

### THE SIXTH CHAPTER.  Won's Failure —Grace Calls on Sexton Blake —"It's Gone!"

HIS MAJESTY'S mail proved a much safer and much quicker carrying agent than either Harry Graham or Dr. Huxton Rymer, for although Harry had lost his little piece of pencil in Melbourne, and Rymer lost his in New York, the registered package which Harry had addressed to Grace Lansing, and which contained his draft and the Diamond Dragon arrived safely, having come by the same fast mail steamer which had brought that old Celestial, Hang Lee.

Had the old Chinaman known that the Diamond Dragon was so near to him for the whole journey, and yet so impossible to get at, it is hard to say what scheme his cunning brain would have conceived to reach it. But he was saved this exercise of his brain, for he was in ignorance of the fact.

But he had at least one controlling string in his wrinkled yellow hands, for he had gained possession of one half of the lead pencil, and even if Won failed to get the other half from Rymer, and that son of a pig succeeded in presenting it to Graham, Harry could not deliver up the Diamond Dragon without his own half.

Having been broken, and not cut, the broken ends of the pencil were jagged, and without his half to see if the piece presented fitted all right, it would be impossible for Harry Graham to tell whether the half presented were really the genuine half or not.

The method of the broken pencil, which Rymer had adopted instead of a written receipt, was well known to Hang Lee, and when Tommy, the Chinese gardener, had mentioned the fact, he knew at once what it meant. For in his young days, many, many years ago, when piracy was rampant in the China Sea and the Malacca Straits, Hang Lee, a leading light in the piracy game, had often adopted the same method with his confederates, only then he had used a piece of broken bamboo instead of a pencil.

Consequently his knowledge of the method, and his further knowledge of the integrity of Englishmen of Harry Graham's class, told him that the piece he had secured gave him a certain advantage, for he knew that Harry would not give up the package until both halves had been produced.

With his true capacity for building only on certainties, he laid his plans, without counting on Won securing the other half from Rymer.

If he did, so much the better, for then he would hold a still stronger hand in the game.

On his arrival in London he had gone at once to a certain quiet, shuttered house in the Chinese quarter in Limehouse. Not even the denizens of that murky district knew that the quiet old Chinaman was the powerful and dreaded Hang Lee himself. Only his agents were well aware of this, and there was little chance of it leaking out from them.

Hang Lee had wasted no time in getting down to business. In a back-room behind the opium den, which was the chief excuse the shuttered house had for existing, he sat with the same inscrutable expression, rolling his eternal yellow cigarettes, and listening without comment to the reports of his agents. But for the difference in the appearance of the two rooms, he might have been sitting in the secret room above the gambling den in Little Bourke Street, and certainly the old Celestial gave no indication that he had just arrived from the other side of the globe.

There, while he smoked and smoked, he listened to the report of Wang Ho's movements. The next man informed him of the real identity of the man whom Sexton Blake had gone to see at the Embassy, and who passed under the name of Li Hong.

For a bare second Hang Lee's eyes narrowed to slits, and his wrinkled face grew, if possible, even more wrinkled, but he made no comment on what must have been a stupendous surprise to him. A third came hurrying in with the information that Wang Ho that very afternoon had gone up to see Sexton Blake; and a fourth, who had been keeping watch on Grace Lansing's home, reported that the postman had that afternoon delivered a brown-paper package which corresponded to the description which Hang Lee had cabled from Melbourne, of the package Chan and Won had seen Harry Graham address in the Melbourne post-office.

After hearing the last report, which placed him in possession of all that had happened in London, the old Chinaman waved them away, and smoked in solitude for an hour.

No one knew that he was in London except his trusted agents, and no one seemed to imagine he would come, except Sexton Blake. Blake had intuitively felt that the Diamond Dragon might be magnet enough to draw the old Celestial to London; and be it said that Hang Lee's concentration was at that moment not centred on the great Li

Hong, the traitorous Wang Ho, the unsuspecting Harry Graham, or Grace Lansing, nor the Rymer who had dared to steal the Sacred Dragon, but on a man who as yet knew only a few points in the matter—the great detective, Sexton Blake.

Hang Lee knew what to expect from Li Hong and Wang Ho. It would be Oriental cunning of the deepest, yes; but there were no points in that game which Hang Lee didn't know, and he could fight them with their own weapons. To Harry Graham and Grace Lansing he gave no thought, but Sexton Blake was different. He had felt the temper of Blake's steel once in China, and he realised, with the true insight which made him such a dangerous foe, that the biggest danger-flag flew over Sexton Blake. That being so, the biggest danger must be wiped out first, and with a grunt he tapped on the floor with his foot.

The door opened to admit one of his Celestials who had previously reported to him, and Hang Lee motioned to him to draw near.

"You say you saw that traitorous dog Wang Ho go to Sexton Blake's?"

"Yes, Excellency."

"You know Sexton Blake when you see him?"

"Oh, well, Excellency!"

"Have you a man watching his house?"

"Yes, Excellency."

"Very well. Go at once, and don't lose sight of Sexton Blake for a moment. He must be dealt with at once. You understand? Kill him! Whether it be in his house or in the street I do not care, but don't fail."

"I will do as you command Excellency."

"See that you do!" replied Hang Lee. "You won't find it as easy as you anticipate; but, remember, I want him put out of the way."

"It will be done, Excellency."

"Very well. Go! Let me know at once when you have accomplished it."

The Chinaman backed out, and once more Hang Lee sank into meditation. He was roused by a faint knock at the door, and, grunting permission to enter, he looked up to see Won enter. For once the old Chinaman permitted himself to smile, but only himself knew what about.

"You have succeeded?" he said, without greeting, as though Won had merely been round the corner to surreptitiously buy some opium, instead of chasing a man half round the globe.

"Yes, Excellency," replied Won in a low tone. "I succeeded in New York."

He held out the broken piece of pencil which he had secured from Rymer, and Hang Lee laid it down on the table beside him.

"What did you do with him?" he asked.

Won made a comprehensive movement with his hands, which was evidently understood by Hang Lee, for he nodded slowly.

"Good, Won; you do well. From now you will enter the upper council."

Won bowed, but little did his attitude suggest that he had that moment achieved the ambition of his life. To sit in the upper council and assist in the plans of the organisation of which Hang Lee was the head was indeed an honour and a fitting reward for his successful work. But any glowing thoughts that filled his yellow head were quickly cast aside as Hang Lee spoke again. He picked up the piece of pencil which Won had brought from New York and held it out.

"Take this," he said, "and wear the European garments you have on. Go to the address of this Englishwoman" —and he held out Grace's address, which Chan had secured in Melbourne. "Tell her you gave Graham a package in Melbourne for safe keeping, which was to be delivered to you on presentation of this piece of pencil. He is supposed to have the other, and she will probably object. But tell her it is urgent. Describe what is in the packet, if necessary. Do your best to get it. She may be persuaded to give it up. If not, get it in some way. It seems certain that the Diamond Dragon is in that packet."

"Very well, Excellency, I will go at once," replied Won, as he tucked the piece of pencil in his pocket. With a bow he departed, and Hang Lee again buried himself in smoke while he awaited the result of his latest moves.

Won lost no time in calling on Grace Lansing, and that young lady looked up in astonishment as the well-dressed Celestial was ushered in.

"I must apologise," said Won in almost perfect English as he bowed. "I would not have intruded on you, Miss Lansing, before the arrival of my dear friend Mr. Graham, but the matter is urgent, and as I see by the papers his ship was compelled to put back to Australia, I took the liberty of calling."

Grace, who had been inclined to be a trifle frigid at first, thawed when she heard him refer to Harry Graham as his dear friend.

"Won't you be seated, Mr. Won?" she smiled pleasantly, glancing at the card she held. "For what reason did you wish to see me?"

Won bowed again and sat down.

"I will be brief, Miss Lansing," he said. "In Australia, just before my dear friend Mr. Graham left for England, a mutual friend, Dr. Hutton, gave to him for safe keeping a little packet which he was to post to England for him. At the time I did not expect to be able to get away, or I would have brought it myself, but unexpectedly found it possible, and came by way of America.

"On my arrival here I looked up at once to see if his ship had arrived, and saw with surprise that it had been compelled to put back to Australia on account of the gale. When Dr. Hutton gave him the packet, Miss Lansing instead of a receipt he broke a pencil in half, giving Mr. Graham one piece, and keeping the other himself.

"In case Dr. Hutton was unable to claim the packet personally, he was to send his piece of the pencil, and the bearer was to receive the packet."

Here Won smiled an expansive smile, redolent of innocence, as he felt in his pocket, although he was watching Grace as a cat watches a mouse, to see how she took the story. He took out the piece of pencil and held it up.

"Here it is, you see, Miss Lansing. Dr. Hutton gave me this before I left Australia, and as the packet must have reached here by now, I will be greatly obliged if you will give it up to me. I would have preferred waiting until my dear friend himself arrived, but it is important."

Grace was in a state of doubt. Won's story certainly had the ring of sincerity in it, but in one little point it disagreed with the letter Harry had enclosed in the packet. This she was sure of; hadn't she read it over and over, and didn't she know it word for word? And while Won fished for the piece of pencil, she rapidly ran over the letter in her mind.

"Darling girl," it had run, "just a note to tell you the glorious news. Have won the capital prize. Tat's lottery, and am sailing the day after to-morrow on the Martah for dear old England. The prize is ten thousand, darling, and in case anything should happen, I am sending the draft by registered post to you. Am enclosing a packet which a chap by the name of Hutton gave me to bring to England for him. He acted so mysteriously over the whole business that I have decided to post it, too, as I've got an idea it must be valuable.

"He broke a pencil in half, and gave me one half, and kept the other half himself. Odd, wasn't it? It seems a silly idea to me. I'm not to deliver the packet to anyone unless the half of the pencil they present fits with the broken half I have. I'm not sending that to you, but am sticking it in my luggage. Take care of the jolly things for me like a good girl until I arrive, which I hope will be sharp to the minute. If you can, meet me at the dock. I'm crazy to see you again. —With heaps of love, in haste,

"HARRY."

Yes, she knew it word for word. But the discrepancy was in Won's statement that Dr. Hutton had asked Harry to post the packet, and Harry's statement in the letter that Dr. Hutton had asked him to bring the packet. From Harry's letter she gathered that the posting was entirely his own idea, and, besides, how did she know the piece of pencil this Chinaman held matched the piece Harry had.

No, the man's story might be all right, but it certainly looked odd, and whoever owned the packet would have to wait until Harry himself arrived. As she came to this decision she looked up at the still smiling Won.

"That piece of pencil may be the right piece, and it may not, Mr. Won," she said, looking straight at him. "But, in the first place, I can't prove it, for I haven't the other piece, and in any event I would not deliver the packet until Mr. Graham himself arrived."

"Then the packet has come?" asked Won, smiling.

Grace flushed with chagrin, for she had meant to be entirely non-committal about the arrival of the packet. But she knew that the Chinaman read the truth in her eyes, so she passed it off lightly,

"Oh, yes, a packet has come, but I will send it on to the bank until Mr. Graham arrives. I am sorry to disappoint you. Mr. Won, but I really can't do as you ask."

"I am sorry, too, Miss Lansing," said Won, hiding his disappointment at not finding the English girl as plastic as he hoped. "But I suppose I must wait until my friend arrives. However" —and he laughed carelessly— "I don't think I'd trouble to send the packet to the bank. It's not valuable in that way, and would do no one any good. It's only valuable to the owner."

He rose as he spoke, and bowed, and Grace wrinkled her brows as she walked to the window and watched his retreating figure down the street.

"He may be genuine, and he may not," she said to herself, "but I'm not going to deliver that packet to anyone until Harry arrives. There comes a messenger boy. I wish he were coming here with a message from Harry. What a nuisance his old ship having to put back. But I suppose I ought to be very thankful it was no worse. Oh, that boy is coming here! I do hope it is news from Harry."

Grace waited expectantly until the maid entered with a cable on a tray, and her heart leaped.

"It is —it is from Harry!" she gasped, tearing it open. It was very brief, and very different from what she expected.

"Am starting again. Pencil stolen from luggage. Deliver packet nobody; any excuse. —Love,

"HARRY."

That was all, and Grace read over the words again and again, hardly able to believe her eyes.

"Oh," she breathed, her eyes flashing, "if this had only arrived while that suave Celestial was here I'd have given him a shock! But I wonder what can be in this wonderful packet? Perhaps I really ought to send it to the bank. I'll just go up and take it out of my dressing-table, anyway, and lock it in my trunk"

She left the room, and ran lightly up the stairs to her bedroom. After pressing her lips to the cable, she tucked it inside her dress, and then approached the dressing-table. Opening the drawer, she drew out the packet, which, though untied, was still wrapped loosely in the brown paper. The draft had been already locked away with Harry's letter, but she had thrust the leather packet away without looking at it.

As she undid the paper and reached in, her hand hit the corner of the dressing-table, and she gave a smothered exclamation as the packet fell heavily to the floor, flying off as it did so. Reaching down, she picked tip the leather belt and peculiar-shaped pouch, and her brow wrinkled with concern as she saw the fall had broken the seals.

The flap was hanging open, but she did not see it as she was holding the pouch by the bottom. As she began to roll it up again, the weight of the heavy Diamond Dragon forced the flap open, and before she had noticed it, the great gold Dragon, studded with its myriad of priceless, glittering gems crashed to the floor.

To say that Grace was amazed was to put it mildly. As her eyes fell on the blazing, scintillating Dragon, she gasped and gurgled inarticulately. Never in her wildest dreams had she ever imagined such a priceless collection of jewels could be brought together, and there before her very eyes lay the wonderful spectacle.

She dropped to her knees in speechless admiration, and, true daughter of Eve, lifted the huge cluster, and held it at different angles lost in amazement. But her first feeling of admiration gave place to one of intangible fear as she looked at the two gigantic solitaires which formed the Dragon's eyes. Circled as they were with emeralds, they seemed to gleam with a baleful light, and she turned away with a shudder.

"Ooh," she said nervously, "the thing seems to be almost alive! It frightens me. There must be something odd in such a thing being given to Harry to bring home. And —oh," she cried, as a sudden thought flashed across her mind, "that Chinaman said not to trouble sending it to the bank as it wasn't valuable! He lied, for it's worth untold wealth!"

As she lifted the glittering mass, and slipped it back in the leather case, her intangible feeling of fear intensified, and when she rose a vague, nameless dread had seized her.

"Oh, what shall I do?" she said distractedly. "I'm frightened. It's too late to take it to the bank to-day, and the Chinaman said not to do so. Oh, what can I do? Suppose they intend trying to get it from me. It may have some mysterious meaning that Harry knows nothing of, and we may both be in danger over the thing. Such a priceless article must have some hidden meaning, and such a peculiar shape —a dragon. Oh, I see it now! The dragon is the Chinese emblem, and that Chinaman wanted it. What can it mean?"

She was getting more nervous every minute, and by the time she had locked the packet away in her trunk she had worked herself into a state of nervous dread. For the rest of the afternoon Grace worried over the matter, and evening brought no relief. She had a tiny revolver, and decided to load it in case of anything occurring, when the thought of Sexton Blake flashed across her mind, and she jumped up with a cry. Her father was dead, and her mother, an invalid, rarely left her room, so, late though it was, Grace could manage to slip out without disturbing anyone.

Acting on her thoughts, she hurriedly donned a hat and coat, and then the thought that a pair of almond eyes might be watching outside made her quail. She took off her things, and, returning to the drawing-room, wrote busily for a few moments. Then, ringing, she sent for the house boy.

"Here, Briggs," she said, as that worthy made his appearance, "take this to the nearest office, and send it to this address. If you can't find an office open, take it to a messenger office, and send it from there. But be sure to send it urgent. Here is some money. Take a taxi and hurry, I will wait up until you return."

"Very well, miss," replied Briggs, "if I can't get it sent, I'll take it myself."

That Briggs was able to send it has been seen, for it was that urgent message, prompted by the events of the day, which led Grace to seek an interview with Sexton Blake.

Grace found sleep out of the question that night. She dozed by fits and starts, but the slightest sound sent her into a state of nervous fright, and she spent most of the interminable night sitting up staring with great frightened eyes into the darkness.

Morning, which seemed years in coming, finally made its appearance, and as the furniture took on ghostly, but friendly shape, in the grey, creeping dawn, she managed to snatch a little sleep. She was up betimes, however, and, barely touching her breakfast, was speeding along in a taxi by half-past eight in order to be prompt for her appointment. It was just on the stroke of nine when Grace rang the bell in Baker Street, and Tinker, according to Blake's instructions, received her in the consulting-room.

"You are Miss Lansing?" asked Tinker, as he drew up a chair for her.

"Yes," nodded Grace, "but, Mr. Blake, isn't he at home?"

"Er —I am his assistant Tinker, Miss Lansing, and am authorised to hear what your trouble is, providing you wish to tell me. Haven't you seen the morning papers regarding Mr. Blake?"

"No," replied Grace, looking puzzled. "I came straight here, and haven't seen a paper yet."

Tinker reached over, and picked up a morning paper from the desk.

"There it is," he said, pointing to a big headline, and passing it to Grace.

"Why!" she gasped. "Attempted Murder of Sexton Blake! Oh, how terrible!"

Rapidly she ran her eyes down the lines, which were a verbatim report of the statement issued the previous evening to the reporters by Blake himself, in the guise of the old professional man.

"I am awfully sorry to have troubled you," she said, handing the paper back. "I wouldn't have come had I known of this, but I am so worried. I don't know what to do."

"Would you care to tell me what it is?" asked Tinker.

"Oh, I don't know! I feel it will need the advice of Mr. Blake himself, and now I'll have to just wait. It relates to a packet which my fiance sent me from Australia, and since receiving it, there has been an attempt to get it by people who, I feel sure, are not the owners. I see its awful eyes everywhere!" And she shuddered.

"Its eyes," said Tinker, "what is it —an animal?"

"No; that is, not a real animal. It is a jewelled dragon; but, I will be going now, and thank you for your kindness."

Long training under Sexton Blake had taught Tinker to pretty well mask his emotions under any circumstances, and although he managed to conceal his amazement, he nearly fell out of his chair with surprise when Grace mentioned the jewelled dragon.

"Wait, please, Miss Lansing," he finally managed to jerk out, in fairly steady tones. "You say a jewelled dragon. Is it by any chance a gold dragon set with immense diamonds?"

"Yes, why?" exclaimed Grace, raising her brows in astonishment.

"Wait here for two minutes, please!" gurgled Tinker, as he slid from the chair and hurried to the laboratory where Blake sat smoking.

"Guv'nor, come quick!" gasped Tinker. "This Miss Lansing wants to see you about what she called a jewelled dragon, and crikey, I asked her if it was set with big diamonds, and she said yes! It must be the missing Diamond Dragon we are after!"

Blake was as amazed as Tinker, but made no comment as he rose and followed the lad back to the consulting-room.

"Good-morning, Miss Lansing!" he said, holding out his hand. "I must apologise for permitting you to get the impression that I was lying at death's door. I am on a very important case at present, and as an attempt was made last evening to murder me, I deemed it just as well to let that impression get abroad. It will make my investigations easier, and consequently I must ask you to keep it a strict secret that you have seen me."

"Oh of course I will, Mr. Blake!" smiled Grace. "I am so glad I have been able to see you! I am so worried."

"What is it?" asked Blake, seating himself. "My assistant says you mentioned something about a jewelled dragon."

"Yes, Mr. Blake; it is this way."

Grace gave Blake a detailed account of the packet which she had received from Harry Graham and the letter he had written. Then she told him of the Chinaman's call, and his attempt to gain possession of the packet by giving her the missing piece of pencil. Of Harry's cable, which arrived immediately after the Chinaman had taken his departure, and her subsequent accidental discovery of the real nature of the contents of the packet.

Blake's eyes glittered drily as he heard her story.

"Just answer me a few questions, Miss Lansing," he said, as she finished.

"Firstly, have you Mr. Graham's letter to you?"

"Yes, Mr. Blake, I brought it with me." She passed Harry's letter over, and silence reigned while Blake rapidly scanned the contents.

"H'm!" he remarked. "You are positive the Chinaman said this Dr. Hutton asked Graham to post the packet, not bring it?"

"Yes, positive."

"Was it after your final refusal that he suggested your not taking the trouble to send it to the bank?"

"Yes."

"Which end of the pencil was it the Chinaman presented?"

"It was the end which had been sharpened, although the point had been broken off."

"I see of course, Graham, doesn't mention which end he was given, so for the present that doesn't help much. Now listen, Miss Lansing. There are big forces at work to secure possession of this diamond dragon which you hold, and I think it best you should know that they will stop at nothing in order to get it. It happens that the attempt on my life was made by one of the parties, so you can see what they are prepared to do. It would be foolish to say your position is not dangerous, for it is. In some way they have discovered you have possession of the dragon, and will do all they can to get it away from you. My suggestion is that we go to your house, get the dragon, and put it in the bank until Mr. Graham arrives. Then leave matters to me, and I will see the proper owner gets it. Are you prepared to trust me to this extent?" asked Blake, looking up with a smile.

"Oh, of course, Mr. Blake!" exclaimed Grace. "I'm only too grateful for your trouble. It will take such a worry off my mind to feel you are looking after it!"

"Very well, Miss Lansing; I think we had better lose no time in carrying out our plan. They are quite capable of forestalling us. By the way, have you looked at it since yesterday?"

"No; I locked it away. It frightens me with its blazing green-rimmed eyes!"

"It's a pity it doesn't have the same effect on others!" laughed Blake, rising. "Excuse me for one moment while I make a few changes in my appearance. And one word more, Miss Lansing, don't breathe to a soul that I am mixed up in this matter. A great deal hangs on it!"

"I won't, I promise you!" replied Grace.

Blake bowed and entered the dressing-room, from which he emerged a few moments later with the same white beard he had worn the previous evening.

"Now, Miss Lansing!" he said; and Grace rose.

Grace ushered Blake into the drawing-room on their arrival at her house, and, telling him she wouldn't be a minute, ran lightly upstairs in order to get the dragon.

Five minutes passed before she returned, and when she did, Blake sprang forward with a sharp exclamation as he saw her deathly pale face and shaking hands.

"What is it?" he said quickly, supporting her.

Grace essayed to speak, and only after several attempts was able to gasp out:

"It's gone —it's gone!"

RYMER SUDDENLY SPRANG UPON THE CHINESE ATTENDANT.

THE CORD WAS DRAWN TIGHT CUTTING OFF HIS STARTLED EXCLAMATION.

SILENTLY HIS GUIDES LED HIM OUT INTO THE DARKNESS.

"HERE IT IS GRAHAM" LAUGHED HUTTON

## THE SEVENTH CHAPTER.   Rymer's Escape —In England — The Diamond Dragon Disappears.

WHEN Won and his two companions in New York lifted Rymer's bound, insensible body, and carrying it along the mud-walled passage, dumped it into the river, they felt quite certain in their deep, Celestial minds, that was the finish of the man who had dared to steal and trifle with the Sacred Diamond Dragon.

It will be remembered that a stone at the end of the underground passage opened over the waters of the East River, and through this opening, bound and still unconscious, had Rymer been thrust. But, instead of sinking like a stone and not coming up again, the cold plunge into the water revived him.

Still dazed from the blow, he had no idea what was happening to him. The rushing waters, which closed over his head, however, soon told their story, and, as his lungs threatened to burst as he went down, down into the black depths, he gave a few feeble twists of his body.

As he felt his downward course checked he struggled harder, and fought with all his will-power to hold out, when he realised he was rising slowly. His ears were full of a thundering roar, his eyes were starting from his head, and his lung's threatened each moment to burst.

If unconsciousness claimed him once more he knew that even the most slender chance was gone, and he gave one last spasmodic struggle as he felt his senses reeling.

But his last effort sent him up until his head came above the surface of the river, and as the blessed air rushed into his outraged lungs, he struggled again to keep afloat.

To make any headway was impossible. An expert swimmer, he knew every trick of the water, but with legs and arms bound, he realised his position was well-nigh hopeless. But life was dear to him, and that eternity of suspense in the water had frightened him. The thought of the great unknown beyond had inspired his last frantic struggle which had driven him to the surface.

Throwing himself on his back, he filled his lungs, and lay half afloat and half submerged, threatening each moment to sink, but kept partially afloat by the frail buoyancy of the air-filled lungs and his restricted twistings.

And, on the very brink of death, the current gradually seized him and carried him out into the middle of the river.

It was then that Fate took a hand, and in this case Fate was represented by the blazing spectacle of a burning warehouse at the edge of the river.

By the lurid glare which it cast out over the water could be seen the puffing, hurrying fire-tugs, which keep watch and ward over New York's river-front, and which do such effective work in the saving of lives and property.

Whistles were going on every side, and the engines on the shore got their water going almost simultaneously with those of the fire-tugs, the curving, whip-like streams meeting to form the apex of a thin watery arch, falling a moment later with a hissing roar into the seething inferno beneath.

Shooting about with hasty turnings, were several speedy motor-boats containing river-police, who darted into every spot in search of river thieves and scavengers, who, vulture-like, lurked about waiting for what chance or their own ability might give them from the burning warehouse.

It was into this hurrying, whistling, clanging pandemonium that the almost exhausted Rymer was carried by the current, whose edge had almost thrown its eddying grip about him.

On an ordinary night the almost submerged body would have passed without notice, any inward bound or outward going ship nosing it for a drifting log from a rotting wharf.

But Fate, in its prank, chose to send him into the glare cast by the burning warehouse, and as his numbed senses felt the heat, and his water-deafened ears heard the faint echoes of the pandemonium, he renewed his struggles, knowing that where such events were occurring there must be other human beings.

At first his efforts to raise his white face seemed doomed to disappointment, and he sank back again with a choking gurgle of despair.

His last shred of will-power was fading away; the rushing waters were claiming their prey, his feeble twistings stopped, and as he went under a roaring, crashing sound beat down his senses, and he remembered no more.

But a scurrying police-boat had seen that white face as it rose above the fire-lit surface of the water, and a sharp command had sent it tearing off its course in that direction. With a wide generous sweep it turned with canted gunwale, and came along broadside on the log-like body, which at that moment had gone under.

A blue-uniformed, peak-capped policeman bent over as they floated past, and before the sinking body had hardly left the surface his hand gripped Rymer's collar.

With a mighty heave he dragged it up and over the gunwale; the motor was again started, sending the boat on its interrupted errand, while Rymer's rescuer and another policeman began untying his bonds and giving first aid to the drowning.

No word was spoken until they had loosed his bonds and started to chafe his wrists.

"Something crooked here," growled Rymer's burly rescuer. "Evening clothes and well dressed. He's probably been slugged for his money."

"Yes," growled back the other; "and, take my word for it, it didn't happen far away. No man could float very far bound as he was, and by this bump on the back of his head, I guess his brain wasn't too active."

"That's a cinch," replied the first speaker; "and, believe me, I wouldn't be surprised if some of the yellow-faced pirates in those 'Chink' joints over there could throw some light on the matter. But his lordship is beginning to show signs of life. Give a hand here, Bill, and we'll turn him over. By the time he gets some of that water out of him, and a stiff swig of whisky into him, he'll feel better. Shove us over the flask, Bill."

"Bill" did so, and turning Rymer over, the other policeman poured a generous dose of the raw spirit between his lips.

Rymer grunted and opened his eyes, and, had the gunwale of the boat not thrown a shade over his face, his rescuers would have seen a quick look of fear fill his eyes as he saw the police uniform.

It passed almost at once, however, as he realised the reason he was where he was, and, with a low moan of pain as he lifted his pounding head, he sat up.

"Well, sir," exclaimed his rescuer, who gloried in the name of Pat Maloney, "you had a close shave of it this time."

"I did, officer." exclaimed Rymer huskily, "but, thanks to you, they didn't get me."

"They didn't get you?" said Maloney sharply. "Do you know who did it sir? We thought some of the Chinks had done it."

Rymer had been trying to gather his wits together for some plausible story to tell the police, and Maloney's remark gave him just the lead he wanted. Seizing on it, he nodded his head.

"You're right, officer. It was a couple of Chinks. They got me in a taxi near Houston Street, and took my roll. I don't remember what happened after that, but it's pretty easy to imagine."

"They're gettin' too fresh," growled Bill. "What they need is another raid."

"Aw, gwan!" snapped Maloney. "Little raids don't do no good. Until the chief makes a clean sweep they will flourish like the dirty yellow weeds they are. But if you can give us any idea where they took you, sir," he added, turning to Rymer, "I'll report it, and maybe we can grab some of them."

But Rymer had his own reasons for desiring as little publicity as possible, and he shook his head.

"I haven't the faintest notion, officer. I'm afraid I'll have to consider myself lucky to escape with my life. But I would be very grateful if you could set me ashore. My head is aching terribly, and these wet clothes aren't doing me any good."

"Sure, sir, we'll set you in at the nearest landing-stage. If it hadn't been for the fire yonder I guess you'd have been down with Davy Jones now," he concluded cheerily.

Rymer made no reply, but huddled against the gunwale, shivering. At that moment a flickering glare of the fire spread out as the roof fell in, and as the bottom of the little motor-boat was illuminated he gave a sharp exclamation.

For the first time he had seen his heelless shoes, and he knew only too well now the true reason of the attack upon him.

The policeman turned and regarded him curiously as he cried out, but he swallowed his feelings for the moment and smiled weakly.

"My head," he murmured. "I hit it against the side of the boat."

The policemen regarded him sympathetically, but made no comment, and a moment later the boat nosed the landing-steps.

Rymer stumbled out and felt in his pockets.

"They left me a little," he said, as he pulled out a small roll of wet bills. "It's lucky I had these in another pocket. Would you permit me to make you a little present?"

Maloney and Bill indicated that their permission would not have to be forced, and into their ready hands Rymer slipped a few wet notes.

"If you'll give me your name and address, sir," said Maloney, as he tucked the notes away, "I'll see what I can do about this affair, and let you know."

"Oh, it might as well be dropped now!" smiled Rymer, turning. "Thanks to you and the fire, I'm getting off with some lost money and a sore head, when I might have been at the bottom of the river. No; I think we'll say no more about it, officer. Good-night to you, and again thanks for your timely assistance."

"Don't mention it, sir!" they chorused. And Rymer walked briskly up the steps to search for a cab.

"I say, Pat," remarked Bill, as they pushed off and started the motor, "doesn't it strike you as funny that he had money on him? If it had been money they were after, they had him long enough to take all he had. And did you notice both heels of his shoes were missing? There's something deeper than just robbery, my son."

"Oh, shut up, Bill!" growled Pat. "What the blazes do we care? he treated us well enough."

And with this concrete remark they dismissed the matter from their minds.

Rymer walked past several warehouses before he was able to find a taxi, but just as he turned out of a narrow street he saw one and hailed it.

"The Breslin Hotel," he said, as he opened the door and sank back to give himself up to gloomy, foreboding thoughts.

"By heavens," he muttered, as he glanced once more down at his heelless shoes, "who would have thought such a thing? They must have had me spotted away back in Australia! But how in thunder? Oh, by heavens, I have it. That smooth Chink who crossed the Pacific with me, and said he was in the Diplomatic Service, must have been following me. Certainly the pencil is what they were after. Its discovery was no accident. But how on earth did anyone know I had it, and that it was of any value?

"By Jove, I wonder if that Chinaman in the pub yard saw me give young Graham the Dragon and break the pencil? This attack couldn't have emanated from young Graham. He left Australia before I did, and must be just about reaching England. No, it must have been that Chinaman. But who would have thought Hang Lee was so clever? By heavens, I'll have to reach England and get hold of that Dragon from

Graham as soon as he arrives. He'll give it to me, I guess, without the pencil.

"Oh, my head! They must have it in for me all right, and if it hadn't been for that police-boat I'd have been a goner."

He smiled grimly at the thought how little his late rescuers dreamed that the big-bearded man they had rescued was Dr. Huxton Rymer, wanted very much at Mulberry Street and Scotland Yard.

"Graham will wonder why I haven't got the pencil," he muttered, as the taxi pulled up in front of the Breslin, "but I can tell him I lost it. However, I'll have to get there before the man who has got that pencil, for I've just remembered I told Graham to deliver it to anyone, no matter who presented it. Oh, thunder," he groaned in a sudden wave of despair, "suppose they reach Graham first? He's so confoundedly punctilious he'll hand it right over. I'll have to catch the first steamer."

He opened the cab-door and stumbled out, not noticing nor caring for the curious glances which followed the wet, bedraggled figure which entered the dignified portals of the Breslin.

He hurried through the lounge to the lift, and a minute later stood in his room.

A hot bath made him feel better, and afterwards he lost no time in looking up the sailings for England.

He discovered that the Lusitania left at noon the following day, and began immediately to make arrangements.

Sore, tired, and gloomy, he crept into bed, but while his money lasted he would fight for the possession of that glittering Diamond Dragon, the temporary possession of which had inflamed his old love of wealth. And the pity of it was that Dr. Huxton Rymer, at one time a leader in his profession, and one of the most skilful surgeons who ever wielded a knife, preferred to seek ease and luxury without honest toil, and with all his brilliant mind couldn't see the inevitable result.

Had he been of a superstitious turn of mind, that night of fevered dreams would have been sufficient to increase his feeling of gloomy foreboding. The Diamond Dragon seemed to suddenly come to life, and was swimming up and down in the dark river.

Its green-rimmed eyes blazed balefully about, and as Rymer tore along, with a screaming horde of frenzied Chinamen at his heels, he saw the Dragon turn and grin with a ghastly grin as Rymer, terror-stricken, fell shrieking with fear over the end of the wharf into its great gleaming jaws, which were held open ready to receive him. He could feel its hot breath, and, looking up, could see its great diamond teeth were coming down upon him, but just as they closed on him he awoke in a cold sweat from the effects of the nightmare.

Rymer lost no time the next morning in getting to the steamship office, and was fortunate enough to secure a berth. As his funds were not too great, he deemed it wise to travel second-class, and, all unknowingly, did a wise thing, for on the same ship, travelling first, was Won, in all the glory of the latest-cut European clothes, with Rymer's little piece of pencil in his pocket.

As the great steamer moved with slow, graceful dignity down the harbour, Won looked at the green waters, and permitted himself a slow Oriental smile as he thought of the man he had sent to the bottom, and who, by the ruling of the great Confucius, might at that very moment be far beneath him with the fishes.

Even Won's ingrained self-control would have received a shock did he know that his victim was indeed beneath him, but not as deep down as Won thought. At that moment Rymer, very much alive, was standing on the deck beneath smoking and planning.

Consequently, by another whim of Fate, it was decreed they should travel to England together, as they had travelled from Australia to New York together, only on the last stage neither knew that the same ship sheltered the other.

It has already been stated how, on Won's arrival in England, he hastened to report his success to the likewise newly-arrived Hang Lee, and how with the piece of pencil he had secured from Rymer he tried to bluff Grace Lansing to give up the Diamond Dragon.

Rymer, on the other hand, lost no time in seeking a quiet hotel, where he settled down with a file of newspapers and spent some time poring over the shipping news.

He gave a sharp exclamation, and leaned forward as he read of the putting back to Australia of the Martah, which carried Harry Graham as a passenger, and his blood ran cold as he thought of the fate of the Diamond Dragon if the ship had gone down. Little did he know that at that moment the thing which was causing such a scheming and planning on the part of such powerful forces was lying where it had been carelessly placed in the drawer of Grace Lansing's dressing-table.

"Nothing for it but to kick my heels around until Graham reaches

London!" grumbled Rymer, as he hung up the file of papers and lit a cigar. "But in case I run into those Chinks again, and should be recognised, I guess I'd better make a change in my appearance."

Suiting the action to the word, he hastened out of the hotel into a near-by barber's, and emerged twenty minutes later minus his heavy beard and moustache. A search of his luggage brought to light the white beard and moustache of an elderly man, with its attendant wig.

When he had put these on and slipped on a pair of blue spectacles, his appearance was little like that of the man who had that day arrived. He slouched his shoulders and walked up and down in front of the mirror with the dragging gait of age. After half an hour of steady practice, he smiled with satisfaction.

"I guess that'll do!" he muttered. "Scotland Yard wants me pretty bad, but I can keep clear of them all right. But I might run into Sexton Blake, and I'm too busy to settle old scores with him now. Besides, I guess this will fool even those clever Chinks."

Removing his disguise, he rang for the boy and demanded his bill, after which he sent his luggage downstairs.

Five minutes later he was in a taxi, taking advantage of its friendly shelter to once more assume the disguise which he had tested in the hotel bedroom.

"I'll go to another hotel and enter in this disguise," he muttered. "Then they won't get curious. Might as well go on from there and look up old Morris. When I get hold of the Dragon again he'll come in handy to dispose of the stones through some of his underground channels on the Continent. Mustn't let the old beggar get too much commission on it, though. The old thief got too much on the last stuff he disposed of for me."

With this decision, he leaned out and directed the driver to a certain quiet hotel in the West End, and, bidding him wait on their arrival, entered the hotel, with his aged gait, and secured a room.

After sending his luggage up, he re-entered the cab and told the driver to drive into the City, where he intended leaving the cab and walking to the resort of Morris, the old fence whom he had decided to look up.

As they drove slowly along, Rymer leaned back, planning his conversation with Morris, when something came within his range of vision sending all thoughts of Morris scurrying from his mind and causing him to sit up, with a muffled remark.

What he saw which caused him such consternation was the figure of a man walking along on the footpath. He was dressed in the conventional frock-coat and silk hat which autocratic fashion orders, and from behind, as Rymer saw him, presented no cause for remark to the casual observer.

But Rymer knew the style of walk, which no veneer of civilisation could entirely efface. It was the shuffling step of the Celestial; and, although, in the case of the man in question, it had been almost entirely effaced, still, there was enough left for Rymer's sharp eyes to place it.

But that was not the full reason of his exclamation. As the walking man slightly turned his head, Rymer recognised the suave, impassive features of Won —the supposed member of the Diplomatic Service who had travelled with him as far as 'Frisco, and, unknown to Rymer, the rest of the way as well.

"By thunder!" he gasped. "That's my friend who left Australia, with me, I'll bet anything! And I'll wager he's the same gentleman who got the piece of pencil from me in New York! Now, how, in the name of all that's mysterious, did he get here so quickly? Is it possible he came on the Lusitania?

"Good gracious, if that is so, what a chance I missed to get the pencil back! But what is he doing here in the West End? Surely it can't have anything to do with the Dragon? Ah! He's going up the steps of that house! I'd give something to know who lives there!"

It was true Won was the pedestrian, and at the moment when Rymer saw him he was on his way to call on Grace Lansing on his mission which failed so thoroughly. As he rang the bell and fumbled for his card-case, Rymer's cab drove past, and, through the little window at the back, Rymer watched the door open and the Celestial disappear within.

"By thunder, I've got to see what he's after!" muttered Rymer, rapping on the window. "I'll send the taxi round the next corner to wait, and investigate."

In response to his rapping, the cab pulled up, and Rymer descended.

"Here's half-a-sovereign," he said, thrusting his hand into his pocket. "Drive on around the corner and wait there for me. I may be five minutes, or an hour —I can't tell."

"Very good, sir!" responded the man. "I'll wait, never fear!"

And, as the cab drew away, Rymer walked slowly back along the street on the side opposite Grace Lansing's house. As he passed, a big "To Let" sign on the house opposite hers gave him a sudden idea. If he could gain its interior he could command a view of the house opposite, and although he might be able to see nothing, still, it would look suspicious hanging about the street.

Barely pausing in his walk, he swung round and mounted the steps of the vacant house as he made the decision.

"It will be a pretty mess if one of my skeleton-keys won't open it." he muttered as he drew out a bunch of all sizes. "However, if anybody gets anxious enough to ask questions, I'll bluff that I'm the agent, and if my keys fail to open it I can always say I must have lost the right one."

Taking in the character of the lock with the eye of an expert, Rymer began hastily fitting one key after another. In the glass panels of the door he could see mirrored, Grace's house, and could easily tell if Won left before he got inside the vacant house.

But fortune favoured him, for he hadn't tried more than half a dozen likely keys when he heaved a heavy sigh of relief as the lock slipped back.

Once inside and the door closed behind him, Rymer lost no time in entering the bare front room; and, standing well back from the window, commanded a view of Grace's drawing-room.

He had a perfect view of Won, but as yet could not see Grace, and, consequently, had no idea as to the identity of the individual to whom Won was speaking.

"It's probably got nothing to do with the Dragon at all!" he grunted, as he saw Won talking rapidly. "However, I'll watch the yellow villain and see just what his game is."

"Ah!" He gave the exclamation, and his eyes glittered as he saw Won reach in his pocket and draw out a short piece of pencil, and, even at that distance Rymer recognised the piece which had been stolen from the heel of his boot in New York. "So it was you, after all, was it?" he muttered savagely. "By thunder, I'll get even with you for that, you slippery heathen! I'd like mighty well to get a glimpse of the person you are speaking to. You don't seem over pleased, either, my friend. Ah! Putting the pencil back in your pocket, are you! Now, what on earth is your game? Now you're leaving, and —Oh! It's a lady, is it —and young, too! I'd like to know what she's got to do with that pencil."

He drew back as he saw Won leave the room in the house opposite, and then saw Grace approach the window and watch the departing Chinaman.

Rymer was puzzled. He was undecided whether to follow Won or stay and watch events in the house opposite. It was really Grace's presence at the window which decided his course of action, for he decided it might look strange if he walked out of the vacant house just then.

At that moment the messenger-boy arrived with a cable from Harry Graham —the cable which was to kindle the first flame of real fear in Grace's mind and cause her to send a telegram to Sexton Blake.

Rymer watched her uninterestedly as she read the cable, but her subsequent agitation roused his curiosity. As she hurried from the room he stood puzzled; but happening to glance across the road again, he saw Grace throw up the blind in the room over the drawing-room. Quickly he wheeled and hurried up the stairs of the vacant house, entering the upstairs front room.

Grace was at that moment taking the packet from her dressing-table, with the intention of locking it away in her trunk.

Rymer forgot his surroundings, and gave a startled cry as he saw what followed. With dry lips and chest heaving with emotion, he watched, with clenched hands, while Grace picked up the packet, which had dropped to the floor, and made her accidental discovery of the real contents.

While she gazed in startled fascination at the glittering Dragon, and finally thrust it back into the leathern case in a panic of fear, she little dreamed that Dr. Hutton, of whom Harry Graham had written and her recent visitor had spoken, was in the upstairs room across the road watching with intense agitation her every movement.

He strained forward, with eager, greedy eyes as Grace thrust it back and locked it in her trunk.

As she left the room and descended the stairs, Rymer staggered back against the wall, white and shaking.

"My heavens! How has she become possessed of the Dragon?" he muttered, mopping his brow. "By all rights it should be with Graham aboard the Martah, and, instead, I find it in the possession of a young girl in a house in the West End of London. Even if it came by the quickest route, it could barely reach here; and yet that villainous Chink knew it!

"What on earth has happened since I left Australia? What is the Dragon doing here, and what has happened to Graham? Is it possible that girl across the road is the girl he said he was engaged to, and — By Jove, I have it! The only way it could possibly get here by now is by the quickest mail steamer. Graham must have posted it to her. But how on earth has that Chinaman discovered the fact so soon? At any rate, it's a certainty that they will be too shrewd for her. His call must have been to endeavour to get it by the pencil, and having failed in that they will adopt other methods. But I'll fool you this time, you yellow heathen! I'll get that Dragon by hook or by crook, if I swing for it!"

Muttering savagely, Rymer, after a long, comprehensive look at the house opposite, passed out of the empty room and down the stairs. With an unconcerned air, he opened the street door and passed down the steps, his eyes narrowing under lowered lids as he caught sight of a strolling Chinaman in English clothes far up the street.

"They don't intend to lose sight of her or the Dragon, he muttered under his breath. But you can put on twenty of your heathens, and I'll get that Dragon yet under your very noses!"

He walked, with his assumed stiff gait, until he reached the taxi, which had pulled up around the corner. Then briefly saying "Hotel!" he lay back, with closed eyes, bringing into definite form the germ of an idea which had been born while he stood in the vacant house.

•     •     •     •     •

Darkness had just fallen, and the first creeping fog of autumn was accentuating the gloom of evening. The street lamps shone with a sickly glare, their feeble light restricted to a small circle.

Several hours had passed since Rymer had watched with astonished perturbation the scenes which had been enacted during the afternoon in Grace Lansing's house. Risking any occurrence, he had waited for darkness before putting into operation the plan which he had elaborated in the taxi. He knew the Chinaman he had seen would stay on watch right along, and he also knew that Won's failure and the watching man's presence indicated that the Chinese had by no means given up their attempt to get possession of the Dragon.

Diplomacy had failed, and he knew the Celestial mind well enough to know that cunning, and, if necessary, force, would be adopted quickly and without compunction. It was a race between them, and he was determined, cost what it might, he would not be the loser.

As he walked slowly along the dark street during early evening, he was dressed exactly as during the afternoon, excepting that his hands were encased with a pair of thin rubber gloves, and his boots had been exchanged for a pair with felt soles. Thus equipped to guard against the leaving of suspicious traces, he sallied out on his dangerous mission.

As he drew abreast of Grace's house, he knew from a presence of a light in the drawing-room that it was occupied; but the room above, where he had seen Grace with the Diamond Dragon, was unoccupied, and that room was his objective.

How many occupants there were in the house he had no idea. Grace had been the only one he had seen. There might be several men, and, of course, the servants, but he tapped the automatic revolver in his pocket significantly as he muttered, "Men or no men, I'd risk the whole of Scotland Yard for that Dragon, and if anyone tries to stop me I pity him!"

He counted the houses as he walked along until he came to the next corner. Then, turning around it, he walked down the side street until he came to a narrow lane, which ran at the rear of the houses whose fronts he had passed. He walked along the dark lane until he counted the seventh, then peered over the high fence at the dark, silent windows.

"Don't seem to be exactly a party on in there!" he muttered grimly. "However, while I'm wasting time out here, those Chinks may be operating from the front, so I'd best lose no time."

It was the work of a few minutes to pull himself up and drop over on the other side of the fence. Then, with stealthy footsteps, he crept across the soft turf until he stood under a dark window.

At that moment, a sound caught his ear which caused him to drop to the ground in the shelter of the wall, and hold his breath. A door had opened near him, and barely had he dropped down, when a white shadow flitted across the ground in the direction of the lane. A soft whistle followed, and a moment later down the lane came the long, heavy stride which Rymer's ears had recognised only too well.

A maid slipping out on the sly to have a talk with the bobby.

"By Jove, if she's left that door open. I'm a good mind to chance it! If I'm discovered, the policeman is good and handy, but what a chance!"

He began creeping stealthily along in the shadow until he reached a dark square which indicated the presence of a door. Slowly passing his hand along, he chuckled softly as his hand felt a narrow opening between the frame and the door which the maid had left slightly open.

He paused, undecided for a moment whether to risk it, but just then a soft laugh reached him from the direction of the lane, and, with suppressed breathing, he pushed open the door and stepped inside.

He closed the door as far as it had been, and stood for several moments listening. No sound reached him, and pulling out a small electric torch, he began creeping along, guiding himself by the wall.

When he thought himself free from discovery by the policeman and maid, he pressed the button of the torch and peered around. He was in a long passage, with a door at the further end. A door led off from each side, but that was all.

Cautiously turning, he threw the light back along the way he had come, and smiled grimly as he saw he had passed a stairway in the dark.

Turning off the torch, he crept back, and began cautiously mounting the stairs, holding his breath tensely as they creaked from time to time.

He reached the top safely, and once more used the torch. A passage similar to the one below ran along, and once more trusting to the wall for guidance, he went ahead.

On reaching the door at the further end, he softly turned the handle, and found himself standing in a large upstairs hall. It was in darkness, but the hall below was lit up, and through a half-open door he could see another light.

"That's the drawing-room," he muttered, "and it's the room over that I want."

At that moment a boy hurried along the lower hall and knocked, and Rymer drew back in the shadow listening.

It was the house boy being sent with Grace's urgent telegram to Sexton Blake, which, it will be remembered, reached Blake immediately after the murderous attack on him in his dressing-room.

Rymer smiled as he heard Grace tell the boy she would wait up for his return, and as the front door closed, he began again to steal along. He turned up the dark hall, past a closed door where the invalid

Mrs. Lansing lay sleeping, all unsuspicious of the intruder so close to her. Rymer reached Grace's room in safety, and softly turning the handle, a moment later he stood safely inside.

"So far, so good!" he breathed. "Now to see if her keys are in that drawer where I saw her toss them this afternoon. If not, I'll have to try my own, but it will be mighty risky."

But fortune was with Rymer that evening. Grace had not taken her keys from where she had placed them during the afternoon, and a moment later, while she sat nervously awaiting the house boy's return, Rymer was fitting her key in the trunk.

His hand shook with emotion as he threw the light of the torch into the trunk, and saw the leather belt and case. A moment served to convince him that the Diamond Dragon was safe inside.

With shaking fingers, he crushed belt and all in his pocket, and closed the lid of the trunk. Locking it, he returned the keys to the drawer of the dressing-table, and with his revolver in his hand began his retreat.

Back the way he had come he went, until he reached the bottom of the stairs. His heart beat suffocatingly as he crept back along the passage to the door at the rear. He sighed with relief when he found it closed and locked, for now there was little risk of running into the arms of the law, and he didn't care a farthing what surprise might be occasioned in the morning when it was found unlocked. Turning the key, he slipped out, and closed it behind him, and a few moments later was standing in the lane outside, breathless but chuckling.

As he reached the street in front, he saw a slow, moving figure, whose walk he recognised, and he chuckled as he passed it.

"Go it, you yellow heathen! Keep a good look out for the Dragon!"

Still chuckling, he hurried along, with one hand pressing against his precious burden.

But the shadowy figure had heard that chuckle, and was standing pondering over it. At that moment another shadow loomed up, and a hasty consultation in guttural Chinese took place, with the result that before he turned the corner, Rymer was being shadowed.

And it was the events related above which caused Grace Lansing to fly down from her room, with white face, and breathlessly inform the waiting Blake that "It was gone!"

## THE EIGHTH CHAPTER. *Blake Ferrets Things Out.*

WHEN Blake saw Grace's white, frightened face, and heard her startled words, he turned and spoke sharply.

"It's gone!" he snapped out. "The Diamond Dragon gone! Are you sure?"

"Only too sure!" cried Grace. "Oh, how could it have gone? Who could have taken it? I can't understand it"' she almost moaned. "I am frightened —frightened of I don't know what. There seems to be some sinister force at work about me which I can't see but can feel. Oh, what can I do, Mr. Blake? What will Harry say?"

"Calm yourself, Miss Lansing!" said Blake sternly, seeing she was in danger of breaking down. "If it is gone, it is gone, and we must lose no time in trying to get track of it. Sit down, please, and answer my questions."

Grace sank into a chair, while Blake walked up and down with a heavy frown on his face.

He was keenly disappointed, and more than irritated at the sudden dashing of his hopes to the ground. He had counted more than he realised on bringing the case to a sudden conclusion on making the discovery that the Diamond Dragon had fallen so strangely into the possession of Grace Lansing.

It would have been so simple to take it and leave it in the bank until Harry Graham returned. Then he would explain to that young man just how Dr. Hutton had no claim to it, and although neither of the Chinese parties had the more right to it, how it would be better for the welfare of the Chinese Republic to pass it over to the quiet old Celestial who called himself Li Hong.

Blake had anticipated no trouble in persuading Harry Graham to see his point of view, and this sudden set-back to his plans was irritating. His head was still sore from the blow he had received the previous evening in the dressing-room, and although he expected and took a hundred risks every day of his life, he had no fancy for a continuation of the vendetta which had evidently been declared against him by Hang Lee.

That Hang Lee's agents had in some way entered the house and secured the Dragon, he had no doubt, and never for a moment did he consider the possibility of the thief being the so-called Dr. Hutton. That personage was, as yet, a shadowy figure in the case, and since he had heard from Grace a couple of hours before of his connection with the Dragon, he had not attempted any deductions on the matter. But now that he had been forestalled, he saw that he would have to give every faculty he had to the solution of the matter.

As he paced up and down, his eyes roving about, he came to a sudden stop.

Across the street he saw the figure of a Chinaman in English clothes hurrying along. The sight caused him to think rapidly. Was it one of the men shadowing him, or was it another one who was keeping a watch on Grace's house.

If the latter was the case, why —good heavens! —the Dragon, after all, couldn't have been stolen from Grace by Hang Lee's agents! Then who —was it possible that this fellow Hutton had entered into the case? He swung around quickly as the Chinaman disappeared from view.

"Now, Miss Lansing, if you are sufficiently composed, answer my questions, please, and try to remember every detail of what I ask you. In a matter of this kind, and with the foes we have to reckon with, it is the apparently trivial and unimportant details which count."

"I will do my best to answer you, Mr. Blake!" cried Grace. "Please proceed!"

Blake drew up a chair and sat down facing her.

"Firstly, what time was it yesterday afternoon when you put the packet in your trunk?"

"Late in the afternoon. Five o'clock, I should say."

"How long before that did your Chinese visitor leave?"

"Between twenty minutes and half an hour."

"Did you go to your room at once on his departure?"

"Not at once. I walked to the window and watched him down the street. Then I saw the messenger-boy coming, and stood until I saw him come up the steps."

"Did you notice anything else as you looked out of the window?"

"I don't remember anything else."

"Then you went to your room?"

"Yes. Immediately after I had read Har —Mr. Graham's cable message."

"How long were you in your room?"

"Just a short time. After locking the packet in my trunk I came downstairs."

"Did you bring your keys with you?"

"No. I put them in the drawer of my dressing-table. But nobody would touch them there. The maid was about up there almost all the time until nearly eight, when she left my mother for the night."

"Is your mother a sound sleeper?"

Grace nodded.

"Were you in your room again during the evening?"

"No, not until I went up to bed."

"I'd like to finish my questioning up there if you please," said Blake; and Grace, rising obediently, led the way.

Blake stood inside the door as they reached the room, and gave a comprehensive look around.

"What I want you to do, Miss Lansing," he said quietly, "is to control your nerves and forget as far as possible that I am here. Then start at the door here, and as far as possible repeat in detail your movements when you came up yesterday afternoon and put the packet in your trunk."

"I'll try," laughed Grace, in embarrassment; "but I'm afraid I will be clumsy over it."

"Don't be self-conscious," replied Blake, with a tinge of sternness in his tones.

Grace backed up to the door, and began walking forward. Stopping at the dresser, she opened the drawer, and in lieu of the packet used a handkerchief for her illustration. With truly credible acting she went through the mimicry of her movements the previous day, even to the extent of her ejaculations of amazement at the discovery of what the leather pouch contained.

Then, rising, she walked to the trunk and opened the cover, winding up by returning to the dressing-table and placing her keys in the drawer.

Blake nodded in approbation.

"Very well done, Miss Lansing. That is all here, thank you! By the way, I notice a vacant house across the road. I can't read the agents on the 'To Let' board from here. Do you know who they are?"

"Oh, yes!" replied Grace, in surprise. "Potter and Potter. They handle most of the houses on this street. Most of them belong to one estate."

"Ah, I see! We will go downstairs now, I think. You have a telephone, haven't you?"

"Yes; did you wish to use it?"

"If you please."

They descended the stairs, and Grace led the way to the rear of the hall where the telephone had been attached.

Without troubling to look in the Directory, Blake lifted the receiver and gave the number of his apartments in Baker Street.

"Is that you, Tinker?" he said to the voice which came over the wire.

"All right. How is Pedro now? Quite recovered from the blow, has he? Very well, bring him at once to Miss Lansing's house. Take a taxi and hurry. What? Don't ask questions. Make haste!"

And Blake, with a slight frown, hung up the receiver. Disregarding Grace's puzzled glance, he picked up the Directory and turned to "P." A moment later he had again lifted the receiver and given the number of Potter and Potter.

"Is that Potter and Potter's?" he asked. "Is Mr. Potter in? Which one? Either will do. Yes —at once, please!"

A short wait, and then:

"Is that Mr. Potter speaking? Sexton Blake at this end. Yes. Quite well, thanks. I am speaking from Miss Lansing's. I see you have a vacant house to let in Duke Street. Can you send a man along immediately with the keys. I'd like to have a look through it? What? Am I going to be married? No thanks, not yet!" And Blake's frown relaxed as out of the corner of his eye he saw Grace turn away smiling.

"Tell him to take a taxi and I'll pay for it. You will, all right. Thanks!"

He rang off, and turned to Grace.

"Now, Miss Lansing, we will continue our questions, please."

They walked back to the drawing-room and sat down.

"You say you sent the house-boy out last night, with your telegram to me!"

"Yes; I was going myself, but was frightened."

"What time did you go to bed?"

"Nearly midnight."

"Did you go right to sleep?"

"Oh, no! I tossed about all night long. It was daybreak before I dozed off!"

"Ah, didn't you doze all that time?"

"No; I tried hard, but I was awake the whole night. In fact, I was so frightened, Mr. Blake, I sat up in bed half the time. Every little noise startled me."

"What servants were out during the evening besides the house-boy?"

"None, I think."

"Aren't you positive?"

"Practically; but I have on one or two occasions discovered the housemaid slipping in from talking to the policeman on this beat. They are to be married, and consequently, as long as her work is done I don't mind."

"I see. Will you kindly send for her?"

"Is that necessary? I'm sure she would know nothing."

"I don't expect she does," replied Blake shortly. "Please send for her, though."

Grace rose and rang the bell, and a moment later Alice the housemaid knocked and entered.

Grace started to speak, but a look in Blake's eye silenced her, and she stopped.

"Are you the housemaid?" asked Blake, turning to the girl.

She looked inquiringly at her mistress, and at a nod from Grace, answered:

"Yes, sir."

"What time did you leave the house last evening?"

The girl grew red to the roots of her hair, and looked first at Blake, and then at Grace, and finally at the door; but the cold eye of her interlocutor conquered her inclination to fly, and she stammered in embarrassment:

"What time did I leave the house, sir? I don't understand."

"Yes, you do," said Blake sternly. "You went out to speak to the policeman on the beat, didn't you?"

There was nothing for it but to own up. That cold eye seemed to read her very thoughts, and with flaming cheeks the maid whispered a hesitating:

"Y-e-s, sir!"

"Ah, and what time was that?"

"Just after ten, sir."

"How long were you out?"

"I didn't leave the yard, sir. I just stood at the fence. Only about half an hour altogether, sir."

"Did you see or hear anybody about while you were there?"

"No, sir, not a soul."

"I suppose you were too taken up with each other to notice anything," said Blake. "Think well, my girl. Nothing of any description happened which was out of the ordinary? Don't be frightened. It is to help your mistress that I ask."

"Well, sir, I don't know what right you have to ask. But this morning the house-boy remarked, sir, that he found the rear door unlocked. I was the last to come in, sir, and I'm positive I locked it after me!"

"Ah!" said Blake; but in that simple expression there was a world of meaning.

He smiled at the maid, and nodded.

"Thanks —that will do."

Glad to get away from the ordeal of that compelling eye, she cast a hurried look of appeal at her mistress and fled.

But Grace was quite as mystified as the maid, and was even more so when Blake walked to a large picture of Whistler's which hung on the wall and began chatting on the artist and his works with a depth of knowledge and interest in his subject which left Grace staring in amazement.

The detective kept up his discourse on art until a taxi pulled up outside, and from it descended Tinker and Pedro. Then, dropping his manner of the salon, he once more assumed his cold, analytical air, and again Grace marvelled at the versatility of that complex man whose name was a byword in every home in the kingdom.

She turned as the door opened to admit Tinker and Pedro holding out her hand to the lad, and patting Pedro's great head.

"I came right along on getting your message, guv'nor. What is it —some new development?"

"Wait and see, my lad," replied Blake briefly. "I'm expecting a man from Potter & Potter's, and then we'll make a move. Ah, I hear a taxi just outside! It is probably our man."

Blake was right. It was the man from Potter's in the person of Mr. Potter himself.

"Ah, Blake!" he exclaimed, as he was ushered in, "Morning, Miss Lansing! How is your mother keeping?"

"Fairly well, thank you," smiled Grace.

"What's the matter, Blake?" asked Potter, turning to the detective. "I thought when you first rang up about a house that one of the fair sex had at last captivated you, and that we were to have the honour of providing you with a house."

"Nonsense!" laughed Blake. "I haven't time for anything like that. I want to make a short examination in that vacant house across the road, if you don't mind. I'll explain why later."

"Certainly; with pleasure!" answered Potter, getting to his feet. "Do you wish to go over now?"

"Yes. I don't want to lose any time. Will you wait here until I return?" asked Blake, turning to Grace.

"Yes, of course, Mr. Blake."

"Thank you. Come along, Tinker, and bring Pedro."

The little party bowed to Grace and departed, watched by the worried and mystified girl as they crossed the road. Potter threw the door open, and they stepped inside.

"Hold Pedro," rapped out Blake, "and don't either of you move forward just yet. Ah, luck is with us! This house has been vacant for some time, I see, Potter!"

"About three months," answered the agent. "But what's all the mystery?" he asked in amazement, as Blake drew a magnifying-glass from his pocket and dropped flat on the hall floor.

But the detective made no reply. For the time being he was deaf, dumb, and blind to everything but the faint footprints left in the thin dust-coating on the floor, and probably Pedro appreciated as much as anyone the true worth of that all-seeing gaze as it picked up the scent.

Moving slowly, Blake crept along the hall, stopping twice where the marks were particularly distinct. There he took from his pocket a sensitive print-mould of his own invention, and made two careful casts of the prints. Then, rising to his feet, he held out his hand for Pedro's leash, and waited patiently while the dog nosed the cold scent.

He gave the animal his head while he followed the trail into the drawing-room from where Rymer had watched Won hold up the piece of pencil the previous day.

"The conditions are perfect in here for the picking up of a cold scent," explained Blake to the puzzled Potter, "and the longer he noses it the more certain will he be. I am giving him a most difficult task, but he has picked up cold scents before now, and I'm in hopes he will this one."

As he reached the drawing-room he walked behind Pedro as the hound went straight to the spot where Rymer had stood, and then he passed out to the hall again and over to the foot of the stairs.

As he began to ascend Blake pulled him back and passed the leash to Tinker, who was following his master's methods with breathless interest, for although he had seen Blake at work times out of number, he never lost interest in the trailing of a scent.

Again Blake had recourse to his magnifying-glass. Starting at the bottom, he began working slowly up the balustrade, using the glass over every inch. The balustrade, like everything else, had had a coating of dust, but its scraped appearance indicated that someone's hand had recently rubbed along it as they ascended the stairs.

He was in hopes of getting a cast of a finger-print, or perhaps part of the hand, but the rubbing condition seemed to preclude any such possibility, until he had worked nearly to the top. There he peered through the glass for several minutes, studying several faint minute marks which had been left near the edge of the rail.

With infinite care he applied the delicate print-mould, and when he raised his hand again he had on the sensitive surface of the mould an exact reproduction of those faint marks.

Nothing else was found to be on the rail, however, and he signed for Tinker and Potter to follow up.

Pedro led the way along the upper hall to the empty front-room over the drawing-room, and again Blake called a halt at the door.

Entering alone, he once more dropped to the floor and began creeping about with the glass. Over he went to the spot where Rymer had stood when Grace discovered the real contents of the leather pouch.

Then the detective turned and followed the faint dust recorded prints over the wall, where, it will be remembered Rymer had staggered in agitation on seeing the Diamond Dragon. With a smothered exclamation as he rested on his knees, Blake swung the glass up, and began a minute examination of the wall. Up he gradually worked pausing from time to time, but always going higher, until he stood erect, with the glass on the wall on a direct level with his own eyes.

Finally he returned and retraced his steps to where they stopped in a line with the window. Looking across, he could see the dressing-table and the trunk in Grace's room and in a line between the two the door which led out to the upstairs hall.

"That is all," he said briefly, turning and holding out his hand for Pedro's leash. "We will return to Miss Lansing's house, and I will explain matters to you there Potter."

"Good heavens, I should think so!" laughed the agent. "Of all the mysterious performances I ever saw this beats them all! Is that the way you usually work, Blake? I should think you'd get housemaid's-knees!"

"It isn't always I'm able to pick a trail as well as this," he said, leading Pedro over, and allowing him to nose the footprints again.

"Well if you have to pick up a trail on much less I don't see how you can do it," said Potter incredulously. "Do you mean to say you can guess what the movements were in the house here of some person whose footprints you seem to be able to follow with that glass?"

"I'll tell you more, than that," laughed Blake shortly. "Wait until we get across the road."

Tinker smiled pityingly at Potter's ignorance of his master's ability.

"You've never seen the guv'nor at work on a really difficult trail, Mr. Potter," he remarked as they turned and descended the stairs.

On reaching Grace's house Blake gave that mystified young lady another surprise by asking to be taken to the yard at the rear, but she had had enough experience with him that day to obey without question.

When they emerged from the back-door Blake took off Pedro's leash and turned the hound loose, while he stood in the doorway and watched the dog's movements. For a moment Pedro stood undecided, sniffing the ground in perplexity.

"Find, find!" called Blake sharply, and with nose down Pedro began running about the yard. Around and around he went, until his course took him over near the fence. There he paused suddenly, and worried about for a few moments, but finally turned and begin approaching the house. Twice he stopped in perplexity, but caught the scent again. Blake watched him with tense gaze, until he reached the very wall of the house, where he paused and began running around in a small circle.

As he persisted in sticking to the same spot, Blake, signing to the others not to follow, hastened along the wall and knelt down where the dog was working. Pulling out the magnifying-glass again, he spoke to Pedro, and then went to work. Ten minutes passed before he raised his head, and when he did it was only to creep inch by inch along the ground beside the side of the house, until he reached the back-door. Then, getting to his feet, he called Pedro, and put him on the leash.

"Now we will go back to the drawing-room," he said briefly.

As they trooped in again Grace remarked:

"Oh, I've got something to tell you, Mr. Blake! My mother —"

"Wait, Miss Lansing," said Blake. "Tell me after. I know Mr. Potter is anxious to get away, and I owe him some explanation for imposing on his kindness. It's this way, Mr. Potter," he continued, turning to the agent. "There has been a theft here, and Miss Lansing asked my assistance. The article was taken from her room, and I had reason to think her movements had been watched from the vacant house across the road. I investigated, and find I was right, and the scent which Pedro got over there was the same one which he got in the back-yard."

"Well, I'm blest!" remarked Potter. "You are the limit, Blake; but it was worth the trip to see you work. I was glad to be of use, and hope you find the rascal. My condolences, Miss Lansing!" he said, turning to Grace and holding out his hand. "So long, Blake! Good-bye, Tinker!" And away he went.

"Now, Miss Lansing, I know a little more than I did." remarked Blake as they re-entered the drawing-room. "In the first place, the man who stole the Diamond Dragon from you watched you from the drawing-room opposite when you were talking with your Chinese visitor.

"Then as you went to the room above he did likewise, and saw the Dragon when you discovered it in the pouch. I also know that he was puzzled and agitated enough to stagger back against the wall.

"He left the vacant house, and during the evening, entered the yard at the rear of this house. He reached here a little after ten, and was disturbed by the maid slipping out to see the policeman.

"He dropped to the ground against the wall of the house, and lay there for some little time, but finally perceived the maid and the policeman pretty well taken up with each other, and decided to take a risk.

"He stole along, and found she had left the door open. Slipping through, he made his way upstairs —probably by the back way — until he reached the upper hall, and thence along to your room.

"To secure your keys where he had seen you place them in the afternoon was the work of only a few seconds, and from that to the possession of the Dragon was an easy step.

"On his returning the way he had come, however, he discovered the maid had re-entered the house and locked the door. He unlocked it and passed out, and that explains the reason the house-boy found it unlocked this morning.

"Lastly, he was about six feet high, and yesterday afternoon wore a number eight shoe, with three small horseshoes on the outside edge of each heel. He also wore a frock-coat, and I presume a silk hat, and carried a stick. His age I can't tell you. Last evening, when he entered your house, he wore felt shoes. That is all I can tell you yet. Whether he was white man or Chinaman I don't know, but I am inclined to think he was white."

"Well, Mr. Blake," gasped Grace, "I really think you must be a wizard. How you know all that I fail to imagine. But listen. You remember my telling you I had something to tell you?"

Blake nodded, and frowned at Tinker, who was grinning with delight at his master's deductions.

"Well, it is this," went on Grace. "My mother, as you know, is an invalid, and we have fixed the bed in her room so she can look out of the window. When she saw you all going into the vacant house this afternoon, she sent for me and asked me what was going on. She said she had seen a man go into there yesterday afternoon. Naturally, I pricked up my ears since you seemed so interested in the house, and I asked her if she remembered what he looked like. Well, Mr. Blake, your description is exactly the same as hers, excepting that she said he was an elderly gentleman, with white beard and moustache. But beyond that there is no difference."

"Ah!" exclaimed Blake quietly. "Thanks to your mother, that information will save me some work. It also endorses what I say, and once more proves the value of mathematical analysis."

"But tell me, Mr. Blake, please, how did you know how tall he was, and such things?"

"I think it is all very obvious," smiled Blake. "When he staggered back against the wall he left his imprint against the dust. I knew from the marks about knee high that it was caused by the brushing against the wall of the bottom of either an overcoat or frock-coat.

"Well, it was too warm yesterday for an overcoat, so I naturally deduced that it must be a frock-coat. When I had you go through the same actions you had gone through yesterday afternoon, I saw at once that a man standing in the vacant house across the road could watch your every movement. That is what induced me to investigate over there.

"I knew from the answers you gave me that the robbery must have taken place during the evening and before you went to bed. Pedro proved that to my satisfaction, and the unlocked door this morning confirms it.

"That is all, Miss Lansing. It's very simple, you see. But we've got the hardest work of all to do yet, so I must be moving. Rest assured I will do all in my power to get back the Dragon, but on no account do anything without consulting me. Do you understand thoroughly?"

"Oh, yes, Mr. Blake!" cried Grace gratefully. "And thank you so very much for being so kind!"

Five minutes later Blake, Tinker, and Pedro were whizzing along in a taxi to Baker Street, where Blake hastened to the laboratory with the imprints he had taken.

BLAKE'S deductions regarding the movements of the man who had succeeded in stealing the Diamond Dragon were, we know, correct in every detail up to the point where he had left Grace's house. After that Blake knew nothing of his movements, although he settled down in his laboratory for a close study of the finger-print he had, in order to discover if it belonged to anyone whom he could place. For it will be remembered that as yet he had no trace as to the identity of the thief.

Rymer's movements, after getting safely away with the Diamond Dragon, were full of excitement which he had not anticipated.

As he strode, chuckling, down the street in the murky gloom of night, he was totally unaware of the silent Chinaman who followed him so noiselessly. He had noticed one of the Celestials watching Grace's house, but never dreamed that his chuckle had aroused suspicion in that mind, and that another Chinaman had sped along after him.

He passed several streets before the fog-shrouded shape of a creeping taxi appeared, and stumbling into the road, Rymer held up his hand. Giving the address of his hotel entered and sank back, totally unaware that, concealed by the blanket of the fog, the following Chinaman had stood on the edge of the kerb and had distinctly heard his order.

As Rymer's cab drew away, the watching man on the side-walk dashed along after it. He gained rapidly, but Rymer's driver, seeing a clear run, put on speed, and the racing shadow dropped back. At that moment another taxi wheeled into view along the street, and the Chinaman dashed up to the startled driver. He jerked out the name of Rymer's hotel.

"Reach it before the cab that just passed," he jerked in perfect English, "and I will give you half-a-sovereign."

The chauffeur needed no further inducement. He threw in the clutch, and risking sudden death in the fog-filled streets, he threaded his way through by the short cuts, and pulled up in front of the hotel just as another taxi turned the corner a hundred yards away.

As the Chinaman stepped out, the light from the hotel fell on the features of Won, Hang Lee's able lieutenant. He tossed the driver the promised half-sovereign and strolled slowly along, stopping to gaze in a near-by shop-window.

Rymer's cab drew in to the kerb and discharged its fare, who walked across the pavement to the hotel entrance with the aged walk of his disguise.

The watching Won gave an almost imperceptible start as his cunning mind stripped that tall, bearded figure of its disguise and read thereon the features of the man whom he thought at the bottom of New York Harbour.

He turned back to his scrutiny of the shop-window, and gazed in silence for some minutes. Then he strolled casually up the street until he saw another taxi, which he hailed. He gave an address in Limehouse, and settled back to mentally arrange his report of this new phase of the affair to Hang Lee.

Rymer had stepped from the taxi and entered the hotel in an unconcerned manner, but coming down the street he had seen Won's face as the hotel light fell momentarily on his features. In a flash he had recognised the Celestial, and a cold feeling coursed through him from head to foot.

"Curse those yellow fiends!" he muttered. "Am I never to shake them off? I wonder if that persistent Chink has any idea that I have secured the Dragon? But I'll fool you yet, you wrinkled heathen!"

He entered the hotel office, and ascended at once to his room. There he lost no time in packing his bags, and on finishing, rang for the boy. As that worthy entered, Rymer pulled half-a-sovereign from his pocket and held it carelessly between finger and thumb.

"I want my bill sent up at once," he said shortly. "And I say, my lad, I suppose there is a back way from the hotel?"

"Oh, yes, sir," answered the boy. "Most of the gents use that way to reach the billiard-room."

"Do you know of a nice bright lad around the hotel who would get my bags out that way without anyone seeing him?"

"I know the very boy for the job, mister," grinned the lad, with one eye on the disc of gold.

"Will you send him up?" asked Rymer, smiling.

"I don't need to, mister," replied the boy. "He's here now."

"All right, sonny. Bring up my bill, and then get busy with these bags. If you do the job properly there's half-a-sovereign for you.

"It's mine, sir!" said the boy briefly, as he turned and sped away.

Once again that day Rymer changed his hotel, and fifteen minutes later, while he kept guard over his bags in the dark lane behind the hotel, the boy hurried away for a taxi.

Barely had Won, Chinaman, thinking his man safe in the hotel for the night, sped away to inform Hang Lee of his discovery, when Rymer was also speeding away to a quiet hotel in Fleet Street.

He went straight up to his room and carefully locked the door behind him. Then he turned the window-catches and drew down the blinds. Going over to the table, he opened his coat and drew out the precious Diamond Dragon, his eyes glistening with greed as the brilliant, scintillating mass threw back the rays from the electric light like a myriad blazing coloured shafts, each shaft piercing through Rymer's reserve and searing him with its potent flame.

His hands shook, and he licked his dry lips as he picked it up, fondling and caressing it in an ecstasy of joy.

"Oh, you beauty!" he muttered thickly. "Wealth, ease, power — everything is mine! Who would think you had such a power in your cold, hard stones? If those yellow fiends succeed in getting you away from me now, they'd earn you all right. But take your last look at this old world, my beauty, for very soon those eyes will come out, and then the rest of those lovely shimmers, after which you will go into the melting-pot.

Was it only his fevered imagination that made him think those green-rimmed, baleful eyes glared at him with sinister menace as he announced its fate to the Dragon? He shivered slightly, and then laughed harshly.

"You're enough to make anyone nervous!" he growled. "But blessed by Confucius or not, into the melting-pot you go!"

He lifted the scintillating monster and thrust it back in the leather case. Then he set to work. First he emptied the water-bottle and set it on the edge of the dressing-table near one of the windows. Opening his bags, he thrust his hand in and drew out a long piece of cord, from which he cut a short length. One end of this he tied securely around the curved neck of the bottle, and the other end he attached to a strong pin.

With this end in one hand, and a slipper in the other, he approached the window, and as the string grew taut placed the point of the pin against the lower frame of the window. A few blows with the heel of the slipper were sufficient to fix the pin firmly, and when he stood back, the string between the pin in the sash and the bottle on the edge of the dresser was taut. He duplicated these movements at the other window, this time using a glass tumbler in lieu of a bottle. When he had finished both windows, he stepped back with a chuckle.

"In case anyone has managed to track me, and should take a fancy to call on me during the night, I guess that will announce their arrival all right. If either of those windows are raised an inch, it will pull the bottle or the glass over, and I don't think there's any danger of my sleeping through the crash that will follow. Now for the door!"

He swung around to pick up a chair. This he balanced on two legs, and then leaned it back against the door. Again he brought the string into requisition, this time tying the soap-dish to the top of the chair.

Then he grunted when he had finished.

"I'll bet ten to one the Chink doesn't live who can get past that without noise enough to waken old Confucius himself!"

He slipped off his clothes, and after placing the Diamond Dragon and his automatic revolver under the pillow, turned out the light.

"To-morrow," he muttered, "I'll finish my interrupted trip to old Morris; but, by thunder, it was the luckiest chance and most profitable interruption I could desire! I really think, Huxton, my boy, that your luck has turned. First, the melting-pot for his nibs, and the Continent for the stones, and Paris, my boy, for you!"

And with this pleasant reflection, Dr. Huxton Rymer, polished rogue, fell into a sound sleep which was worthy of the just.

. . . . .

Rymer was first awakened from a pleasant dream by what he at first thought to be a miniature gatling-gun, followed by a thundering crash. Instinctively grabbing his revolver, he leaped out of bed on to the bare floor, on which chinks of the morning sun had crept from under the drawn blinds. He looked first at the windows, and then at the door, and saw in the fallen chair and shattered remains of the soap-dish what had caused the startling crash.

He knew by the fact that it was day that the cause of the racket was no stealthy visitor; but being a man to whom the police had a warm desire to extend their hospitality, he was naturally a little nervous. Again the thunderous pounding sounded on the door, and Rymer tiptoed softly across.

"Who is it?" he asked, in a sleepy voice. "What is the matter?"

"It's the chambermaid, and it's half-past eleven," came a voice from the other side. "I thought you had died, sir."

"Oh, that's all right!" replied Rymer, immensely relieved. "I'll be out in half an hour. Is my shaving water there?"

"Yes, sir; I'll leave it at the door."

"Very good. Gad," he murmured, as the maid's footsteps withdrew, "I'll be glad to get out of London! It's too trying on the nerves here for me. I thought Confucius was after me when I heard that crash. By Jove, I wonder if the Dragon is safe?"

He strode over to the bed, and lifted the pillow.

He gave a sigh of relief as he lifted the flap of the yellow pouch, and saw the Diamond Dragon still safe.

"That's no dream, anyway," he muttered, with a grim smile. "I fancy, Rymer, my boy, you did this little job as neatly as you ever did anything in your life. Not a trace except that unlocked back door, and that couldn't be helped."

Little did he know that at that very moment Sexton Blake, by the aid of a magnifying-glass, was examining the footprints in the vacant house opposite Grace Lansing's, and that a few minutes later he was to take an imprint of a fingerprint made by that hand which wielded the razor so blithely.

But he didn't know this, and, in fact, hadn't the faintest suspicion that Sexton Blake was mixed up in the matter.

Even if he did, it is doubtful if he would have altered his plans, for the madness of lust was on him, and every look at that blazing mass of jewels only intensified the madness.

He finished his toilet about the same time that Sexton Blake finished his investigations at Grace Lansing's, and while Blake, Tinker, and Pedro were on their way to Baker Street to make a test of the finger-print, Rymer was speeding east in order to effect a suitable disguise at a certain den he knew before calling on old Morris, the fence!

Poring over the finger-print in his laboratory, we leave Blake. Speeding eastwards, we will leave Rymer, while we follow Won's movements the previous evening, from the time he left the taxi after recognising Rymer to go and report to Hang Lee.

Like unchanging fate, the old Chinaman sat in the same room at the back of the gambling den in Limehouse. He seemed indefatigable, for barely had he moved since his arrival in London earlier in the day.

Many of his agents and spies had come and gone, bringing reports, and leaving to carry out fresh orders; but through it all Hang Lee sat rolling his eternal yellow cigarettes, unmoved and expressionless.

When Won had returned from his futile attempt to bluff the Dragon out of Grace Lansing, by presenting the piece of pencil stolen from Rymer, Hang Lee had said nothing, one way or the other. Lighting a fresh cigarette, he stared into vacancy, and for a few moments silence reigned. Finally, he spoke briefly:

"Take a man, Won, and return. Watch everything well. If any chance presents itself, act. If not, return here. In the meantime, I will give it my thought."

With a murmured. "Very well, Excellency," Won had departed, and it has been seen that the result of his return was first his suspicion of Rymer in the fog, and his subsequent recognition in front of the hotel.

And now he was back, facing the old man, and making his startling report that, after all, the white pig he thought at the bottom of New York Harbour lived, and not only lived, but was in London. Still, worse again, he had been in the neighbourhood of Miss Lansing's house, where, as Won thought, the Diamond Dragon reposed.

Hang Lee spoke just three words, but Won flinched under them as though they had been tongues of fire.

"You have bungled!" said the old man.

Won bowed submissively, and stood expecting to receive his sentence, but Hang Lee did not pronounce the expected decree.

"I give you another chance," he said. "I have been thinking. We have failed all round. We have failed to kill Sexton Blake, we have failed to get the Dragon, and now you tell me this white pig still lives!

"Go back to the house where the Dragon rests. Keep watch to-night. To-morrow, go to this English girl and offer to buy this sacred Dragon. Offer her anything, no matter how much. It will be paid for. Go!"

And Won went.

All night did he and the man he had left keep guard. Early the next morning, at the time Grace was breakfasting, previous to her call on Blake, Won had hastened away to freshen himself up for his second call on her. Even his impassive countenance was not proof against the chagrin he felt when, on his return half an hour later, his companion told him Grace had departed in a taxi.

Undecided what to do, and not daring to go back to Hang Lee with such a report, he sent his companion off, and waited with Oriental patience for developments. He had not long to wait, for shortly after he saw Blake and Grace return to enter the house. Won was the Celestial whom Blake saw pass along the street as he stood at the drawing-room window, and Won viewed from a safe distance the subsequent arrival of Tinker and Pedro, followed by Potter, the house-agent.

He was puzzled when he saw the party cross the road and enter the vacant house, and still more puzzled when he saw their return to Grace's house. He could make nothing of it, and decided his best plan was to watch developments.

He saw Potter leave, and then watched Blake, Tinker, and Pedro drive away.

Now was the time to make his call, and offer Grace any price for the Dragon, as Hang Lee had ordered him to do. But he knew events were taking place of which he knew nothing, and to call now might be disastrous. It would be safer to risk Hang Lee's displeasure now, than perhaps to bungle matters and face it then. With this decision, he hailed a taxi, and told the driver to drive to Limehouse. He arrived there to find Hang Lee still sitting in the back room, as though he hadn't changed his position all night, which, in truth, he had not.

"Well," he said shortly, "will she sell?"

"Excellency, I have not made the offer. May I explain?"

"Speak!" said Hang Lee, in tones of ice, and Won obeyed with alacrity.

Quickly, and in deep, guttural tones, he explained what had occurred, and his desire to consult with Hang Lee for fear of bungling matters.

Dead silence reigned for some minutes before the old man spoke.

"You did right, Won," he remarked. "This Sexton Blake is the biggest danger. It is bad that he and the girl have talked together, and she may even have passed the Sacred Dragon over to him. But they must not meet again. The girl is becoming troublesome. I will think."

Won stood patiently while Hang Lee closed his eyes, slowly nodding his head the while. Finally, he lifted his lids, and spoke with decision.

"I see but one thing. It is risky, and may fail, but we can try. San Lo, the silk merchant, has a large motor-car, with a white driver. I will give you a note to him, which will place it at your disposal. Sexton Blake has evidently talked with the girl about the Sacred Dragon, and on that supposition we will take the risk. Go to a telegraph-office and send a telegram to the girl. Word it like this:

"Complications have suddenly arisen. Wish to see you at once. Cannot come. Am sending car for you. Urgent.

"S. B."

"She will take the initials for Sexton Blake, and there is a chance that it will work. If the driver gets her, have him pick you up afterwards, and bring the girl here. With her in our hands, we will have one difficulty the less, and a weapon as well. Send several men out, and try to locate the man who stole the Dragon. He escaped last night, and has disappeared. That is all. Go, and don't fail!"

Won departed, knowing that his last chance to retrieve himself lay in the success of his efforts, and determined that if risk would bring that success he would get it.

He hastened along to the premises of San Lo, the wealthy silk merchant. That opulent Celestial was only anxious to do as Hang Lee suggested in his note, and five minutes later Won stepped from the luxurious limousine and entered a telegraph-office.

Then he re-entered the car, and while the chauffeur headed west. Won gave him his orders.

"You are to go to this address," and he handed him a slip of paper on which was written Grace's address. "A telegram will reach her in a few minutes, which she will think comes from Sexton Blake, the detective. Stop outside, and then ring the bell. Ask for Miss Lansing, and tell her you have come to take her to Sexton Blake. I will get out around the corner, and when you get her, pick me up. Then drive to the address in Limehouse, which I will give you, and leave the girl to me."

"That's all very fine," growled the driver; "but I'm paid to drive this car, not to mix up in dangerous games like that. What do I get out of it?"

"How much?" asked Won shortly.

"Well, I don't know what your game is," replied the driver, with a shrewd look, "but it looks like kidnapping to me. I won't do it under fifty pounds."

"All right," answered Won at once. "Here's twenty-five now.

You get the rest when you get the girl."

The driver was sorry he hadn't asked for a hundred since it came so readily, but he mentally concluded the job was good for a little gentle blackmail from his opulent master, and he pocketed the notes without further comment.

Blake and Tinker had been gone from Grace's house less than two hours when she received an urgent telegram saying Blake needed her at once. Her first inclination was to ring up on the 'phone and ask him what had occurred, but she reflected that if the 'phone would have answered the purpose he would have used it instead of telegraphing.

That the telegram was a forgery never dawned on her mind. It seemed natural that something might occur, or that he had remembered further questions to ask her, especially as they had been talking about the case so short a time before.

She then decided that she wouldn't wait for his car, but take a taxi and hurry along. Just then she noticed the telegram was sent from the City, and she concluded Blake must be making inquiries there.

"I'll get my things on and be ready," she reflected. "I'll miss my lunch, but that can't be helped. I can get something to eat in a restaurant after I see what Mr. Blake wants."

Hastening up to her room, she donned her hat and coat, and barely had she descended again when she heard a motor stop outside.

She walked over to the window and gazed out on the luxurious limousine which stood at the kerb.

"Mr. Blake certainly believes in comfort," she smiled to herself, as she swept her gaze over the rich upholstering. "But here comes the chauffeur. I'd better not keep him waiting."

She hurried to the door and opened it before San Lo's chauffeur could ring the bell.

"I saw you coming up the steps!" smiled Grace. "I received Mr. Blake's telegram just a few minutes ago, and got ready at once!"

"Very good, miss." responded the chauffeur, smiling inwardly at the ease with which he was earning his fifty pounds. "If you'll step in, miss, we'll get right along."

Grace tripped down the steps, and stood while the chauffeur threw open the door. Then she sank back into the corner and revelled in the smooth, noiseless movement of the big car as it swung around and headed towards the City.

She sat up puzzled as it pulled up after covering a short distance, but sat back again as she saw the chauffeur lean down and apparently do something to the driving-wheel.

The side door swung back so noiselessly that the man who opened it was half in the car before Grace saw him.

She looked up in puzzled surprise, and felt a sudden grip of fear when she recognised the well-dressed Chinaman who had called on her the previous afternoon.

All too late she saw the trap, and reproached herself bitterly for falling into it so easily. With a determination not to be taken without an appeal for help, she dashed up and pushed against the Chinaman.

"What do you want? What is this?" she said quickly. "Open that door, or I will scream for help!"

At that moment the car had started again, and Grace opened her mouth to scream.

Surely at noonday some of the passing pedestrians would hear her and come to her assistance. But Won was too quick for her. With the silence and quickness of a panther, he leaped, and his hand covered her mouth.

As she realised that his hand held a chloroform-saturated handkerchief, she struggled wildly, but Won was not taking any chances. Without any attempt to be gentle, he threw her back in the corner and held her firmly until her struggles grew gradually weaker and weaker, and she finally relaxed.

The drug had done its work. Slightly panting, Won sat up and stuffed the handkerchief in his pocket. Then he opened the windows to let in some air, and, picking up the speaking-tube, gave the chauffeur the address of the gambling den in Limehouse.

That worthy nodded, and sent the great car on at a faster pace, with Chinese captor and unconscious captive inside.

It was nearly an hour later that the car pulled up in the narrow street before the shuttered gambling-den. No time was lost in transferring the unconscious girl from the car to the back room, where Hang Lee sat, and even if any comment had been caused in that district, it would have been quickly suppressed when it was seen into which house the captive was carried.

A rude couch was brought in and placed before Hang Lee. On it Grace was laid, and Won, with the assistance of another Celestial, began restorative action on the unconscious girl.

Grace opened her eyes, and gazed about vaguely, not realising for the moment what had happened to her. As her eyes came round and gazed into the deep, menacing orbs of the impassive, wrinkled face, it all came to her with a shock, and she sat up in horror.

"Oh, how dared you bring me here?" she gasped, shaking from head to foot in nameless terror. "This is an outrage, and you will be punished for it! What do you want of me?" she cried wildly.

"Peace!" said Hang Lee gravely, and at his compelling tone Grace paused. "You have been brought here," went on the old man, "at my orders. You know what I want!"

"I don't —I don't!" cried Grace. "What do you want of me?"

Hang Lee pointed at Won.

"For what reason did he call on you yesterday?"

Grace turned and looked at Won.

"Oh, is it that terrible dragon!" she cried. "I haven't it! I swear to you!"

"If you haven't it, you know where it is," replied Hang Lee coldly. "You have given it to Sexton Blake."

"No, no! I swear to you I am telling the truth! I had it yesterday! But last night it was stolen. That was why I sent for Mr. Blake. I am telling you the truth. I don't know where it is!"

"And Sexton Blake is looking for it?" inquired Hang Lee suavely.

"Yes —that is all I know. Let me go, please, and I will promise I will say nothing about this outrage. And you know kidnapping is serious in London."

Hang Lee snapped his fingers.

"You babble like a babe. Don't talk so much, and listen to me. You say the Diamond Dragon was stolen? You may be telling the truth, and you may be lying. If you are telling the truth, you must suspect someone."

"No" answered Grace wildly, "I don't! I went to Mr. Blake to get him to advise me, and was going to give him the Dragon to keep for me. When we arrived at my house, and I went to get it. I found it gone. That is all I know."

"Does Mr. Blake suspect anyone?"

Grace paused before replying. Would she be doing Blake's cause any harm by telling her captors about the vacant house. No; she decided she wouldn't, for Blake had seen all he wished for there.

"Mr. Blake said it was someone who had stood in a vacant house across the street and watched me while I talked with you," she said, turning to Won.

"After you left I went to my room and locked the Diamond Dragon in my trunk, and he saw where I put the keys. During the evening a man got into the house and stole the Dragon. That is the truth, I swear, and all I know. Now, will you please let me go."

"You are telling me the truth," said Hang Lee slowly, "but Sexton Blake is still searching for the Dragon. For that reason you must remain here a prisoner. If you don't act rashly no harm will come to you. Won, take her to the room upstairs and see that she wants nothing. Send a woman up to look after her, and if she escapes, I will hold you responsible."

In vain Grace pleaded for mercy; in vain did she speak of her invalid mother. Hang Lee was deaf to every plea, and, sobbing wildly, she was led away and turned over to a Chinese woman.

When Won returned to the room where Hang Lee sat, he stood with bowed head waiting for the old man to speak.

"Won," came the slow, guttural tones, "the white pig you thought dead has the Diamond Dragon. Find him!"

And Won, with a low, "Very well, Excellency!" stole silently from the room.

RYMER'S DREAM.

ALL unsuspicious of the drama being played in the East End of London, Sexton Blake had sat in his laboratory ever since his arrival at Baker Street.

On his right hand were powerful glasses of different sizes, and on his left a most comprehensive illustrated record of finger-prints, and under each record the name (and in many cases the prison number) of the owners.

Before him lay the reproduction of the finger print he had found on the dusty stair-rail in the vacant house. Slowly and methodically he had been working through the illustrated record, skipping for the moment the prints of those he knew to be still in prison, and studying those of the "released" or "wanted" owners.

Fully half the leaves in the big book had been turned over, and still he had had no success, but at the moment in question he was deeply studying a print halfway down a certain page, comparing it particle by particle with the print before him.

His eyes glittered drily as each curve found its mate in the book, but not content with the proof of his eyes, he reached for an extremely delicate-looking measuring instrument, and began proving his comparison by an infallible method. Point by point, line by line, curve by curve, it again responded to the test, and as the final point was proved, he leaned back and stared thoughtfully at the wall.

"Well, I must confess this is a surprise!" he muttered. "I thought Dr. Huxton Rymer had dropped out of sight for good. But if the finger-print system doesn't lie, and I've never known it to do so yet, he must be the Dr. Hutton mentioned by Graham. I heard he went to Australia after that last affair in New York, but heard afterwards he had gone to the dogs. Hutton! Of course, that's a natural contraction of Huxton. Drop the 'x' and stick on another 't.' And then the doctor. By Jove, I think I am right!

"I wonder what Scotland Yard would say, if I told them Rymer was in London? They'd smile with their usual incredulous smile, I suppose. But they won't be informed just yet. He's tackling a pretty big proposition when he trifles with the Sacred Dragon, but his successful stealing of it last night shows he hasn't lost any of his old cunning. This complicates matters, too. I thought the thief was some criminal of a lower calibre who had stolen the Diamond Dragon,

118

ignorant of its real meaning and value. I've got enough on my hands with Hang Lee and his gang of cutthroats, without this complication of Rymer. One thing is certain. Unless they have secured it to-day, Rymer must have the Dragon, and it's a case of find him at once."

Curiously enough, at that same moment Hang Lee was using almost the same words to Won in the back room of the gambling-den in Limehouse, and the words uttered by both referred to the same man.

Rymer, unconscious of the decision of the two arch-enemies to find him, was just leaving a shabby, tough-looking den near the river front. His elderly disguise had been changed to that of a beggar. A ragged suit covered him, his tall figure was bent nearly double, a rough wooden crutch supported him, a dilapidated cap was pulled down over his eyes, the white beard and wig had given place to straggly red, and a long, vivid scar decorated one cheek.

As a disguise it was a masterpiece, but the wildest stretch of the imagination could not call it a thing of beauty. In this fashion he began hobbling slowly along, to call on Morris the "fence," and in his inside pocket was the Diamond Dragon of priceless worth.

If Blake could only have known this, what a capture he could have made, and what complications and worries he could have saved. But even his analytical mind, brilliantly deductive as it was, could not do the impossible, and he sat in deep thought in the laboratory viewing from every point the new element which had been introduced into the case.

"The only thing I can see is to adopt my first plan. I'll have to get into my Chinese disguise and go into Chinatown. It will be a case of live and smoke with those yellow cutthroats and wait patiently for some clue. It is just possible that Hang Lee's crowd may have a line on Rymer, and if I can spot their game, I may reach him before he has succeeded in disposing of the Dragon. Wang Ho will come in useful there, and I'll send word to him."

Rising suddenly, he strode into the consulting-room, where Tinker sat writing up the notes of the morning's work.

"Any luck, guv'nor?" he asked, sitting up.

"Yes, my lad!" jerked Blake, walking to the desk and picking up his old black pipe. "I know the man who stole the Dragon from Miss Lansing's trunk last night."

"Great Scott, guv'nor!" exclaimed Tinker. "Did you find his print in the 'record'?"

Blake nodded.

"Yes; it is Dr Huxton Rymer, and it happens that he is wanted pretty badly, too."

"Crikey! There are some shining lights in this game!" murmured Tinker, with a grin.

"We haven't any time for hilarity," replied Blake shortly.

"We may discover, before we are through, that one of these 'shining lights' will get away with the shining Dragon. If we are to get it before Hang Lee does, or Rymer digs the stones out and dumps the Dragon in the melting pot, we've got to move. I want you to get into a disguise and go at once to the Chinese Embassy. See either Li Hong or Wang Ho. Either tell Wang Ho or leave word for him to come on here at once, as I can make use of him now. Look sharp, Tinker; we're playing a swift game from now on."

Tinker jumped up and hurried to his room. Throwing open the wardrobe door, he stood for a moment considering what disguise he would assume.

"I haven't had this one on for a time," he said to himself.

"I guess I'll use it to-day." He pulled out a pair of worn corduroy trousers, and a shabby black velvet coat. From a drawer he took a wig of heavy straight black hair.

This he spent some time in adjusting to his satisfaction, and then he started on his face and neck. He spread a dark stain over them, even to his chest, and then did likewise with his hands and wrists and arms. After that he put on a flannel shirt, and then donned the trousers and coat. A loosely-knotted handkerchief completed the job, and when he had finished he looked as much like an Italian boy as though he had been born there.

He had picked up a wonderful vocabulary of Italian, and under Blake's guidance had mastered the correct accent. Consequently, when he adopted the Italian disguise, he passed exceptionally well in it.

"May I take Pedro with me, guv'nor?" he asked, on his return to the consulting-room.

Blake stopped in his pacing, and his face relaxed.

"You are certainly coming along, my lad. That Italian disguise is a masterpiece. Yes, take Pedro if you wish."

Tinker's face lit up with pleasure at Blake's remark.

Praise was rare with his master, but when he did praise it meant something.

Calling Pedro, he started out on his message, leaving Blake to his maze of deductions.

Tinker found on his arrival at the Embassy that their first intention was to show him off without ceremony, but on his mentioning the simple name Li Hong, the clerk's attitude changed at once.

"Come in!" he said, in very bad English. "What you want?"

"I want to see either Mr. Li Hong or Wang Ho at once," replied Tinker.

"We don't know any Li Hong or Wang Ho," answered the young Celestial cautiously.

"Don't waste time, young fellah!" said Tinker. "I want to see either one. I don't care which, and I want to see him quick."

"Who you come from?" inquired the clerk.

For answer Tinker merely looked at him, and slowly winked.

The young Chinaman smiled expansively.

"You velly smart young fellah. But Mista Li Hong not here. Wang Ho not here either."

"Can you tell me where I can find either of them?" asked Tinker.

"I give you address in Limehouse where you find Wang Ho if you want."

"Right-ho, my son! Cough it up, quick!" replied Tinker; and the clerk scribbled an address.

Tinker, with the address in his pocket, left the Embassy and called a taxi. Giving the driver the address, and holding the door for Pedro to get in, he settled back for the long ride.

"That wasn't a bad sort of chap for a Chink," he thought, referring to the young clerk. "I wonder what Wang Ho is doing in Limehouse? Probably over in some joss-house. Funny beggars, these Chinks; but the guv'nor seems to think a lot of this mysterious Li Hong. He speaks of him almost as though he were a Royal personage. Crikey, things do look mixed up! I'd like to know just what the guv'nor thinks, but I daren't risk asking him now. I'll just keep my eyes open, and see what I can."

He sat absorbed in thoughts of a similar nature until they reached the narrow turnings of Limehouse. Then he sat up and began sizing up his surroundings as they drove through.

"Not a very lovely place!" he muttered. "It looks Chinese. I wouldn't want to be stranded down here on a dark night without a gun, would you, Pedro, old chap?"

Pedro pounded his tail, but gave no indication as to what he would do with a gun on a dark night, or any other kind of a night.

After innumerable turnings, the taxi pulled up with a jerk before a shabby, murderous-looking house.

"I say, cabby!" said Tinker, as he alighted. "I've got to look up a Chink in here, and it seems a murderous joint. If I don't come out soon, just raise a tattoo on the door, will you?"

"Sure thing, kid!" grinned the driver "Better leave the dog out, here. They might put him in the steam-pot in there and eat him for dinner."

"I guess they'd find him a tough proposition!" laughed Tinker. "However, I'll leave him outside."

Rapping loudly on the door, he waited for some moments, and was just about to give a second summons when he heard shuffling steps inside. He drew back as the door opened, but he had no need for caution. Standing back so he could not be seen from the street was a tall, well-dressed Chinaman, and Tinker knew enough to know he was a pure Manchu.

Tinker stepped closer, and spoke in a low tone:

"Is Wang Ho here?"

The man looked at him closely for a moment, and then beckoned him in.

"Do you come from Sexton Blake?" he asked, as he closed the door.

Tinker nodded.

"I am Wang Ho," replied the Celestial.

"Mr. Blake wants you to go to Baker Street at once," went on Tinker. "New developments have taken place, and he wants you to help him."

"Good! I will go at once. Will you have some refreshment before you go?"

"No, thanks," replied Tinker. "I don't care for anything."

He hated to refuse what was evidently offered out of kindness, but the musty odour of the place sickened him, and he wanted to get out in the air again.

Wang Ho probably read and understood the lad's reason, but he gave no sign, and only smiled.

"Very well. I think it wiser we should go to Baker Street separately. I will leave after you and get a taxi farther along."

"All right," replied Tinker, turning to go.

"Well, did they threaten to cut your throat," grinned the driver, as Tinker emerged.

"No; they wanted to poison me," he answered. "Get out of here as soon as you can, cabby, and stop at the first telegraph-office you come to when we reach the City."

They returned a slightly different way from which they had come, and Tinker would have been more than astounded had he known one of those gloomy, shuttered houses had only an hour before enfolded Grace Lansing as a prisoner within its sinister wings. And how desperate Grace would have been in that upstairs room had she known a friend was so near, and yet so irrevocably removed from her.

The driver lost no time in reaching the City again and pulled up in front of a telegraph-office.

Tinker descended, and with Pedro at his heels went in to send a wire to Blake saying that Wang Ho was going right along. For he knew from Blake's manner that matters were very urgent, and even if a wire only reached there a short time before his own arrival, the few minutes saved might be of value in his master's plans.

He was leaving the telegraph-office, and crossing the pavement to re-enter the taxi, when Pedro stopped suddenly and began nosing the pavement in obvious excitement. Tinker watched him in surprise for a moment, but as the hound began working on the scent he had found, Tinker called him back.

"What is it, Pedro?" he asked, looking at the hound curiously. "What scent have you found?"

The dog only pounded his tail and turned again, and this time was deaf to Tinker's commands to return.

"Now, what on earth has he found?" muttered Tinker, looking up and down the street. "I'd go with him and find out, but the guv'nor may need me for something. I don't see anybody that looks familiar."

He glanced quickly along the street, but failed to identify any of the hurrying pedestrians.

Although it was a fairly quiet street, there were several people about, and the appearance of none was suspicious. At that moment, however, he caught sight of a ragged, crippled beggar, and his brow wrinkled.

"This is a poor street for a beggar to work in. Perhaps, though, he's either leaving his regular spot or going to it. I'll have to do something pretty quick, though. I'll risk it, and see what Pedro has found."

He turned hastily, and paid the driver, and began hurrying along after the dog.

Pedro pulled up when he saw his master was coming, and waited until Tinker caught him up. Then, with his nose once more to the ground, he started on. While they walked on Tinker strove to find out which of the pedestrians Pedro was following, but not until they had covered several blocks did he finally decide that the hound was on the bait of the crippled beggar.

"Hum!" he grunted. "I wonder if it's some criminal disguised whose scent Pedro knows. Crikey, it would be a go if it was the chap that stole the Diamond Dragon from Miss Lansing. Pedro would recognise his scent after this morning. However, now that I've started I'll follow his nibs for a bit."

Calling Pedro back, he sauntered along, not losing sight of his quarry. Finally, the beggar hobbled down a side street and began ascending a shop-lined hill. He stopped about halfway up, and entered one of the dingy shops. Tinker quickened his steps, and as he passed the shop which the beggar had entered, he read the sign:

"A. MORRIS,
Pawnbroker and Secondhand Dealer."

"Now, what does our ragged friend want with old Morris?" muttered Tinker, as he hastened on. "From what I know he wouldn't have much business with beggars, unless —I wonder if I could see anything from the back of the shop?"

He was standing at the entrance of a narrow alley which ran off, and from where he stood he saw that by climbing a fence at the back, he would be standing in the yard at the rear of the pawnbroker's.

To think was to act, and with Pedro at his heels, Tinker, looking like any Italian street-boy, walked boldly up the alley. When he reached the fence, he looked hastily about, and, seeing no one in sight at the moment, began hoisting himself to the top of the fence.

Before dropping over to the other side, he reached down and pulled Pedro after him. Then, with stealthy steps, he began stealing across the yard. One solitary window, thick with dust and grime, was set high up in the rear of the pawnbroker's shop, and towards it Tinker bent his steps.

"If I can get up there," he muttered, "I might be able to hear something. It evidently looks into Morris's office, and if my crippled friend is anybody in disguise, and has business of importance with the old rascal, that's where they will be. I'll just see about arranging a quick retreat in case of accidents before I investigate."

He turned and retraced his steps to the fence into which a gate had been set. It was bolted on the inside, and with a chuckle, Tinker slipped the bolt. Softly ordering Pedro to lie down, he went back and stood beneath the high window. It was fully eight feet from the ground, and, putting his ear against the wall, he could hear the murmur of voices inside.

"They're in there all right," he muttered. "I'd give something to hear that conversation."

He cast about desperately for some method of getting up to the window, and as his eyes lit on a pile of old barrels in the corner, he stole over to them. He picked out one, apparently fairly sound, and, lifting it, carried it over, and set it on end under the window.

Then, climbing on top of it, he slowly straightened up until his head was almost on a level with the window-sill. The voices were more distinct, and he knew from the sound that the window looked down into the office. The murmur was not loud enough, however, for him to distinguish what was being said, and if he peered in through the window his shadow might attract the attention of the men below.

There was nothing else, however, but to risk it, and holding his face back from the window, he stood up straight. His eyes barely reached above the sill, and if he were to see down into the room below he would have to raise himself higher. He was bringing his face closer and closer gradually in order not to cause too sudden a shadow against the window, and had placed his hands on the sill to draw himself up, when the opposite wall of the office became visible through the grime on the panes, and Tinker stopped suddenly at what he saw.

Straight across from him was a large, dirty cracked mirror hanging on the wall. He could just make out that the lower edge rested on a littered mantelpiece, but that was not what caused him to stand breathlessly silent.

Mirrored in the dirty glass were the reflections of two men bending over a desk in the office. Their backs and bent heads were all the lad could see, but one of them he recognised as Morris, the pawnbroker, and the other as the crippled beggar.

But, strange to say, the cripple was moving and gesticulating with a freedom of movement which was in marked contrast to his previous painful actions, and Tinker knew in that moment that the ragged outfit was, in truth, but a disguise.

He watched breathlessly while the two men talked in low tones —the beggar doing most of it, while the pawnbroker kept nodding his head, and grunting from time to time. Then, with a slow smile, and cautious look around, the disguised cripple unbuttoned his coat, and drew forth a leather belt, and pouch. He opened the flap of the pouch, and Tinker nearly fell off the barrel in his excitement as he saw reflected in the mirror opposite the blazing, scintillating Diamond Dragon of which he had heard so much.

"Crumbs —oh, crumbs," he breathed excitedly, "what a beauty! No wonder those Chinks are ready to commit murder for it. And what a lucky thing I followed Pedro. He certainly deserves a medal for this, and won't the guv'nor be pleased. Without doubt this is the man the guv'nor says is Dr. Huxton Rymer, and he's losing no time in getting rid of the Dragon. Oh, he's not going to leave it with Morris, after all! I wonder why not?"

It was true. The cripple could be seen putting the Dragon back in his pocket, and then begin talking with the pawnbroker. Tinker lowered his head, and put his ear against the edge of the sill. The tones grew louder, and he knew from their raised voices that the two men were arguing, and in the heat of argument forgot their previous caution.

Suddenly he heard a full sentence as the cripple raised his voice in finality.

"Ten per cent., Morris —not a penny more. If you want the business at that, all right."

"I tell you," snapped the pawnbroker, "it's not enough! It is robbery. But give me time."

"Time! How much time do you want?"

"Until to-morrow."

"All right. This time to-morrow, then, and let me tell you —"

Tinker could catch no more as the voice trailed away in a lower pitch, and the scraping of feet, accompanied by the pushing back of chairs, told him the cripple was getting up to go.

"I've got enough, anyhow," he muttered, as he leaped to the ground and made haste to put the barrel back. "I'll take Pedro, and follow his crippled nibs to wherever he hangs out, and then I'll make tracks to tell the guv'nor. He will be no end pleased at the news."

Tinker stole back across the yard, and after letting Pedro through the gate, closed it, and pushed the bolt in again. Then he drew himself up, and dropped over into the alley.

The cripple had just left the pawnbroker's, and was hobbling slowly along when Tinker and Pedro reached the street again, and, slouching along in a careless manner. Tinker took up the trail.

On and on they went through narrow streets, and into broader ones, then twisting and turning back again into congested, odorous alleys and lanes, ever getting into a more unsavoury district.

Dusk had now fallen, and still the crippled beggar went on, apparently tireless in his slow, hobbling progress.

Finally, they got into the Limehouse district, and Tinker whistled softly to himself.

"Crikey, he's taking a risk coming through here! If any of these Chinks dreamed he had that Diamond Dragon on him, they'd make mincemeat of him in about two minutes!"

As the darkness grew more intense, Tinker closed up a bit, as in those dark, shadowy streets he was in danger of losing his quarry.

Finally, Rymer crossed a small bridge over a black watercourse, evidently an unsavoury arm which led into the river. Then Tinker saw him turn suddenly, and go down a narrow, dark alley, leading toward the water.

Hastening along, Tinker also turned into the black alley, and began stealthily creeping down it, trying to discover what had become of the now invisible cripple. Half-way down the alley turned, and led on to a small landing, which jutted out into the water, and as it was the only visible course for the quarry to take, Tinker took it also.

With infinite caution, and a warning hand on Pedro, he kept on, knowing from the hound's acquiescence that they were on the right trail. He had started creeping by a small tumble-down shed, and was looking keenly ahead, when from the shadowy doorway of the shed a man leaped out and sprang toward him.

Pedro, with a growl, had leaped clear over the creeping Tinker almost before the lad was aware that the cunning Rymer, knowing he was followed, had purposely led the way to this unsavoury spot.

Tinker leaped to his feet and drew his revolver, as he saw Rymer turn and strike wildly with his crutch at Pedro. The dog dropped with a growl of anger, and Tinker raised his arm. Rymer, however, without even looking, was viciously bringing the heavy crutch around with a swing. It caught Tinker fair on the side of the head, and sent him reeling.

He tried wildly to save himself, but for the moment he was helpless, and, with a gurgling cry, he fell over the edge of the landing into the sinister water below. Pedro had recovered from the blow he had received, and was again advancing to the attack, when Tinker fell into the water.

He stopped hesitatingly, evidently trying in his canine mind to decide whether to go after his young master, or to make another attack on the man who stood viciously swinging the crutch about. Rymer, however, settled the matter for himself.

Leaping forward, he drew back, and delivered a crushing blow at the dog. Pedro saw it coming, however, and leaped just in time to save himself. But if his agility saved him from being either stunned or killed, it settled what he should do, for in his spring he was carried over the edge, and turned a complete somersault into the water. With a mocking laugh, as he saw his two victims swept along into the blackness of the night by the deep, swirling waters, Rymer turned and retraced his steps.

"I don't know who they were," he muttered, as he gained the street again, "but that dog was mighty like Sexton Blake's, and the boy was about the build of his assistant. Where they got my trail I can't imagine, but I've settled them, and I'll guarantee they won't bother me again. This town is certainly getting too warm for me, and as soon as I complete arrangements with Morris to-morrow, I'll get out quick."

If he had dreamed that the lad he had knocked into the water had been a witness of his meeting with the pawnbroker earlier in the afternoon, he wouldn't have been satisfied with only knocking Tinker into the water senseless. But neither Rymer nor Morris had seen the lad at the window, and the rejuvenated cripple went on his way to change his disguise, quite certain that no one knew of his visit.

Tinker's dazed senses balanced on the brink when he hit the

water. One moment his mind was fairly clear, and the next it was cloudy. He must have hit his left arm in falling, for he tried to use it in his struggles to keep afloat, and found it not only helpless, but exceedingly painful at the shoulder joint. He fought hard for strength, and to keep his senses, wondering what success Pedro was having. He looked back, but could see nothing, the current having already carried him along some distance.

Close to him he could see the rear walls of the Chinese houses lining the water's edge, their overhanging ends lending a sinister shadow to the picture. His ears caught the faint sound of a faraway splash, and he dimly wondered if it was either Pedro or Rymer, or was he hearing the actual disposal of someone through a rear window of the gloomy haunts on the shore, a disposal that would be reported a mysterious disappearance.

Faint splashings continued to reach him, growing louder and louder, and finally accompanied by heavy breathing.

Tinker, who had been treading water trying to get back his strength, turned to see what it was, and as he did it was upon him. A great wave of joy went over him as he felt Pedro's wet head, and saw that he was uninjured.

With excruciating pain, and talking all the while to Pedro in a low tone, he raised his injured arm, and threw it over the dog's strong back, which easily supported it. Then, thrusting out his right arm, and paddling slowly, he spoke to Pedro, who began also paddling ahead.

"We'll work our way into the shore, old chap," whispered the lad. "I can't hold up with this arm much longer. We'll take our chances of getting through some of those joints there."

Pedro, naturally, made no reply, but paddled on valiantly, while Tinker gradually steered their way towards the shore.

Nearer and nearer they drew, until finally Pedro was almost touching the buildings on the left. In the dim shadows ahead Tinker could see a window close to the surface of the water, and its overhanging sill gave him an idea.

"If I can make that," he muttered, "I can rest, and maybe get my shoes off. It's wide enough to sit on if I can draw myself up."

He directed every energy towards it, pushing Pedro in close. This was almost Tinker's undoing, for so close had he pushed the dog that, with the weight on his back and the wall so close, he found it impossible to swim.

He began struggling to keep afloat, and it was just then that they began sweeping past the window. Pedro's struggles had sent them too far away for Tinker to reach it with his uninjured arm, and as they threatened to miss it altogether, he lifted his injured arm from Pedro's back, and clutched the fast-passing sill.

The pain was intense, and before he could work around to grasp the sill with his sound arm the current and Pedro's weight threatened to force him to leave go.

But, gritting his teeth to keep from giving in, he hung on with all his strength.

Slowly and painfully the steady pull drew him nearer and nearer. Finally Pedro was close enough to get his paws on the sill, and, with his weight removed, Tinker made it. As he drew himself up, panting with exhaustion, a deafening crash sounded on the inside of the window, followed by the sudden springing of spreading flames.

AFTER Tinker's departure with his master's message for Wang Ho, Blake went back to the laboratory, and once more made a final comparison of the finger-print he had got in the vacant house and the illustrated print in his book of records.

"No," he said, sitting up; "there's not the shadow of a doubt. Now the point is, where is Rymer? He'll do everything in his power to get the Dragon off his hands quickly, and if I am to save it, I'll have to act at once. He usually hangs out around the East End when he is here, except, of course, when he is flush, and then he makes for the Continent. But he must know there is a horde on his heels, and whether he will have the nerve to go to his old haunts or not it is hard to say. However, I think my first plan is the best. I'll go into Chinatown with Wang Ho and try to pick up some clue there."

Blake got to his feet, and returned to the consulting-room as he heard the bell ring. It was a telegram for him, and he lost no time in tearing it open. It was Tinker's message, saying Wang Ho was on his way, and barely had Blake finished reading it when the bell rang again. It was Wang Ho who had followed on at once, and Blake waved him at once into a chair.

"Have you news of the Dragon, Mr. Blake?" asked Wang Ho eagerly.

"Yes, I have news," jerked out Blake. "I know the man who stole the Dragon in Melbourne. He is now in London, and at this moment has the Dragon in his possession. There have been a great many developments since I saw you," he added; "but I haven't time to go into them now. What I wanted you for is this. I find I will have to disguise as a Chinaman and go into the Chinese district. Our only hope now is to try there and get some clue. Are you going to come with me?"

"Of course, Mr. Blake," replied Wang Ho. "Besides. I am bound to do everything in my power to secure the return of the Dragon."

"Very well," answered Blake. "Have you friends there whom you can trust?"

"Yes, several. I was at the house of a relative there this afternoon when your assistant found me."

"Ah! He had to go on there, did he?" remarked Blake. "By the way, he ought to be here by now, but I suppose he has stopped at some place on the way back. But to return to the subject. Where is this house of your relative?"

Wang Ho gave Blake the address, and the detective jotted it down on his cuff.

"Very well. Here is my plan. You leave here and go back at once. When dusk has fallen I will take a cab and follow you. I will not disguise until I get there, and then we will go to work. To start with, we will make a round of the gambling and opium dens, and I needn't tell you to arm yourself well. No man can see the ending of this chase."

"I won't fail to do so," answered Wang he slowly. "I can shoot your British guns and I can handle a kris."

Again the bell rang, and Blake frowned irritably.

"Step into the dressing-room," he said, rising, and throwing open the door. "I don't know who it may be, and I don't want anyone to see you."

Wang Ho slipped inside, and Blake closed the door just as Mrs. Bardell rapped at the outer door and entered.

"Well," demanded Blake irritably, "what is it?"

"There's another one of them furriners on the step. They seem to think this is a Chinese laundry!"

"Do I understand you to mean there is a Chinaman at the door?" asked Blake sharply.

"Yes, and I told him —"

"Never mind what you told him! Show him in!"

Mrs. Bardell flounced out, and Blake smiled as she disappeared. For the landlady classed all foreigners together as undesirables, and in reality covered a fear of them under her grumbling remarks. This Blake understood, and when she began to grow garrulous he found it wiser to speak sharply.

She opened the door again to admit the visitor, and Blake looked up to see the countenance of Won. He was dressed in his immaculate English clothes, and held his silk hat at a jaunty angle.

Although Blake did not know him, he knew Blake, and his opening question was altogether unnecessary.

"Are you Mr. Blake?" he asked politely.

Blake bowed slightly, trying all the time to fathom who the Celestial was, and why he had called.

"I have a letter of importance which I have been requested to

132

hand you. I am to wait until you read it, please, and get your answer."

He felt in the inside pocket of his coat, and drew forth a letter, which he handed to the detective. Blake took it in silence, and tore it open, but so amazed was he at the contents that it needed every ounce of his trained self-control not to show in his face the surprise he felt. These were the words which he read and re-read:

"Dear Sir, —Since your call on Miss Grace Lansing this morning that young lady has fallen into my hands. I am inclined to think you either have a certain thing which I want, or know where it is, so I am holding the girl as a hostage. If you have the object in question you can release the girl by handing it over. If not, you can gain her release by assisting me instead of the other side. I know you can call your police in on a matter of this kind, but if you call them in to release the girl I will act at once. You know me well enough to know how that will be. If you agree to my terms, come with the messenger. If not, beware! For obvious reasons, I don't give the address of the place where the girl is, but it is safe; and, let me inform you, any effort to bring in the police will bring down a swift judgment on her head and yours.

"Your obedient servant,
"Most illustrious one,
"HANG LEE."

Blake had suspected the actual presence of the old Chinaman in London, but the well-known signature did away with any doubts. He knew then that it was indeed a fight of giants, and if he were to come out of the affair at all, he would need every ounce of subtlety he had.

The letter which he had received was the result of Hang Lee's deliberations after instructing Won to send men out to sweep the city of Rymer.

He feared Blake might stumble on Rymer first, and had called Won back. After writing the letter, he had instructed Won in his part.

"Get him some way to come here," said the old man. "If the letter doesn't catch him, try some other way. We must tie his hands and keep him out of this matter until we get the sacred Dragon back."

Won had departed at once, and while Blake read the letter he watched the detective closely. But Blake had succeeded in controlling his surprise, and when he looked up his face was as impassive as the Celestial's.

"Is the writer of this your master?" he asked.

Won bowed.

"It is a very strange letter," remarked Blake coldly. "Your master seems to forget that he is in a civilised country. Do you know this gives me power to arrest you?" he demanded.

Again Won bowed, but said nothing.

Blake hadn't the faintest idea of arresting Won. He knew he might arrest or even kill fifty of Hang Lee's agents, and that deep old Celestial would only shrug, and send out others. He knew that to Hang Lee every man was only a pawn in the greater game, and if they went under —well there were always plenty more to fill their places.

But Blake desired to gain time to think, and had made the remark only in order to get an opportunity to do so. His mind was working like lightning. He hadn't the slightest doubt that every word in the note was true, and that Grace Lansing lay a prisoner in their hands. His blood boiled at the thought of it, and he was tempted to strike down the suave Celestial where he stood.

But he knew he must tread very warily. Grace would be safe enough until he answered Hang Lee's letter. If he refused to reply to it, or attempted to release Grace by force, he knew the old man would carry out his threat in the letter.

No; he must meet subtlety with subtlety. Force was of no use at present. Hang Lee must be fought with his own weapons, and in order to do so he must have time. He would adopt a different attitude, and try bluff. Again he picked up the letter and read it through slowly.

"This letter," he said, looking up when he had finished— "this letter, I must own, is a great surprise. It is useless to say that Hang Lee holds the trump card. But, on the other hand, it is hard to surrender, and before doing so I will require to think matters over. I will give you a definite answer to-night, not before."

Won bowed.

"Where will you give your answer, Excellency, here?" he inquired.

Blake shook his head.

"I will answer to Hang Lee himself; no one else. You can take me to-night to him, and I will give him his answer."

"Very well Excellency! I will do so. What time shall I call?"

"About seven."

Won bowed, and, with murmured thanks, took his departure. As the door closed behind him Blake leaped across the room, and threw open the dressing-room door.

"Quick, Wang Ho!" he jerked. "Come here to the window!"

He dragged the Chinaman across the room as he spoke, and in the shelter of the curtain pointed out Won, who was descending the steps to the street.

"Do you know who that is?" he asked.

"No, Mr. Blake," answered Wang Ho; "but I have seen him before. I saw him enter a gambling-house of my countrymen in our district."

"You are sure it is the same?"

"Absolutely, Mr. Blake!"

"Then here is what you have to do," jerked Blake, turning and leading the way. "Come with me."

He entered the laboratory, and threw open the window.

"Go out this way and through the back gate. Get a taxi, and drive as fast as you can through to this gambling-den. Get into shelter in some place, and watch out for his arrival. If he reaches there shortly after you do we will know he has gone direct. If he does so, jump in a taxi and come back here at once. Hurry now, or he may reach there before you."

"Why, Mr. Blake, what is it all about?"

"Don't waste time asking questions," snapped Blake; "hurry up! Everything hangs on it."

He pushed Wang Ho through the window as he spoke, and a moment later the Celestial was tearing out the back way.

"It would be useless for me to follow him!" muttered Blake, as he returned to the consulting-room and filled his pipe. "Even Hang Lee wouldn't dare send a letter like that to a man in London without sending men to see if the messenger was followed on his return. If I tried to follow him I'd have half a dozen Chinks on my heels at once.

"But what a nerve that old chap has got. Grace Lansing's position is a bad one, and she must be rescued. But if old Hang Lee thinks I am going to purchase her freedom by giving up the search for the Dragon he is mistaken. It is going to be difficult and dangerous to get her out of their hands, and if things are bungled Heaven help her, for Hang Lee will carry out his threat!

"However, if Wang Ho really did see this Chinaman come out of a gambling-house, it is just possible the place may be one of Hang

Lee's network of dens, and that the old man has his headquarters there. If that is so, I think I see a way to move. But if not, I'll have to use urgent measures. Heaven help them if they harm that girl! But even the Dragon must wait until I free her."

Blake had been pacing up and down the room, with a grim set to his jaw and a hard glitter in his eyes. But now he turned, and; again filling the old black pipe, cast himself into the big chair, to give up his mind to the weaving of plans for the outwitting of the subtle Chinese.

He was irritated at Tinker's non-appearance, for he knew the lad was aware of the urgency of matters since Dr. Huxton Rymer had succeeded in successfully stealing the Dragon. But as his brain seized on the problem, and began dissecting it point by point, Tinker faded from his mind, his irritation passed, and dead silence reigned as that giant intellect worked with the smoothness of well-oiled machinery.

Three hours later Blake came back to earth as the street door bell pealed, and getting to his feet, turned on the light, for it was already dusk.

He glanced up quickly as the door opened, and a look of relief overspread his face as he saw it was Wang Ho.

"Well," he demanded quickly, "did you find out anything?"

"Yes, Mr. Blake. You will be pleased," replied Wang Ho, sinking into a chair. "I drove through as fast as possible, and left the taxi at the entrance to the street where the gambling-house stands. I walked down, and entered the house of a friend which stands nearly opposite. I must have got there quickly, for it was not until twenty minutes later that the man I was looking for drove up."

"Probably held up in a block of traffic," jerked Blake. "But proceed, Wang Ho. What else?"

"Nothing much, Mr. Blake. As you say, he may have been held up in the traffic. I watched him into the house, and his cab drove away. I waited an hour, but beyond a few people entering the house, I saw nothing. Then I came direct back here."

"Good —good!" muttered Blake, pacing up and down. "You being a Chinaman, they wouldn't suspect you so quickly. But tell me," he jerked, coming to a stop, "have you ever been in this gambling-house?"

"Oh, yes, plenty of times when I was in London before!"

"It has an opium-room, of course?"

"Yes; on the left as you enter."

"And the gambling-room —where is it?"

"On the right."

"Is it a pretty good-sized place?"

"Fair. It is two storeys and a basement. The rooms are small, except for the gambling-room and opium-room, which are each formed of two rooms thrown into one."

"I see. Well, Wang Ho, listen carefully, for our lives will depend on it. Go back there, and, early in the evening, go into the gambling-room. Play there a bit, and then go to the opium-room. Some time during the evening I will be in there. I will be dressed as a Chinaman, but if you think you recognise me make no sign. We will have to tackle this thing singlehanded."

"Do you suspect them of having the Dragon in there?" asked the Celestial, in surprise.

"No, they've got a white girl there who is mixed up in the case, and she has got to be rescued at once. If I am to find the Dragon, I expect you to lend me your assistance then to-night. Besides, I think it is just possible your friend Hang Lee may be there, and, if so, I may be able to kill two birds with one stone. However, I can't form any plans until I get there. Watch every man who enters, and when you see one pull his revolver you will know it is I. Now hurry along; I have a lot to do."

And the mystified Wang Ho, who, Celestial though he was, could not follow the subtleties of the detective's mind, hastened away to do as he was bid.

After his departure Blake rang for the landlady.

"Has Tinker been here at all this afternoon?" he inquired.

"I 'aven't seen 'im since 'e came back 'ere with you this noon."

"Very well. Bring me something to eat at once. I am going out, and if Tinker should come in tell him I have left a letter of instructions on the desk."

But Tinker was not destined to get that letter; at least, not that evening, for, with Pedro, he was at that moment trailing the crippled beggar along the narrow, dark streets of Limehouse.

The landlady brought Blake a hasty supper, and while he wrote Tinker's instructions with one hand, he used the other to make a hurried meal.

Then, calling Mrs. Bardell to take the things away, he said: "I expect a caller at seven. It will be the same man who came this afternoon. Admit him at once when he comes."

As she closed the door and departed, Blake walked to his desk and opened one of its many drawers. From it he took a short, heavy sandbag, which was a memento of one of his stirring cases. Slipping this up his arm under the sleeve of his coat, he closed the drawer, and, pulling the big chair out of the glare of the light, sat down to await his visitor.

The clock on the mantel was just chiming seven when the bell rang, and Blake shifted slightly.

A moment later the door opened, and Won entered.

Blake waved him to a chair, which had been set with its back toward the desk.

"I see you are prompt," he remarked, as his visitor sat down, ignorant of the fact that Blake had placed the chair in that exact position.

"Yes. Excellency," replied Won quietly. "My master was angry at the delay, so I lost no time in coming for you."

"Then your master is still determined to carry out what he says in the letter?" asked Blake.

"Certainly, sir! Hang Lee never says anything he doesn't mean."

Blake yawned and stood up.

"Well, I suppose there is nothing else for me to do but to visit your master," he said, walking toward the desk.

But as he walked the arm concealing the sandbag was shielded from Won by his body, and ever so slowly Blake let it slip down until he had grasped it with his hand. By this time he was close beside Won, and, wheeling suddenly as he gripped the sandbag, he lifted his arm and struck quickly.

Won saw the descending sandbag before it reached him, and, with a startled grunt, started up. But so true was Blake's aim that Won's movement only served to make him meet the descending weapon a trifle sooner, and as the soft thud of the sandbag sounded against his head, he rolled out of the chair to the floor without a sound.

"I hate to take advantage of a man like that," smiled Blake grimly, as he opened the drawer and replaced the sandbag. "But Hang Lee must be met with his own weapons, and I have never known him yet to use kid-gloves. I have no doubt he intends a far worse fate than this for me, my unconscious friend; but, thank Heaven, I know his methods, and can at least be on the watch!"

Little did Blake realise how deadly Hang Lee's real intentions were towards him, nor did he realise just what that wily old Celestial had planned.

He dragged Won up from the floor, and set him on a chair. Then, with a deftness born of long experience, he began removing the Chinaman's clothes. It should be stated here that Won had changed his European clothes since the afternoon, and when he came back in the evening was dressed in his native garments.

It was that which prompted Blake to remove them, and when he had finished he picked up the unconscious body of his visitor, and propped him in a chair where the electric light fell full on his face. Then, entering his dressing-room, and bringing out a small handbag, Blake drew up a chair facing the other.

Placing the bag on the desk with his revolver beside it, and drawing forward a mirror, he set to work. From the bag the detective drew several different cosmetics, then a colouring fluid, and a package of fine, almost invisible, threads. With these materials he started to work, and, point by point, inch by inch, line by line, he began making his face a duplicate of Won's.

When he had finished his face he drew forth several pig-tailed wigs, making a careful examination before he decided which one he would use. This he adjusted, and so thorough was his work that he coiled the pigtail and bound it exactly like Won's.

Then Blake slipped off his clothes and donned those he had removed from his visitor. When he stood up and regarded himself in the mirror over the mantel, he smiled grimly.

"As neat a job as I ever did," he muttered; "but I'll need all my neatness to-night if I'm not mistaken. Hallo! My visitor is beginning to show signs of life. I'd better fix him up before he kicks up a row."

He hastened into the dressing-room, and returned a moment later with several lengths of strong cord, and a long silk sash. Won was stirring and muttering, but Blake unceremoniously dragged him on the floor, and went to work. First he securely bound his ankles, and then his knees.

After that he turned him over, and tied his wrists securely behind his back, again shifting him, he rolled the silk sash up into a ball and thrust it in Won's mouth. With a handkerchief he completed this part of the job, and he surveyed his work with satisfaction.

"There, my friend! I'll defy you to work out of those bonds. But just to be on the safe side, I'll strap you to the chair in the dressing-room."

Picking him up, Blake carried him into the dressing-room and carried out his plans.

As he finished Won came to his senses and blinked with puzzled eyes. As he realised how he had fallen into the trap of that big Englishman who stood over him, his eyes blazed not with fear of Blake, for, to do him justice. Won was a brave man, but with fear of that deep old Celestial, Hang Lee. He knew quite well enough what command he would receive when Hang Lee discovered how he had been fooled, and though he did not flinch from killing himself at Hang Lee's command, he, in common with almost everyone else, flinched from the silent scorn and menace of those fathomless eyes. But there was one man going before Han Lee that night who would not flinch, and between those two there would be a battle of wits for victory.

As Won saw how exactly Blake had copied him, his fear gave place to amazement, and unconsciously his eyes paid tribute to the ability of his English adversary. But Blake had no time to waste, and with a parting injunction that it would be useless for him to attempt to escape, the detective returned to the consulting-room and turned out the light.

Then, with his revolver in a convenient place, he started out to attempt single-handed to rescue Grace Lansing, and beat at his own game the wiliest Celestial living.

Barely had Blake covered a hundred yards before a silent figure appeared from a shadowy spot and approached him.

"Couldn't you get the son of a pig, Won?" he asked, in guttural Chinese.

With as good an imitation of Won's voice as possible, Blake replied in Chinese.

"No; to-morrow —not to-night."

"Will we stay on watch?" asked the other.

Blake nodded.

"Yes, of course!" And the figure disappeared again in the shadows.

"By thunder!" muttered the detective, as he strode on. "That was a close shave, but he never suspected. It was lucky, though, in a way, for now I know what my name is supposed to be —Won; I'll remember that."

A couple of taxis were coming towards him, and Blake hailed them both.

"Here, driver," he said in English to one of the men, "here is half-a-sovereign. Go to Victoria Station and wait for me at the Brighton side. If I am not there in half an hour you needn't wait any longer."

"Right you are!" replied the man, and Blake watched him until he had disappeared around the corner. Then, turning to the other, he told him to drive to Limehouse, and entered the cab.

"If by chance that Celestial did feel suspicious, he might have taken the second cab and followed me," he smiled grimly as he sank back. "But I guess my little ruse will settle that, and I don't see any more cabs in sight."

Blake smoked thoughtfully during the long ride to Limehouse, but on reaching that unsavoury district, he tossed away his cigar and sat up. Picking up the speaking-tube, he told the driver which street to stop at, and when the cab pulled up at the corner he stepped out quietly. He pulled out a sovereign and passed it to the man, and then spoke in low tones:

"Listen, my man," he said. "I am going on rather a dangerous mission down here. This isn't a very good place to hang about, but if you care to wait, I will probably want you again. I may want to leave hurriedly, and would want you to be ready to dash off at once if necessary!"

"Right you are!" replied the man. "I'll drive about for a bit, and come back in half an hour. Then I'll wait for you."

Blake nodded.

"All right; that will do," he said.

A moment later he was walking with a Chinese shuffle down the dark, silent, sinister street, all unconscious that Tinker, in the wake of Rymer, had gone down the same street only a little while before.

Blake continued on until he reached the gambling-den at which he had arranged to meet Wang Ho. Going up to the low, shabby door, he rapped sharply and stood back. What he intended to do when he had gained admittance he did not know.

Since he had been so successful in capturing Won, he had a half-formed idea of at once seeking Hang Lee and trusting to opportunity to give him the whip-hand. But, of course, everything depended on whether his disguise were penetrated or not after he got inside. If it were, he would have to call Wang Ho and try to gain his ends by highhanded methods backed up by an automatic revolver; but everything would depend on what happened when he reached the opium-room.

At that point in his reflections the door swung open a few inches. A Chinaman scrutinised him briefly, then swung it wide open.

"Didn't you get him, Won?" he asked quickly.

Blake shook his head, but did not risk a reply.

The man led the way into the opium-room, which was almost completely occupied by the victims of the drug.

Another Chinaman approached him and whispered the same question, and again Blake shook his head.

"I didn't realise Sexton Blake was awaited so eagerly," he thought grimly.

But the second Celestial was speaking again.

"You'd better report to his Excellency at once, then, Won," he said. "He's in there now."

Blake's pulses leaped, for he knew his Excellency could only mean Hang Lee, and he knew his deductions had been correct. Hang Lee was making the gambling-house his headquarters. But the man's remark put Blake in a quandary. He would have acted on the suggestion of reporting with alacrity, but he hadn't the faintest notion of the position of the room where Hang Lee was. If he acted at all strangely, those suspicious minds would at once begin to regard him closely, and once that happened, Blake knew it would only be a matter of a few moments before someone spotted his disguise.

In some way he must play for time, and get an opportunity of asking Wang Ho where the room was. He could see Wang Ho in a bunk at the farther end of the room, and must contrive in some way to speak to him.

That failing, he could, if he had time, form a pretty good idea of the lay of the house from observation of the walls and shape of the rooms and passage; but to do this he must wander from the opium-room to the gambling-room.

He turned with a shrug in lieu of answering, and began moving along past the bunks, most of which contained their drug-saturated victim. But Fate took the matter out of his hands, and before he got near enough to tip off Wang Ho the Chinaman who had last spoken overtook him.

"I am going in," he said, in low tones. "Will I tell his Excellency you are here?"

Blake took the risk and seized the chance.

"Yes," he whispered. "I'll go along, and wait until you come out."

The man nodded, and Blake followed him on through the opium-room. And as he passed Wang Ho he touched the individual on the arm, and knew from the maudlin muttering that Wang Ho had recognised the touch, and would be prepared.

They passed out of the opium-room into a dark passage, and Blake stood still while the other man knocked. For a brief moment Blake had a view of the occupant of the room, and fleeting as was the glimpse, he recognised the old Chinaman Hang Lee.

For the space of a few seconds Blake was tempted to dash up the stairs behind him and endeavour to find Grace Lansing, but before he had time to consider the plan, the door opened, and the man came out.

"He's waiting," he whispered; and Blake, shifting his revolver, strode firmly forward and threw open the door.

Hang Lee was smoking as usual, and barely glanced up as Blake closed the door and advanced towards him.

"Well," demanded Hang Lee, "why haven't you brought him?"

"I did," said Blake quietly; but something in those chill tones made Hang Lee stiffen.

"You are a brave man, Sexton Blake!" he said impassively, for his shrewd brain had read who his visitor was as soon as he had heard those chill tones.

"That is as it may be," returned Blake, coolly dropping his revolver into his hand. "I got your letter, and considered it wiser to talk with you privately, Hang Lee. That is why I came. I want that girl. If you don't give her to me, I will take you instead. Don't try any tricks, for if you do, I promise you I will shoot at once."

Hang Lee's hand dropped to the table, and for a full minute they looked at each other without speaking.

"I will not attempt to try and persuade you to do as I say," he finally remarked slowly, "for I see by your attitude that is useless. You are clever, and there is no question about your bravery, but you have overreached yourself in thinking you could beard me like this. At this moment, Sexton Blake, you are at my mercy."

"Perhaps," replied Blake coolly; "but I can assure you, Hang Lee, if I go under, it won't be before I make you follow me!"

Blake knew a sudden mysterious attack might come from any point, but he could not tell from where. He knew the floor was probably cunningly honeycombed with trapdoors, and he might even then be standing on one. But he could not tell, and to move might only put him into what he was trying to avoid.

He could only try bluff and trust to luck, but all about him he felt the sinister menace of Hang Lee.

The old man put out his hand and shifted the oil-lamp which lit up the room.

"Don't do that!" snapped Blake sharply; and Hang Lee knew he meant it. Back went the old man's hand to the edge of the table, and as his fingers curled under, they rested on a small round button.

With an enigmatical smile he looked at Blake, and then his fingers pressed gently. Blake felt a sudden quiver under his feet, and knew instinctively what was coming. He made a supreme effort to save himself, but the trapdoor had been released, and he began to drop. Clutching wildly, he reached out and managed to grip Hang Lee. It was too late for Blake to prevent himself falling, but he clung to the old man with a death-like grip.

Hang Lee pulled with all his strength to shake off that awful grip, but it was useless, and he gave a guttural cry as he slid toward the yawning hole. He reached out and grasped the heavy table to save himself, but at that moment the full weight of Blake's body went through the hole, and the table upset with a crash. Blake, Hang Lee, and the burning lamp went tumbling into the blackness beneath, to strike with a sickening thud below.

Sexton Blake had kept his word. He had not gone under without taking Hang Lee with him.

THE STRUGGLE IN THE TAXI.

IN A CAREFULLY MADE GROOVE IN THE HEEL WAS THE BROKEN PIECE OF PENCIL.

TINKER DROPPED TO THE FLOOR IN A DEAD FAINT.

RYMER FELL WITH A SPLASH INTO THE RIVER.

TINKER, who in spite of his injured left arm, had managed to pull himself up on the broad windowsill overhanging the water, stared in horror at the scene of which he was a witness, while still in the act of pulling himself up. The light thrown by the rapidly-spreading flames caused by the broken lamp, lit up the strange scene within, and the lad gave an exclamation of horror as he saw the inevitable fate of the two still figures on the floor.

Had he known that the strange waves of Fate had cast him up from the water just in time to witness Sexton Blake's danger, he would have been still more horrified. But he did not know as yet that one of those Celestial-clad figures was his master.

What he did know, however, was that two human beings were in imminent danger of being burned by the spreading flames, and the fact that they were Celestials, and very probably enemies, did not deter Tinker from a determination to save them if possible.

In the stress of the moment he put aside all thought of himself and his injured arm, and gritted his teeth while he forced himself to use the painful member.

Clinging on with his left arm, he raised his right and began pounding madly at the panes.

Crash after crash followed, and the out-rushing smoke threatened for a moment to drive the brave lad back into the water. But praying for strength he kept on, and almost shouted with relief when he succeeded in making a hole large enough to crawl through.

Disregarding the jagged pane, he hoisted himself up and crawled through, reaching out afterwards to pull Pedro through as well. The smoke poured towards him in a cloud, but, lowering his head, he rushed forward.

A moment's glance sufficed to show him where the heart of the fire lay. The lamp had broken on the stone floor of the cellar in the midst of a pile of rubbish, and was in danger of spreading to a littered pile of barrels in the corner.

But Tinker saw that if he could keep the flames confined to the burning rubbish, and prevent them spreading to the walls, the fire would burn itself out on the stone floor. To cast the burning material through the window was his first idea, but he saw such a plan would be futile.

146

The two men on the floor must wait, for if he attended to them now the flames would reach the walls. Tearing off his coat, he rushed back to the window, and dipped it in the river. Then he returned to the fire and went to work. Slowly, steadily, with sweeping gestures, he began walking around the outer edge of the blazing rubbish, forcing the flames back, and cutting off their spreading paths with the smothering of the wet coat. Like a woodsman in the Canadian timber, or the settler on the plains, he swung up and down, working in rhythmic sweeps.

It was touch and go for a few minutes, but when he had been twice round, he saw that he was holding his own, and if he could keep the pace up, would finally conquer. The steady heat had dried his coat, and he risked another dash to the window.

On his return, he stared in surprise as his eyes fell on Pedro. The big hound was never partial to Celestials, but, strange to say, he was muzzling with apparent joy one of the still figures on the floor. Tinker was puzzled, but at that moment the flames grew brighter, and in the flicker they cast he saw the hound licking the drawn features of the still figure.

"Crikey!" he muttered, dashing at the flames again. "I never saw him do that to anyone but the guv'nor or me. If it is the guv'nor, what was he doing here, and what if he should be dead?"

The awful thought lent a furious strength to his arms, and he worked desperately. Circling round on one of his trips, his eyes again fell on the prostrate figures, and he gave a cry as he saw there was only one. The other had been revived by Pedro's attentions, and had staggered to its feet, a dazed, puzzled look in its eyes. But as those eyes met Tinker's, the lad knew whose they were and read recognition in them.

Blake, for it was he, staggered towards the window and took several deep breaths, and then, turning backwards, reached for the coat.

"I'll take a turn now," he said, in husky tones. "I remember all now, and I see what you are trying to do. I'll explain things later. I think from your promptness we can keep the flames down. Go and see how Hang Lee is."

"Is that Hang Lee?" cried Tinker, in amazement.

Blake nodded. He was too dazed yet to speak. He had grasped the situation when he had come to, and with his usual promptness, gathered his strength together to deal with the first danger.

The burning rubbish was gradually growing less and less formidable, and as he saw that instead of barely keeping the flames from spreading, he was now beginning to conquer them, Blake redoubled his efforts.

Tinker came back with a sober face.

"I'm afraid he's done for, guv'nor," he said. "He doesn't show any signs of life."

"You're pretty white yourself," replied Blake, glancing at the lad keenly. "Have you hurt yourself?"

"Oh, I just hit my left arm," replied Tinker evasively, though his exertions had increased the painful throbbing. "But weren't you hurt at all, guv'nor, by the fall?"

"No; I landed on top of Hang Lee," replied Blake. "But here, my lad, take the coat in your right arm, and stand on guard. We've got the flames under now, and they will burn themselves out shortly. I'll have a look at Hang Lee."

Tinker took the coat and stood on guard, while Blake approached the old Chinaman, who lay crumpled up where he had fallen. Pedro followed his master over, and put his muzzle down to the still body. He drew his head up quickly, and backed away with a low growl.

"I guess that's enough to settle what's the matter," muttered Blake. "Pedro wouldn't do that unless he were dead, but I'll just see."

It didn't take him very long to discover that the fall had broken Hang Lee's neck, and Blake straightened up.

"It's a pity you had to go out like that," he muttered, "but you have received a quick punishment. In trying to finish me, you were hoist by your own petard. However, you were a worthy foe, and I am sorry."

He walked across the floor where Tinker still stood beside the dying flames.

"He's dead," said Blake quietly. "And now, Tinker, we must try and find a way out of this hole. I have work to do upstairs yet."

Tinker slipped on his coat, and began examining one side of the cellar, while Blake took the other. But any staircase it may have had had been bricked up long ago, and for the purpose for which Hang Lee used it the old cellar formed an ideal place. Overhead yawned the black hole through which Blake and Hang Lee had fallen, the trapdoor hanging slackly down.

"That's our only way, Tinker," remarked Blake, standing beneath it and looking up. "But the question is how to reach it. Someone is liable to come in the room up there any moment to see Hang Lee, and if they do we will be discovered at once. However, we will have to risk it. Let me see. Ah, I have it, my lad! Give me a hand while I pull over some of those empty barrels and find a sound one."

They hastened over to the corner, and by the dying light of the fire made a hasty examination of the barrels. Tinker found one apparently sound and dragged it forth. Standing it on end he stood on it to test it.

"This one will do, guv'nor," he said. "It seems sound enough."

"All right, Tinker. Bring it over under the hole. We will have to hurry."

Blake set the barrel on end and climbed up, while Tinker stood watching him.

"What's the idea, guv'nor?" he asked. "You can't reach the hole from there."

"No; but you can from my shoulders," jerked Blake. "Have you forgotten our gymnasium practice. Come on, my lad. Climb up me and get on my shoulders. We'll have to risk the barrel holding us."

Tinker grasped the situation, and, setting his teeth, began his perilous ascent. The achievement which they were endeavouring to pull off is not so difficult on the floor of a gymnasium with mattresses round about to tumble on.

But transfer the scene to the top of an untrustworthy barrel with a hard stone floor to fall on in case of accident, and add to that an injured arm, and it will be seen that Tinker's position was no sinecure.

On the top of that there were a horde of cut-throats above who would cheerfully rend them to pieces if they knew what had happened to their chief, Hang Lee, and discovery might come at any moment. To retreat through the window and trust themselves to the river was out of the question

It might have done if they had time to spare, but before they could return with help Hang Lee's fate would have been discovered, and Grace Lansing's position in that event would have been most precarious.

If they were to escape from the cellar and run any chance of yet saving the situation, they must get back through the hole. And both master and lad set themselves, sore and exhausted as they were, to achieve the almost impossible feat.

Slowly and painfully Tinker got on the barrel beside Blake, and began climbing up over the detective's rigid body. Blake, with feet spread apart, swayed gently to keep his balance, holding his hands up over his shoulders for Tinker to steady himself by when he got up.

First one knee went on Blake's shoulder, then another, and pausing momentarily to grasp Blake's hands, Tinker kept on. One foot was placed firmly, then the other, and with a steady movement he stood up.

For a perilous moment Blake swayed dangerously, threatening to crash over, and had Tinker been nervous or lacked confidence in his master he would have precipitated the threatened catastrophe. But he made no movement, only standing rigid, and presently Blake's dangerous swaying ceased.

"Are you all right?" he asked jerkily.

"Yes, all right, guv'nor. I haven't looked up yet, but if you are all right, I will."

"Go ahead," replied Blake. "I can keep my balance now."

Tinker looked up, and saw the hole immediately over his head, raising his hands, he thrust them over the edge, and then spoke again.

"I can get my arms over to the elbows. If you can give my feet a shove up, I think I can make it, guv'nor," he whispered down.

"Hang on, then I'll try," whispered back Blake. "When I say go, draw yourself up at once."

"Right," whispered the lad.

Blake reached to his shoulders, and grasped Tinker's ankles. Then, stiffening himself, he whispered, "Go!" pushing with all his strength as he did so. Up shot Tinker through the hole, his legs dangling for a bare moment over the edge, then they disappeared in the blackness above.

"How about you, guv'nor?" asked Tinker, thrusting his head down through the hole.

"I'll get up all right, but I'll put Pedro through first."

He snapped his fingers, and Pedro put his paws up on the barrel. Reaching down, Blake heaved him up beside him. Then, picking him up, he steadied the hound on his shoulders.

"If I push him up can you reach him, Tinker?" he whispered.

"Yes, all right, guv'nor!"

Blake heaved again, and Tinker reached forth, grasping Pedro by

150

the front paws. The hound was no light weight, but Blake's support below eased the strain on Tinker, and a moment later Pedro also disappeared through the hole. Then came the difficult part, for even if he could spring up to the hole, Tinker would be unable to pull his weight.

Blake jumped down, and got another barrel. Returning to the first one, he climbed up, and, standing with his feet on the very edge set the second on top of the first, then climbed to the top of the second, and stood upright, expecting the frail structure to give way any moment with his weight.

It was cracking ominously, and he lost no time in reaching upwards. His hands came a bare two inches below the edge of the hole, and a slight jump would make it. Gathering himself together, he sprang upwards, his hands barely grasping the edge before the barrels collapsed with a clatter below. But Tinker was ready, and between them Blake managed to make it.

"Whew!" he panted, as he stood erect in the dark room, from whence he had fallen to almost certain death just before.

"Things are strenuous to-night, but we have no time to lose, Tinker. Have you your revolver?"

"Yes guv'nor. What's the plan?

"This" jerked Blake. "Grace Lansing is held a prisoner upstairs here, and I am going up for her. No questions now," he said, as Tinker gasped in astonishment, for that was the first the lad had heard of Grace's capture. "From this room," went on Blake, "a passage runs along and upstairs, but a door opens off into the opium-room on the way. I want you to stand guard there while I slip up and try and release her."

"Right-ho, guv'nor!" whispered Tinker, and followed Blake out into the dark passage. A chink of light shone from under a door on the left, and Blake gripped Tinker's shoulder as they reached it.

"That's it," he whispered. "Wang Ho is inside, but we haven't time to get him now. The only reason they haven't discovered us already is because they think I am Hang Lee's agent Won, and am engaged with him. But hold the door if they come, Tinker. I won't be long."

Blake crept along the passage and up the stairs, until he reached a dark landing. A dim light shone ahead, and he crept towards it. On getting nearer, he saw that it came through the door curtains of a room at the end, and, with stealthy steps, he crept on and peered in.

A Chinese woman sat on some cushions half asleep. But on a large divan over in the corner lay a girl in English garments, and Blake knew, though her back was toward him, that it was Grace Lansing. With a jerk, he drew the curtains aside, and stepped toward the Chinese woman. She heard him, and started up with opened mouth to scream, but Blake clapped his hand over it and threw her back.

Working swiftly, he bound and gagged her, and then approached the sleeping Grace. He laid a gentle hand on her shoulder, and she sprang up in terror ready to cry out. But Blake had anticipated such a contingency, and put his hand over her lips.

"Hush, Miss Lansing!" he whispered. "It is Sexton Blake. I have come to rescue you, but our safety depends on silence."

Grace stared at him with amazed eyes, but though he looked every inch the Chinaman, she recognised his tones. Her eyes filled with tears, and she began to sob.

"Don't!" said Blake sharply, frightened of hysterics in her nervous state. "You must not give way. I can't stop now to explain, but if we are to get out of here you must follow me at once. Keep close behind me, and don't be frightened; we will get through all right."

But though he spoke reassuringly to Grace, Blake looked forward to a hard fight before he succeeded in getting through the opium-room to the door.

Grace rose obediently, and followed him out of the room and down the stairs, where Tinker and Pedro still stood on guard.

"Any signs of anything?" whispered Blake.

"No, guv'nor. I have heard one or two walking around on the other side of this door, but they didn't try to open it."

"Very well. Now, Tinker, stand back here in the shadow with Miss Lansing. I am going to open the door, and I will leave it open. Wang Ho is in a bunk near this door, and I want him to help us get through to the door. When you see him get out of the bunk, take Miss Lansing's arm and come through the door on the run. Wang Ho and I will go ahead to clear the way. Do you understand?"

"Yes, guv'nor," whispered Tinker. "I'll do exactly what you say."

With a warning pressure on Grace's arm. Blake threw open the door and stepped into the opium-room. Several attendants were moving about noiselessly, and most of the victims in the bunks were tossing in a restless sleep. Blake had no doubt of their ability to get past the few attendants, but before reaching the front door they had to go along the passage off which was the gambling-room.

It would be crowded at this hour, and a shout of alarm from one of the attendants in the opium-room would bring the whole bloodthirsty horde out on the run. It would be touch and go, and he stood a big chance of failure; but there was nothing else, and Blake trusted to the pure boldness of the plan to carry them through.

He attracted no attention as he stepped inside, for the attendants merely thought it was Won returning from his interview with Hang Lee. He could see Wang Ho in a near-by bunk, and, stepping softly across, he touched the apparently sleeping man on the arm.

Wang Ho opened his eyes, and looked up quickly.

"Come!" whispered Blake. "Draw your revolver, we will have to fight."

Wang Ho asked no questions, but reached for his revolver, and tumbled out of the bunk. At that moment the watchful Tinker, with Grace and Pedro, rushed through the door, and tore along after Blake and Wang Ho.

The attendants, accustomed as they were to strange scenes had never received a bigger shock in their lives, and for a moment were startled out of their accustomed calm. But the presence of Grace, and Tinker's garb told them what was happening. With one accord they drew their long crooked-bladed knives, and made for the two Chinamen in the lead —Blake and Wang Ho.

"Fire!" said Blake tensely, and both revolvers spoke at once. Two of the attendants dropped, but with a loud shout of warning to the occupants of the gambling-room, the other two came on. Again the revolvers spoke, and taking advantage of the momentary check they had caused, the fugitives gained the passage leading to the front door.

"Quick, Tinker!" cried Blake. "Make for the door, and get it open. Wang Ho and I will hold them back as long as possible."

The gamblers were pouring out of the gambling-room with a pandemonium of curses, thinking evidently that the place was being raided; but the shouts of one of the attendants in the opium-room told them the truth, and they turned with a snarl. Knives flashed, and more than one revolver spoke. Blake had not yet given the word to fire, but as several of the knives came whizzing through the air, Blake spoke.

"Fire, Wang Ho, and keep backing out! I will hold mine until the last. Hurry, Tinker!" he called.

Wang Ho emptied his revolver into the crowd, and at that short range it was impossible to miss. Three of the foremost went down, and those immediately behind stumbled over them. But not for long did it keep them back, and on they came.

Tinker had been working feverishly at the bolts, however, and at that moment he got the door open.

"All right, guv'nor!" he yelled. "It's open!"

"Lead the way up the street, Tinker!" yelled Blake.

"There's a taxi at the comer. I'll keep the dogs back as long as I can. Go with them, Wang Ho!" he jerked; but the Chinaman, though his revolver was empty, had fight in him still.

Braving the flying bullets and flashing knives, he leaned down, and picked up several of the knives which had fallen about them. With great skill he began hurling them back, and at that moment Blake opened fire. They gained the door, and for a moment the horde was checked. Emptying his last chamber, and shouting to Wang Ho to run, Blake slammed the door in their faces. They raced up the street after the others, and Blake heaved a sigh of relief as he saw the taxi-driver had kept his word and waited.

The door of the den opened, and the raging crowd tore out after them; but Tinker had already managed to thrust Grace and Pedro inside, and tumbled in himself, followed by Blake and Wang Ho. The driver needed no spur to move on, and barely had the door slammed behind Blake than he had thrown in the clutch, and the taxi began to move. A few knives followed them through the night, but the cab rapidly gained headway, leaving the baffled crowd behind.

"That was an occasion when discretion was the better part of valour!" panted Blake, with a smile, as he mopped his brow. "How are you, Miss Lansing? About frightened to death?"

"Oh, I was, horribly," she said, in low tones; "but I know it is all right now. Oh, Mr. Blake, how can I ever repay your brave action to-night!"

"By never speaking of it again," smiled Blake. "Permit me to introduce a real Chinaman, Miss Lansing," he said, "and a brave one as well —Mr. Wang Ho."

Grace put out her hand, and Wang Ho's face lit up as he saw the action. He shook hands gingerly, and looked embarrassed, for high Manchu and traveller though he was, he had never before shaken hands with a white woman.

Tinker received a warm clasp and trembling thanks, which threatened to break any moment into sobs, but Blake saw her condition, and dealt with it accordingly. He led the way in jests and light conversation, and by the time they had reached Grace's home she was laughing and chatting like her old self.

Nothing would do but they must all come in and receive some refreshments, and when they reached the drawing-room Blake put his hand in his pocket and drew out something.

"Can you tell which of these was shown to you the other day, Miss Lansing?" he asked, with a smile.

Grace gasped,

"How did you get them, Mr. Blake?"

In a few words Blake told her of Hang Lee's fate, and how he had found the two pieces of pencil in his clothes.

"Now, which one?" he said. "Can you tell me?"

"Why, yes, I think," replied Grace— "yes, I am sure this one is the piece. I remember it had some lettering on it."

"Then," smiled Blake, "I will give you the other, which must be the one belonging to Harry Graham."

Tinker approached, and with an apology began whispering to Blake.

In the stress of events it was the first chance he had had to tell Blake of his momentous day, and what he had seen at the shop of Morris the pawnbroker.

"That is of the greatest importance, my lad," replied Blake. "We will go on to Baker Street at once, and lay our plans. You have indeed done well, Tinker."

Tinker flushed with pleasure, and pleading urgency and a promise to return when matters had been settled, Blake, Wang Ho, and Tinker departed.

Blake dropped Wang Ho in the City, with a request that he should call at Baker Street the following evening, and then directed the taxi to go on to Baker Street.

On their arrival there Tinker gave Blake detailed account of his afternoon's experiences, and, tired though be was, Blake pulled out the old black pipe, and settled down to form his plans for the recovery of the Diamond Dragon.

BLAKE, HANG LEE AND THE LAMP WENT TUMBLING INTO THE BLACKNESS.

BLAKE SPRANG FORWARD AS HE SAW HER DEATHLY PALE FACE.

THE DEATH OF HANG LEE.

BLAKE EXAMINED THE FLOOR CAREFULLY THROUGH HIS GLASS.

## THE THIRTEENTH CHAPTER.   The Final Act—The End.

EARLY the following afternoon Sexton Blake, Tinker, and Pedro emerged into Baker Street and hailed a taxi. They were soon speeding Citywards, and evidently Blake's plans were fully made and indicated to Tinker, for no conversation took place. The cab pulled up at the foot of a narrow street, and the two descended.

Dismissing the cab, Blake led the way along until a little way ahead, on the opposite side of the street, could be seen a sign— "A. Morris, Pawnbroker and Secondhand Dealer."

The detective pulled up, and spoke in a low tone:

"Cross the street and walk by now, Tinker. If there is no one inside signal when you get past."

Tinker was again disguised as an Italian boy, and though he wore his usual clothes Blake had on a heavy grey beard and moustache. He had not adopted an intricate disguise that day, for in the carrying out of his plans it was only necessary to conceal his identity until he entered the shop.

Tinker, with Pedro at his heels, lurched past the shop, whistling, and when on getting by he raised his hand and scratched his head, Blake started across the street and headed for the shop.

A moment later the detective was standing at the littered counter, while the old pawnbroker came out from his inner office washing his hands suavely as he inquired what he could serve the gentleman with.

"I want to look at these bags over here," replied Blake, pointing across the shop.

"Thertainly, sir —thertainly!" smiled the pawnbroker, rubbing his greasy black moustache. "Thome very fine bags, sir!"

He came out from behind the counter as he spoke, and started across the shop. Blake moved over also, and as he got close to Morris he sprang suddenly. His hands met on the astonished man's neck, and he hissed in his ear:

"Not a sound. Morris! If you make a noise it will go hard with you. I'm not in the mood for trifling to-day." Blake released one hand, and with a jerk drew off his beard. The pawnbroker gazed with bulging eyes as he recognised Blake. He protested fervently and tearfully that there was no reason for Blake to suspect him of anything. And if all his protestations had been true, no more innocent or law-abiding citizen ever lived than the pawnbroker.

But Blake evidently had other ideas on the matter, for he whistled loudly and began binding up his victim. Tinker and Pedro came running in, and Tinker assisted his master. After the pawnbroker had been secured safely, Blake gagged him, and with Tinker's assistance drew him into a near-by cupboard.

Then Blake went to work. Using some of the old clothes from the shelves he padded himself out to the rotund proportions of Morris. Then he pulled out a bald wig and black, greasy-looking moustache, which he adjusted carefully. The nose was the hardest part to duplicate, but a little flesh padding here and a touch there, and he knew from Tinker's delighted grin that his attempt had been highly successful. After that he put on the pawnbroker's coat and vest, and the job was complete.

Nodding to Tinker, the lad took Pedro and withdrew into the cupboard. Blake closed the door on them, and entered the pawnbroker's dingy office. He seated himself at the desk, and though there were none to see he did not for a moment relax his imitation of Morris's every attitude.

An hour passed without customers, but at the end of that time Blake stiffened slightly as he heard the thumping of a crutch in the outer shop. Nearer and nearer it came, and as the supposed pawnbroker looked up he saw a ragged, crippled beggar standing in the door.

"All! So you came back —eh, my friendt?" he said, in a perfect imitation of the pawnbroker's tones.

"Of course!" growled the other, dropping his crippled walk and striding inside. "Well" he grunted sitting down on the opposite side of the desk facing Blake, what, is your answer? Will you be satisfied with ten per cent.?"

"Vell, vell, my friendt, you are a very hard man to do bithnith vit, but I suppose I must take ten per thent. Let me see de peautiful article again, and I will tell you finally."

With a grunt the cripple reached in his pocket and drew out the leather pouch. A moment later the blazing, scintillating Diamond Dragon appeared, and Blake caught his breath as it was held out to him.

Slowly he reached out his hands for it, but just as they hovered over it he lunged quickly, and dropping the glittering Dragon to the desk the cripple cursed wildly as Blake snapped a pair of handcuffs on his wrists.

"Sit down, Dr. Huxton Rymer," drawled Blake, drawing his revolver, and laying it on the desk. "It has been a long time since we met, but I assure you I have been very anxious to renew our acquaintance ever since yesterday."

He was rapidly tearing off his disguise as he spoke, and Rymer glared in speechless rage as he recognised the hated features of his old arch-enemy.

"You, Sexton Blake!" he gasped. "I might have known you'd have a lay in on this. Curse you for this! Some day —some day I swear I will get even with you!"

"Possibly." drawled Blake.. "But in the meantime, my friend, you can spend some time in Bleakmoor planning how you will get even when we meet. But I might mention that from the warm welcome you will receive at Scotland Yard your sojourn there will be a fairly lengthy holiday."

Blake picked up the blazing mass of gems, and looked at them closely.

"I must confess my dear doctor," he said, smiling, "that these stones are quite beautiful enough to tempt a connoisseur like yourself. Unfortunately, however, you put your fingers in an important pot, and were bound to get scorched. It might interest you to know that Hang Lee also got scorched, and paid the penalty."

"What, Hang Lee arrested? Impossible!" cried Rymer, forgetting for a moment his own plight.

"Quite right, doctor," replied Blake. "Not arrested —killed! But come, we will just reach Scotland Yard in time for you to take tea with some of your old friends."

He whistled as he spoke, and a moment later Tinker came running in.

"Get a taxi, my lad, and then ring up Detective-inspector Thomas at the Yard. Tell him I will be obliged if he will meet me on my arrival, as I am bringing an old friend of his along."

Rymer glared in speechless rage, and then turned to Tinker.

"So I owe this to you, do I, you young fool? I thought I settled you in the water yesterday."

"It wasn't your fault that you didn't!" threw back Tinker, as he turned away.

Five minutes later a taxi was chugging out in front, and Blake led his prisoner out. He forced the pawnbroker to turn the key in the door and come along, and then speaking to the driver, the cab headed for Scotland Yard.

• • • • •

Three days later, when Harry Graham completed his interrupted journey and landed in England he was met at the dock by Sexton Blake, and a quite recovered, but very excited Grace.

She was looking radiant in a charming costume, and Harry rushed towards her with a happy smile on his face. She introduced him to Blake, and he was greatly puzzled when Grace mysteriously said he must come at once to make a call. Both Blake and Grace smilingly refused to enlighten him, and he grew still more mystified when their taxi drew up before the Chinese Embassy.

They descended and entered, evidently being expected, for a young Chinese clerk came forward and led them at once to a room at the rear. There sat the mysterious and powerful Li Hong, and with him was Wang Ho, who had proved himself brave and loyal in the gambling-den in Limehouse. On the other side of the room sat Tinker, with Pedro at his feet, trying to explain to the puzzled but interested Li Hong the intricacies of English football.

Blake closed the door behind him, and after Li Hong had bowed Grace into a chair he presented Harry Graham all round.

Then Blake turned and addressed that puzzled young man.

"Mr. Graham," he said, "You were given a certain packet in Australia to bring to England for a man. Would you mind telling me the exact conditions of that agreement?"

"I don't know why you ask me," stammered Harry, in surprise, and looking over at Grace, who was smiling and nodding. "There seems to be a lot I am ignorant of, but I don't mind telling you. I did receive a packet, which I posted on to Miss Lansing. The man for who in I brought it —a Dr. Hutton —broke a lead-pencil in half, and giving me one half, kept the other, this agreement was that whoever presented his half to me was to receive the packet. Unfortunately I have lost the piece I had.

"You say 'whoever' presented the piece of pencil?" remarked Blake.

Harry nodded.

"Would you recognise the piece he gave you?" continued Blake.

"Rather!" answered Harry.

160

Blake signed to Grace, and she held out to the astonished Harry the piece of pencil he had lost.

"Why —why —" he gasped.

"Never mind," smiled Blake. "Explanations later. Is that the piece Dr. Hutton gave you?"

"Yes; I am sure of it."

"Very well," went on Blake, thrusting his hand in his pocket and drawing out the other piece of pencil. "Here is the other. Will you hand over the packet to me?"

"Why, I don't know. Did Dr. Hutton send you, Mr. Blake? But of course I'll hand it over to you, since you have the piece of pencil. But Miss Lansing has it. I'll have to get it from her."

"No, you won't, dear," smiled Grace. "I've got it here." She drew the well-known leather pouch from her bag. "Will I give it to Mr. Blake, Harry?"

"Yes, of course, Grace. But what on earth is all the mystery?"

"That is the mystery," remarked Blake, quietly opening the pouch and drawing forth the magnificent mass of gems.

All eyes gazed in silent admiration at the beautiful yet fearful Diamond Dragon, which had been the cause of so much striving. After a moment Blake turned and handed it with a bow to Li Hong, who stood up to receive it.

Then laying it gently down, he turned and signed to Blake who gave the astonished Harry a full account of all that had happened. Grace herself described her capture and rescue, and the young man rushed over and grasped Blake's arm in gratitude.

"To think —Oh, my heavens, to think," he cried, "what her fate might have been if it hadn't been for you!"

But Li Hong was speaking again, and he turned to listen.

"Miss Lansing," said the old statesman courteously. "Mr. Blake flatly refuses to accept the whole reward for the recovery of the sacred Dragon, and, owing to the part which you have played in the matter, insisted that you get part of the reward. I wish to thank you both for myself and my illustrious country, and have deep pleasure in asking you to accept this more material evidence of our gratitude."

Grace mechanically took the pink slip he held out, and gazed, dumbfounded, as she saw dancing before her eyes the words, "Five thousand pounds."

She and Harry Graham left shortly after, to begin turning the pages of their rosy future; and, after a private interview with Li Hong, Blake and Tinker returned to Baker Street.

"Tell me, guv'nor," said Tinker, "who is Li Hong, really?"

"Li Hong," said Blake slowly, "is one of the highest princes of the blood in China. His estates, Tinker, are larger than England. But he believes a republic is the only salvation for China, and has devoted his life and his fortune to that end."

. . . . .

The court-room was packed when Dr. Huxton Rymer was brought up to face a jury of his fellow men.

From some unknown source, friends had come who engaged the best criminal lawyer in the country for his defence.

On technical details, remand after remand was ordered, but even the master lawyer's cleverness could only postpone the inevitable. Juror after juror was thrown out, but finally the panel was made up, and the trial began.

Rymer trusted more than he thought to his lawyer's ability, and when Sexton Blake took the witness stand, a smile passed over the once famous surgeon's features.

That smile quickly passed, however, when Blake calmly produced the impression of the finger-prints which he had taken in the vacant house opposite Grace Lansing's.

Rymer's face went deadly white when Blake proved to the jurors that the print compared in every detail with his own record, and that of Scotland Yard.

Rymer's lawyer bit his lips in surprised chagrin, and, seeing an acquittal was out of the question, fought with all his eloquence for a mild sentence.

The jury, apparently had their minds made up before leaving the court, for they were not absent more than five minutes.

Then, filing back, the foreman gave the verdict, and Rymer, pale as death, but without emotion, stood up to receive his sentence.

When the old judge finished, Rymer, for a bare moment, gave his feelings rein. He swung around on Blake, and said in a low, fierce tone, which carried to the furthermost corners of the court.

"I owe this to you. Don't forget what I said. I'll meet you yet!"

And as Blake rode homewards, he muttered:

"Well, Rymer is given into their hands again, but I doubt if Bleakmoor will hold him. But, if not, I'll be ready for him, I hope!"

. . . . . .

Rymer shivered slightly when the great doors of Bleakmoor clanged behind him. From that moment he was a cipher in the under-life which the law was compelled to keep in durance for the protection of society.

But characteristic was it of the man's indomitable nature that, as he sat with bowed head on his rough bed that night, his thoughts contained no regret, no sorrow, no contrition of spirit. Instead, from the moment he had cast his first, hasty glance about the narrow, bare confines of his future quarters, his mind had taken up the question of escape.

Sexton Blake was right. Bleakmoor would have to keep unceasing vigilance to prevent Dr. Huxton Rymer from once more getting free to exercise his ingenious mind in filching the wealth and ease he craved for from society which, under his daring hand, was a tempting storehouse.

**THE END.**
**[62400 WORDS]**

# The Spy of the School

By T. C. Bridges

A Novel School Story with a well-laid Plot.

*THE SECOND LONG, COMPLETE STORY!*

## The First Chapter.   The Bully of B Dormitory.

"NOW then, Slug, up you go! Mind you beat Wiggins, or I'll make you do it again."

Slug, a small, fat, sleepy-looking boy, was sitting huddled up on the edge of his bed.

"Oh, please, Jarvis," he said, "let me off this time. I can't do it. I've sprained my wrist."

"Rot! You're always shamming," was the brutal reply. "you'd better hurry up, or I'll give you what for!"

Slug began to remonstrate, but Jarvis seized him by the collar of his night shirt, and kicked him out to the end of the room, where Wiggins was standing shivering with fright and cold.

The scene was one of the big dormitories at St. Cyprian's School, a long whitewashed room where fourteen fellows slept. The ceiling was arched like a church, and big iron stays supported it. These ran up one side of the arch and down the other, and it was possible for a strong and active youngster, hoisted on the shoulders of another standing on a bed, to reach the lower end of a stay, and work his way, hand over hand, right up to the apex of the roof, and so down the other side.

It was the favourite amusement of Jarvis, the bully of B Dormitory, as it was called, to make one of the small boys perform this dangerous feat, and if he could secure two, and make them race one against another, his joy was complete. Fortunately for the small boys, it was not often that the bully had his own way, for Jack Owen, prefect and captain of B Dormitory, hated bullying of all kinds, and even Jarvis, big and strong as he was, had so far not dared to challenge Owen's supremacy.

But on this special night Owen had gone out to supper with his uncle, Colonel Forbes, who was head of the great Government Powder Factory at Laston, the town on whose outskirts St. Cyprian's stood, and it was not likely he would be back before eleven o'clock.

164

So Jarvis had things his own way, and he and his ally and toady, Holmes, known in the school as Putty Holmes, were making life miserable for the half dozen lower school boys in the dormitory.

Slug, whose real name was Philpot, had told no more than the truth in saying that he had sprained his wrist; but so great was his fear of Jarvis, and of the tortures he knew were in store for him if he refused to race, that he said no more, and made up his mind to trust to luck to get over in safety.

Holmes hoisted him up, Jarvis did the same with the unhappy Wiggins, and next minute the two were dangling in the air, hanging to the two iron rods.

"One! Two! Three! Go!" yelled Jarvis. And at once the two small boys began to work themselves hand over hand up the sloping bars. Wiggins began to gain at once.

"I'll lay you a shilling on Wiggins," said Holmes.

"Right you are!" replied Jarvis. "Now, then, Slug," he called, "my money's on you. You lose it for me, and I'll half murder you!"

Slug made a valiant effort, and struggled on till nearly level with the other. But he was fat and heavy, and his hurt wrist was beginning to pain him horribly. Soon Wiggins gained again. By this time they were both near the top, and fully twenty feet from the floor.

"You lazy young hog!" shouted Jarvis, as the wretched little Philpot stopped and tried to ease his aching arm for an instant.

Beside himself with rage, he picked up a boot and flung it at the boy. It struck him on the side. With a shrill cry of pain Philpot loosed his hold, and fell with a tremendous crash down upon the washhand-stand, which was exactly below him.

There he lay perfectly still, with the blood streaming from ugly cut in his head.

There was a moment's awe-struck silence, and then a number of boys, too big for Jarvis to bully, but not big enough to interfere, jumped out of bed, picked poor Philpot up, and laid him on his bed.

One started for the door.

"Where are you going?" cried Jarvis.

"To call the matron," replied the other.

"And sneak on me," cried Jarvis. "Not much! You jolly well get back to bed!" And he and Holmes sprang to the door to hold it.

But at that very moment it was pushed open from outside, and in came Owen.

His quick eye took in the whole scene in a second, and his strong jaw set.

"At your old tricks again, Jarvis," he said, very quietly.

Jarvis slunk away, looking foolish.

Owen went up to Philpot's bed, and quickly examined the injured boy.

"How did this happen?" he asked.

The same boy who had been going for the matron told him quickly.

"There's nothing broken, lucidly," said Owen. "But if this gets to the doctor's ears you'll get expelled, Jarvis. Now, I don't want to be the means of sacking you, though you richly deserve it. So we will doctor up Philpot ourselves. But if you think you're going to get off scot-free, my friend" —turning, again to Jarvis— "you're mistaken. I shall call a Sixth-Form meeting to-morrow on the subject."

Then he sent another boy to the matron for warm water and some linen, and proceeded to bandage up Philpot's head. The boy soon recovered consciousness under his care, but Owen sat by him until he was sound asleep. Then he put out the light, and went to bed himself.

## The Second Chapter.   The Punishment of Jarvis.

"SAY Slug, Jarvis is going to catch it. Ain't you glad?" Wiggins was the speaker.

"Rather!" replied Slug, who was tucked up comfortably on a sofa in the school hospital. To the matron a story had been told of an accidental tumble. "But what's happened?" he inquired of his visitor.

"Owen called a Sixth Form meeting after morning school, and they decided that Jarvis should have a fives-bat thrashing from the whole of the Sixth. And they've gated Putty for the rest of the term."

Slug chuckled at the discomfiture of his enemies, and Wiggins trotted off to be present at the Jarvis punishment, for which the whole school were called together in the big schoolroom just before dinner.

Dr. Bushell, headmaster of St. Cyprian's, delegated a good deal of authority to his Sixth Form. A court of the Sixth— that is to say, all the prefects assembled together —had powers almost equal to his own, particularly in respect to putting down cases of bullying. He found the plan to work excellently, having modelled it on the same idea that is followed at Rugby and many other large public schools. At the same time, the doctor was himself very strict with those boys whom he made prefects, and insisted on their having a due regard for the dignity of their position.

Jarvis's bullying propensities were notorious all over the school. He had arrived first, at the rather late age of fifteen, but looked even older. He was a big, powerful fellow and a good boxer; but he was disliked almost by everyone, masters and boys alike, except a few of the latter, like Holmes, who were his toadies, and helped him to spend his plentiful pocket-money, and one master, Mr. Shafer, the teacher of French and German.

Owen, as he had promised, had laid the case before a Sixth Form meeting, and after the examination of a number of witnesses, it had been decided that Jarvis should undergo a public fives-bat thrashing. This meant that each prefect was to inflict one stroke, and the punishment was to take place before the whole school.

The big schoolroom was a sea of eager faces, when the head prefect called the roll at half-past twelve. Then, "Jarvis," he said, "stand up!"

The big bully, looking sullen, and half inclined to make a fight of it, stood up. He was hoisted on the back of one of the captains of the school, and the head prefect took up the wooden fives-bat and administered the first stroke.

Brady, he called, as he stood aside, and the second, in alphabetical order, gave Jarvis a stinging blow. There were twelve prefects, and Owen's name was the eleventh on the list.

Owen would have been only too glad to get out of the business. But he could not help himself. He was a prefect, and had to do a prefect's duty. So he took up the bat, and stepped forward.

As he did so, Jarvis, who had up to this taken his punishment in sullen silence, made a furious struggle. Throwing the boy who was holding him flat on his face, he sprang up, and, before anything could stop him, had flown at Jack Owen, and struck him a savage blow in the face.

Owen staggered back, but recovered himself, and the boys looking on, held their breath, for Owen's fists were clenched, and it looked as if a fight were imminent.

But with a strong effort, he mastered himself, and stood there white with anger, but perfectly calm. Jarvis looked at him evilly.

"Coward!" he hissed.

Everybody heard the insult —the deadliest that an Englishman can receive.

The head prefect spoke up sharply.

"Take hold of Jarvis, two of you!" he said. "Owen, kindly finish your share of the punishment. What further punishment Jarvis will receive for the insult, will be decided later."

"I refuse to touch him —now!" said Owen, very quietly. Tony Gordon, Owen's best chum, who was sitting near the platform on which the scene was taking place, well knew those quiet tones, and that queer flash in Owen's grey eyes. He had seen the same once before, when Owen thrashed a gipsy for bullying a child.

The head prefect looked his amazement; but he was wise enough not to prolong a painful scene.

"You may go!" he said to the school. "But I must ask the Sixth to meet again this afternoon at half-past four."

The dinner-bell rang at the moment, and the boys trooped out, talking eagerly. Only Tony Gordon waited, and presently Owen joined him. They walked together across the quadrangle.

"Tony," said Jack suddenly, "will you be my second?"

"Your second! What on earth do you mean? You're not going to fight that sweep?"

"I am!" said Jack curtly.

"Don't be a fool, Jack!" put in Tony. "If the doctor hears of it, you'll lose your prefectship."

"Possibly?" observed the other, still more shortly. Then: "Can I depend on you?" he asked again.

"Of course you can, old chap! But, I'm hanged if I like it! A prefect can't fight a fellow who's only in the Upper Fourth —can't fight at all for that matter!"

"It will be this afternoon," went on Jack, as if the other had not spoken— "at least, if he doesn't funk it. Immediately after dinner, behind the fives-courts."

## The Third Chapter. A Fight to a Finish.

"KEEP out of his reach, Jack," was Tony Gordon's last injunction as Owen, stripped to his shirt, stepped out into the ring, around which stood almost every boy in the school. Only the other prefects were absent. They knew well enough what was happening, and they sympathised with Owen, but felt it was best to let him wipe off the insult offered him in his own way.

Jarvis looked much bigger than Owen. He was a heavy, square-set fellow, whereas Owen was rather slightly built. No sooner was his adversary in the ring than he ran at him like a bull. He meant to knock him out in a single round.

It was lucky for Owen that he dodged the first blow. Jarvis's fist missed his jaw by a hairsbreadth, and Owen was nearly floored by the furious assault. But he managed to keep away for the first few seconds, and then, when Jarvis began to get blown, he got in twice on his body.

Learning caution, in the next round Jarvis used his superior knowledge of boxing.

Three times Owen countered, and then, with a left-arm drive, Jarvis got in a crashing blow on the other's forehead, and knocked him down.

Dead silence reigned. But Owen was on his feet again in an instant, so quickly that Jarvis, who thought he had delivered a knock-out blow, was unprepared. Owen got under his guard, and crack, crack! hit him twice just under the left eye.

At that moment "Time!" was called.

"Jack, for Heaven's sake, be careful!" whispered Tony, as he sponged his man's face. "If he hits you again like that you're done. Keep away, and wait till his eye closes. He won't be able to see out of it in another three minutes."

When Jarvis came up, it was quite plain that he, too, realised how much he was damaged, and meant to force the fighting.

He made another ugly rush. But Owen dodged him, and, keeping away to the right, succeeded in coming off with hardly a scratch.

By this time Jarvis was losing his wind, and getting every instant more and more furious.

Again he rushed, and this time he got home. Luckily for Owen, it was only a body blow. But the sound of it made Gordon shake his head. Owen staggered.

Jarvis came on, intent on following up his advantage. As he did so, Owen made another of his quick feints, got away once more to the left, and put every pound of his lean muscular body into a right-hander, which broke through the other's guard, and crashed full on his left jaw.

Jarvis went over as if a mule had kicked him, and lay flat on his back.

"Cave! Cave!" cried at that moment two small boys who had been posted as scouts in case of any masters interfering, and the ring melted away as if by magic. Only Owen, too proud to disclaim responsibility, and Gordon, his second, remained beside the prostrate form of Jarvis.

"What is the meaning of this disgraceful scene?" said a harsh voice. It was Mr. Shaler, the language-master.

"You, Owen, a prefect! And fighting!" he went on, with an ugly sneer which brought the blood to Owen's cheek.

"Yes, sir," put in Gordon "Owen has given Jarvis the licking which he richly deserved!"

"Be silent, Gordon, until you are spoken to!" ordered Mr. Shaler angrily. "Owen." he continued, "you are aware of the doctor's views on the subject of prefects fighting. I shall consider it my duty to report this disgraceful business to him."

"Yes, sir," was all that Owen said.

Meantime, Jarvis had come to, and was struggling to a sitting position. Gordon stepped forward to help him.

Jarvis repulsed him.

"Leave me alone!" he growled. "You and Owen will be sorry for this!"

Gordon merely smiled at the very un-English sentiment. To the surprise of him and Owen, Mr. Shaler proffered his assistance, and helped Jarvis to his feet.

"I shall see him over to the hospital," he said, as if to explain his action.

And, holding Jarvis by the arm, the two left the scene together.

"Rum start, that, Jack!" observed Gordon.

Owen looked thoughtful, and said nothing.

"Fancy that old sweep Shaler turning up," went on Gordon. "I expect Butty Holmes went and sneaked to him. I say, Jack, it's a bad look-out for you! You'll lose your prefectship."

"Probably I shall," returned Owen. "But I'm blessed if I care, Tony. I've given that skunk the licking he ought to have had a year ago. I don't think he'll try any more of his tricks again."

"H'm!" muttered the other, half to himself. "I wouldn't be too sure of that."

## The Fourth Chapter.   Fishing in the Factory.

"ANY luck yet, old chap?" The speaker was Alec Gordon, Tony's younger brother.

"Yes; I've got three fat perch out of this pool. Come along and try it. But lie low, for I believe there's a policeman or water bailiff in those trees over there."

Alec slipped cautiously down under the bank beside his brother, baited his hook with a fat white grub, and dropped his line into the water.

The brothers were both keen anglers, and every available hour was given up to their favourite sport. They knew every inch of water round the county, public or private, and were a couple of the most accomplished poachers imaginable.

The finest fishing stream in the county was the River Leat, which ran through the great testing grounds of the Government cordite factory at Laston. The land was Government property, and big notices threatened serious penalties to anyone found trespassing upon it. All round it ran high walls and fences, and only the Government officials were allowed inside.

A series of most important experiments were in progress at the time with a view to testing several new forms of explosive, and the usual vigilance in keeping off the public was therefore all the greater.

But for the two young Gordons neither walls nor policemen possessed terrors. A few months before they had discovered that, by crossing the marshes to the south of the factory, they could get into the river-bed, and, sheltered beneath its high banks, walk calmly up to some of the best fishing pools.

At night a water-gate was dropped across the stream, so they were always careful to leave before dark. Once or twice every week the brothers visited the place, which was about two miles from the school, and enjoyed most excellent sport, the secret of which they kept religiously from everyone else in the school.

"Beastly bad luck on Owen, isn't it?" observed Tony, as he pulled his hook out and baited it afresh.

"Rather!" replied Alec. "I didn't think old Bushell would really have bagged his prefectship. By Jove, though, wasn't it ripping the way he laid Jarvis out?"

Tony chuckled. Then he added:

"But we ain't seen the last of that beauty yet, or I'm mistaken. I'll bet he's planning mischief in that ugly head of his. He scowls at me in a way to turn milk sour!"

"That swab Shaler's got a down on you, too, Tony!"

"Yes; he kept me in all Saturday afternoon. That reminds me, Alec. It's getting late, and there's German class at six o'clock. I mustn't be late. Pack up your rod, and come along!"

The bank was slippery with recent rain, and as Alec moved his foot slipped. He made a vain effort to recover himself, and fell with a sounding splash into the water, six feet below.

He came up next second, and Tony pushed out his rod to him and helped him ashore.

"You've done it now," he said. "If there was anyone within half a mile they'll have heard that splash."

So they had. A sound of heavy footsteps running came along the towpath from the north. The two boys, knowing that concealment would be useless, resolved to trust to speed of foot. They sprang up the bank, and ran.

Shouts arose from behind. A policeman and another man were in full pursuit.

But the boys ran twice as fast as their pursuers, and rather enjoyed the fun. Besides, they knew that work was over for the day in the only buildings they would have to pass, so there was no danger of their being cut off.

These buildings stood quite near the towpath, and were the new ones erected for the purpose of the secret cordite trials. A long passage ran through them at right angles to the towpath, and connected them with a covered way leading to another building where the new cordite was being made.

As they passed the end of this passage, Tony seized Alec by the arm.

"Someone there!" he uttered.

"I see." said Alec, and they redoubled their speed.

In a very few minutes they were within sight of the boundary wall.

Both pulled up suddenly.

"Done, by Jove!" cried Tony.

The water-gate was closed, and escape cut off.

"We shall get expelled, or worse, if we're caught here!" said Alec, in despair.

"There's a chance still, old chap," replied Tony, "Are you good to try a dive under the gate?"

"I'll try anything rather than get nabbed!"

Both boys were thinking of the grief it would cause their father and mother if they were expelled from school.

"Come on, then!" cried Tony.

He took a short run, and dived head foremost into the deep river. Alec followed him. Their pursuers watched with stupefied dismay.

But the next instant they uttered cries of rage as they saw two heads bob up beyond the gate, and realised how neatly they had been tricked.

Long before they could reach the nearest gate the boys were far out of sight, and jogging at a steady trot up a lane which led to the back of the school.

Neither spoke a word until they had reached their dormitory, and were rapidly changing their wet clothes. Then Tony turned sharply to his brother.

"Did you see who that was in the passage, Alec?"

"It was Owen," returned Alec.

"Sure?" inquired the other.

"What's the good of asking me again?" returned Alec crossly. "You saw as well as I did. He had his face turned away; but if that wasn't Owen's black-and-white striped flannel suit, and Owen's cricket cap, with the Eleven badge, I'll eat it!"

"But what on earth could Owen have been doing down there?" put in Tony thoughtfully. "They don't allow a soul in the place except the workmen and the experts, and they're all sworn to secrecy."

"Well, he's Colonel Forbes's nephew, you know, and goes down there pretty often."

"He hadn't any business in those buildings, though." persisted Tony. "I wish I knew what it meant. Do you know, I've hardly seen him to speak to ever since the fight?"

"Hallo! There goes the bell, and I ain't half-dressed yet. Old Shaler will give me toko. Lucky for you, Alec, you haven't got to go to him next hour!"

**The Fifth Chapter.   Owen's Victory.**

"LATE again, Gordon!" was Mr. Shaler's sarcastic observation, as Tony entered the class-room fully five minutes after the lesson had begun. "Pray, where have you been? Out of bounds again, I suppose, as usual. Really, a boy of your age might set a better example to his juniors!"

With skilful spitefulness he had touched Gordon on the raw. Tony's brains for German were not up to the standard of his athletic capabilities, and he was quite the oldest boy in the class. He sat up very straight, and looked his tormentor full in the eye.

Shaler, delighted to have made an impression, went on: "You have not answered my question, Gordon. Kindly inform me where you have been this afternoon."

"Out for a walk, sir!" said Gordon shortly.

"And what part of the country have you been honouring with your presence?"

No reply. Gordon, too proud to lie, took refuge in silence.

"Answer me at once!" thundered the master, losing his temper.

Gordon merely sat and looked at him.

"Very well, Gordon, you will take a note to the doctor at the end of the hour."

Everyone knew what this meant. But Gordon could take a caning and forget in half an hour. The only thing that troubled him was the thought that he would get another bad report, which would grieve his people. His father, a half-pay naval captain, had great ambitions for his sons, and sacrificed much to keep them at a good school.

The note was penned, and at the end of the German lesson Gordon took it across to the doctor's study.

"What is it now?" asked that functionary, as Gordon knocked and entered. "What, another note? You're always in trouble, Gordon. Mr. Shaler says that you defied him before the whole class, and refused to give him the reason of your being late for school," went on the doctor severely, when he had perused the note. "Why would you not tell him where you had been?"

"I told him I had been for a walk, sir."

"Well, where did you go?"

Again Gordon remained silent. He could but get a caning, he thought. Much better that than confess where he had been, and perhaps get his brother, and Owen, too, into trouble.

"Why don't you answer me?" went on the doctor, "Am I to suppose you were out of bounds again?"

No reply.

"Very well, I shall have to cane you, I suppose. And, mark my words, Gordon, if I have any more trouble with you I shall write to your father, and advise him to remove you. You are doing no good here, and getting other boys into mischief. Stand up!"

•　　　•　　　•　　　•　　　•

Tony didn't mind the licking; but he felt very sore in mind when he left the doctor's study to find that half-past six had struck, and that he was too late for tea. He pictured Alec tucking into bread-and-jam, and felt in his own pockets to see if his resources were equal to a feed at Walker's, the tuckshop.

But he had not so much as a threepeny-bit.

"Perhaps old Walker will let me go on tick for a feed," he said to himself, and he strode off across the playing-field to the little shop which Walker, an ex-butler of Dr. Bushell, had started solely in the interest of the boys of the school.

"I want a slog of cake, Walker, and a cup of tea," he said. "Will you give me tick for them?"

"Can't do it, sir," replied the old man. "You and Mr. Alec owes me over a pound, and that's more than the pocket-money you'll get for the rest of the term."

Knowing argument was useless, Tony turned and went off in a very bad temper.

Half-way across the playing-field a violent storm of rain broke. Tony bolted into the cricket-pavilion for shelter. It was now almost dark. As he entered the place, he was amazed to hear voices. All the school were still in at tea, and it struck him as very odd that anyone should be in the pavilion at this hour. He pulled up and listened.

At first the drumming of the rain on the roof made it impossible to hear words distinctly, but after a few minutes the downpour slackened, and he plainly recognised Owen's voice.

"It's no good, Claud," he was saying, "I've done all I could for you. You've had all I could raise the past two years. The governor thinks I'm frightfully extravagant, and I simply can't ask him for any more."

"What rot Jack!" sneered the other voice. "The old man will shell out anything you ask for. You, the model son, have only to ask and receive."

"All the more reason why I'm not going to impose on him," was the reply. "Upon my word, Claud, you ought to be ashamed of

175

yourself. You have your allowance. Most fellows' fathers wouldn't give them anything after bringing disgrace on the family in the way you have."

"I'm hanged if I'm going to stay here and be lectured by a kid like you!" was the angry reply. "Once more, are you going to shell out, or get the governor to do so?"

"No. I'm not!" was the curt answer. "And, if that's all you've got to say, I'm going back to the school."

Gordon heard Jack Owen get up; but the other evidently pulled him back.

"Wait a minute. Jack," be said; "don't be nasty. Look here, I've got a plan that will give me a lump sum, enough to go to America on. But I want you to help me. Listen." His voice sank to a whisper, and the only words Gordon heard, were:

"Go to the colonel's often —quite easy —yourself—cordite."

"By Jove!" muttered Gordon to himself, as the thought that he was wilfully eavesdropping suddenly struck him. "This is a little too much for me. I'm off!"

Turning up his coat-collar, he slipped out into the rain, and away as hard as he could go to the study he shared with his brother.

## The Sixth Chapter.   Feasting and Fighting.

"TONY, you ass, where have you been? I've been hunting everywhere for you!"

It was Alec who spoke. He came rushing into the study, his face beaming with delight, and frantically waving above his head a foreign-looking letter.

Tony, who was feeling hungry and cross, looked up from his Latin exercise with a grunt.

"What the dickens is up, Alec? Can't you see I'm trying to do some work?"

"Work be hanged! Look here!"

Alec advanced upon his brother, holding out the letter. The letter he unfolded in front of him. Then, very deliberately, he opened it, and pulled out a letter, and from it took a piece of crisp white paper, which he planked down on the desk in front of Tony's astonished face. It was a five-pound note.

"Great Scott!" was all the latter could feebly observe, he turned it over and felt it. "Have you been robbing a bank, Alec?" he inquired, turning an amazed gaze on his brother. "Where did you get it? Who does it belong to?"

"It's ours!" shouted Alec. "Yours and mine. Read!"

Tony took the letter.

"My dear boys," it began, — "I wonder if you have quite forgotten your poor old Uncle James. I dare say your father talks of me sometimes. I am tired of this country, and think of coming home to spend my old age in England. Give your father my love, and tell him so. I have written to you rather than to him, because I knew you were at St. Cyprian's through a friend of mine, George Byron, whose son left last term, and I don't know whether your father is still at Southsea. The enclosed for you with hopes it may be useful. —Ever your affectionate uncle.

"JAMES ASHWORTH."

Tony sat up straight, and gazed at Alec.

"My wig, Alec, it's too good to be true. A fiver! What everlasting luck! We'll settle our tick at old Walkers, and have a dormitory feed. But I thought Uncle James was dead long ago. I haven't heard father mention him for ages. Good old chap! This is decent of him. And look here, Alec, I haven't had a mouthful of tea. Old Bushell kept me late for Hall, and Walker wouldn't give me any tick. Like a good chap, cut down and get me something to eat. And bring up a cake with you. I've got to finish this exercise for old Staler."

It was a gorgeous feed next night in the Gordons' dormitory. Pork pies, sausage-rolls with the flakiest of pastry, tins of sardines, and a couple of big lawn-tennis cakes with an inch of almond-icing on the top. Raspberry wine and water, mixed with a generous hand in tooth-glasses, and bottles of ginger-beer, washed down the repast.

"Finish it all up, you chaps," said Tony, as he carved a cake. "If Mother Griffin finds any crumbs in the morning there'll be an awful row. Hallo! What's that?"

"That" was a sponge heavy with water which whizzed over Tony's head and splashed on the wall behind him.

Tony chucked down his knife, grasped up his pillow, and made a rush for the door.

"Come on, you fellows!" he yelled. "It's B Dormitory on a raid."

Next instant the fun was fast and furious. Owen's dormitory, scenting the spoils of E (Gordon's) room, had laid a plan to get their share. Forcing the wretched young Slug and other youngsters to head a forlorn-hope armed with sponges, the rest had hidden among the flannels in a changing-room near by. As the E forces swept out in a frantic pursuit of Slug & Co., the B reserves slipped in behind them, and before E found out the ruse, had laid hands on all the remaining provisions, and were bolting back to their room. There the robbed ones turned and met them.

Putty Holmes had the rest of the tennis-cake under his arm, and bolted up the dormitory, intent on hiding his spoil. He did not see that Alec was hard at his heels. Whack! came Alec's pillow on his head. Holmes stumbled, dropped the cake, which rolled under a bed, and grabbed blindly at something to save himself. This happened to be a big water-can, which was on the edge of the washhand-stand. Over it went, and down went Putty on top of it, and lay there in the middle of a drenching puddle of cold water.

Most of the defenders had reached their beds by this time.

"Give it 'em, you chaps!" shouted Jarvis, aiming a heavy blow at Alec Gordon's head. It missed his head, but hit him on the shoulder and floored him.

Tony saw the cowardly act. Jumping over the bed, he rushed up through a storm of pieces of soap and slippers, and, grabbing up the first thing that came handy, which happened to be the bolster from Owen's bed, he brought it down on Jarvis's head with all his force.

The bolster split, and a cloud of feathers filled the air. At that moment there was a cry of:

"Cave! Bates is coming!"

Bates was one of the assistant masters.

The invaders melted away instantly.

"Here, help me to pick up these confounded feathers!" muttered Tony "There'll be an awful row if Bates sees them."

He and two or three others began hurriedly picking up the masses of feathers which littered the floor, and sweeping them under a bed.

Among them lay a thin roll of paper, tied together with red-tape. Jarvis, who had picked himself up, made a dive for it.

"Here, that's mine!" he said.

"Get out!" growled Tony. "It's Owen's, I believe."

He seized up the roll, and, just as Bates came in, dodged under the bed, and lay there still as a mouse.

"Much too much noise here!" said Bates. He was quite a young master, and a decent fellow, and privately had no objection to an occasional bolster fight. "Get to bed, all of you, at once! If the lights are not out in five minutes, I shall know the reason why."

He stumped off again, and his steps were heard ascending the stairs which led to the next floor. Tony seized the opportunity to slip out and dart away unperceived. He took the papers with him, not because he thought they were of any importance, but simply to score off his pet enemy, Jarvis.

When he got back to his dormitory, he slipped the papers into his locker with his clothes, tumbled into bed, and was fast asleep in five minutes.

That night Owen was sitting up in his study. He had special permission to sit up from the doctor, as he was working for his Army examination.

His books were open before him, but he was not looking at them. His eyes were fixed on a typewritten letter, which he turned over and over, and examined with the utmost care, as though he would wrest from it some information which was not among its written words.

**The Seventh Chapter.   The Stolen Secret.**

THREE mornings later an excited crowd stood round the school notice-board.

"What's up? Do you know?" cried someone, as Alec Gordon joined the group.

"Haven't an idea." returned that youth. "What's the notice?"

"Whole school to meet in big schoolroom immediately after dinner," rejoined the first.

"Phew!" cried Alec. "Someone's going to get the sack!"

"Quite likely," observed Putty Holmes, in an unpleasantly suggestive manner. He looked at Alec as he spoke.

"What are you looking at me for, you putty-faced baboon?" inquired the latter.

Some of the youngsters sniggered. They all hated Putty. Putty, big as he was, had no idea of risking a fight with Alec. The Gordons were both noted for being able to use their fists.

"I wasn't looking at you particularly," he said. And with a sickly grin he edged out of the crowd and moved off.

"Pity it ain't him," observed Alec, looking after him. "He and his lot don't do much good to St. Cyprian's."

A hum of excited conversation was checked by Dr. Bushell's entrance into the big school-room. He made his way to the dais at the end, turned, and faced the two hundred boys. He looked more worried than any of them had ever seen him.

"I have a very unpleasant duty before me," he began. "Yesterday I received from Colonel Forbes, of the Cordite Works, a letter informing me that there has been a very serious crime committed at the works. You are all probably aware that experiments of the greatest national importance have been in progress at Laston, with the result that a form of cordite has been discovered infinitely superior for use in rifles to that possessed by any other nation in the world.

"Colonel Forbes informs me that a copy of the specifications of this new invention, together with details of the trials, has been stolen from the works.

"For some days no hint of this theft has been allowed to reach the public. Private researches have been made, however, and there is unfortunately no doubt whatsoever that a member of this school is the criminal.

"That any boy under my charge could be so base a traitor is beyond my conception, yet the proofs set before me leave no doubt on the subject.

"I have only one thing to say. If that boy will come to me privately any time between now and tea-time this evening, give up the papers, and fully explain his motives, I am permitted to assure him that he will merely be sent away from the school. But if he does not do so, the law must take its course."

There was a hush of awed silence. Tony Gordon's glance fell on Owen. He noticed that his friend was sitting gazing at the doctor with white face and eyes full of misery.

Tony felt horribly uncomfortable. The remembrance of the words he had overheard in the cricket pavilion four nights ago, and of the day he had seen Owen in the works, returned to him suddenly. Could the criminal be that rascally Claud, and —horrid thought —could the other be shielding him?

The doctor turned and walked out of the school-room, and again a buzz of voices rose. Everyone was asking questions.

Tony went out into the playing-fields, and walked round by himself for a long time thinking things over and trying to get them clear in his head. Finally, he made up his mind to go to Owen's study afterwards and have it out with him. He could not go on with this suspicion between him and his chum.

Just as he came to this conclusion the school bell rang, and he had to hurry in to his class-room.

Everyone had taken their seats by the time he arrived, but, luckily, the master was not yet in the room. Tony hurried to his place, which was as usual, near the bottom of the form. Tony was a most popular fellow, and his appearance was always a signal for a certain amount of good-natured chaff. But this time everyone was strangely quiet and solemn. Tony noticed that they were all looking hard at him, and actually felt a trifle uncomfortable.

When he reached his seat, instead of having to squeeze in between the boys just above and below him, he found, to his amazement, fully a yard of bench left to him.

"Lucky Bates ain't in yet!" he said to the fellow next him.

Jackson, the boy he had addressed, turned his head away, and said nothing.

"What's up, Jacky?" inquired Tony.

Jackson looked uncomfortable, but said nothing.

Tony turned to the boy below.

"Hart," he said, "what the mischief is the matter with you all?"

Hart preserved a stony silence.

Then a horrid conviction burst on Tony. For some unknown reason he was in Coventry.

The master came in at that minute. Tony sat up straight, and kept a stiff lip. He was desperately hurt, but much too proud to show it.

When school was over Tony marched out of the room, head in air. He went straight over to Owen's study, knocked, and entered.

Owen got up, looking so thoroughly uncomfortable that, for an instant, Gordon imagined that he was about to cut him. But, no.

"Come and sit down, Tony," he said, "I haven't seen much of you lately."

"Perhaps you don't want to see me now," he replied bitterly.

"Oh, rot, Tony! Don't talk that way!" cried Owen.

"But, for Heaven's sake do explain things! You might, to me."

"Explain!" uttered the other sharply.

"That's just what I came to you for —an explanation."

"Me! What am I to explain?"

"Why you were in the factory on Thursday last."

"In the factory! I wasn't in the factory on Thursday. You must be dreaming."

"Hang it all, Owen! What's the good of lying? Perhaps you'll tell me next that you were not in the cricket pavilion on Tuesday night!"

"What do you mean by calling me a liar?" cried Owen, jumping up. Then, restraining himself by an effort, he sat down again. "I don't want to quarrel, Tony, particularly with a fellow in such a fix as you are. As for my being in the pavilion on Tuesday night, that is quite true. But what has it to do with you?"

"I shouldn't think you need ask me after what the doctor said this afternoon."

"Surely that has more to do with you than with me," returned Owen coldly. "I don't want to —indeed, I don't believe half of what I've heard. But I tell you straight, if you don't know it, that at present you are in danger of immediate arrest."

"Hang it all, Jack, you'll drive me mad! First I'm put in Coventry, and then you spring this yarn on me."

"Well, will you kindly tell me how the specifications got into your locker, where they were found this afternoon?"

"Specifications! What specifications? All this mystery is enough to drive a chap crazy."

"Look here, Tony, old chap, it's no good trying to humbug me like this. It isn't worthy of you. You've already acknowledged you were in the factory on Friday. The stolen specifications are found in your locker. What can I or anyone else think?"

"I think you're as much of a cad as the rest!" cried Gordon, in a rage.

He jumped to his feet, flung open the door, and, disregarding Owen's cry of "Tony! Tony!" ran down the stairs, out into the quadrangle, and across to the study on the other side, which he and his brother shared.

And as he entered it a tall man stood up and said:

"Anthony Gordon, I arrest you in the King's name!"

## The Eighth Chapter.   Tried and Convicted!

THE Laston Police Court was crowded when the brothers Gordon were placed in the dock, charged with stealing from the cordite factory the specifications of the new Government explosive.

The boys stood there in a sort of dream as, first of all, a policeman identified them as the two whom he had chased on that memorable Friday afternoon, when they had been fishing. He described how he had seen them first, how they had run, how he and one of the water bailiffs had chased them, and how they made their desperate dive under the water-gates.

Then Walter, the sweet-shop keeper, appeared in the witness-box. He told how much in his debt the boys had been, how they had not only paid off the whole amount at once, but spent thirty shillings more in various delicacies. They had changed a five-pound note, he said, and the magistrate shook his head as if he thought that in itself a most damning point against them.

He was followed by the postman who took the school letters, and he gave evidence of a foreign letter addressed to Anthony Gordon, Esq.

The amazement of Tony and Alec was changed to rage when they saw the smug face of Putty Holmes next appear. With a malicious glance at the two in the dock he began to tell with apparent reluctance how he had lost his cricket-pads, which he said were exactly like a pair the elder Gordon possessed, that he had imagined it possible that they might have got mixed up after the last match with those belonging to Gordon, and had therefore gone into E Dormitory to ask if Gordon had had them.

"Gordon not being there, he had asked the captain of the dormitory if he might look in Gordon's locker, and receiving his consent had opened it, and found not only his pads —"

"That's a lie!" cried Tony. "I never had your pads!"

"Silence!" ordered the magistrate angrily.

"Not only my pads," repeated Putty venomously, "but also a roll of paper, the one lying before his Honour. This," he continued, "he would have paid no attention to, but for the startling statement about stolen papers which he had just heard that afternoon from Dr. Bushell. Under the circumstances he had considered it his duty to take it to the master. He had done so, and it had proved to be the very specifications themselves."

Tony stood staring at the roll which lay on the magistrate's desk with paralysed amazement. He recognised it now. It was the very bundle he had picked up on the floor of B Dormitory, close to Owen's bed, on the night of the pillow fight. They must have been Owen's, then, and hidden inside his bolster. There could no longer be any doubt about his guilt.

He felt positively sick. What awful net was weaving round Alec and himself. For now, without implicating Owen, he could make no effort to clear himself.

The rest of the proceedings were a mere nightmare. All he knew was that he and his brother were committed for trial at the assizes.[2] Bail was refused, and the two Gordons were marched off to a cell.

•　　•　　•　　•　　•

That night was a dark one, and no one saw Jack Owen as he slipped out of the quadrangle and up to the cricket pavilion.

His brother was waiting for him there. The two stood and looked at one another for a moment. Then Jack burst forth savagely:

"I knew you were an infernal skunk, Claud; but, at any rate. I thought you had decency enough to do your own dirty work!"

"Hang your heroics, Jack! What are you after now?"

"Do you mean to tell me you don't know what happened this morning?"

"I heard that one of the kids from your school was had up for sneaking those identical papers I told you I had my eye on. Pretty smart of him, even if he did do me a shot in the eye."

Jack was shaking with suppressed fury.

"I don't want to hear any more of your lies!" he said very quietly. "How you got Gordon to do your thieving for you I don't know. Nor have I any idea how you managed to shift the blame on to him. But if you don't tell me, brother or no brother, I swear I'll give you up to justice!"

Claud gazed at Jack for a moment in blank amazement. Then he began to laugh.

"By Jove!" he said. "That's the richest thing I've heard in my time! Do you mean to tell me you believe I hired that youngster to steal those papers? My good chap, you don't give me credit for much sense!"

There was no doubt that he was speaking the truth. Jack was staggered.

"Tony wouldn't have done it himself!" he muttered.

---

[2] a court which formerly sat at intervals in each county of England and Wales to administer the civil and criminal law.
/drf

"Well, if he didn't, you'd better look further for the person who put him up to it. Why, I've never had a word with your pal in my life. And now, look here! What I wanted to see you for to-night was to tell you that I've struck it rich in another quarter. Don't get excited! It's nothing that'll hurt you, or the rest of the precious family. I'm off to the States in a week, and you can tell the governor so next time you write to him. I dare say he'll be as glad as you to get rid of me. So-long!"

Jack sprang after him. But Claud was gone, and the younger brother, his mind in a perfect fog of doubt and amazement, made his way back to his study, and threw himself into a chair.

### The Ninth Chapter.   Fire and Rescue.

"FIRE! Fire!" was the cry which roused Owen from his miserable thoughts. As he rushed out, the corridor was full of boys running full-tilt towards the door leading into the quadrangle.

Outside, the darkness had vanished. Every object stood out in a strong red glare. Great flames were leaping from the upper-storey windows of the masters' quarters, roaring and crackling in a strong breeze.

With the rest, Owen ran across the quadrangle. Already a line of buckets was being formed to pass up water from the bathing-pond. The fire brigade had not yet arrived.

"Hurry up! Hurry!" shouted a voice as two men came staggering up with a ladder. A dozen hands seized it, and began propping it up against the wall.

"They say Shaler is still in his room," said a boy near Owen, in an awed whisper.

"He's cut off if he is," put in another. "The passage and stairs are all alight."

Owen elbowed his way through the throng. As he came to the front there was a crash and a tinkle of falling glass. One of Mr. Shaler's windows was smashed from within, and through the gap Shaler's head appeared. His face was blackened, his thick beard gone, his eyes gleamed with terror.

"Shove up the ladder, you fools!" he yelled "Quick! Quick!"

Those below had got the ladder straight against the wall.

It was nearly six feet too short!

The flames were roaring furnace-like out of the window of Mr.

Bates's room, next to Mr. Shaler's, and through the latter's broken casement volumes of smoke came pouring thicker and thicker.

"Fools! Idiots! Dolts!" screamed Shaler, seemingly beside himself with terror, and stretching his body half out of the window. Then his English left him, and he fell to cursing in German.

Suddenly his head disappeared with Jack-in-the-box suddenness. Another face protruded. It was that of Jarvis.

"For Heaven's sake hurry, you fellows!" he shouted. "And bring a long ladder! We'll all be blown up in a minute!"

"What in thunder's Jarvis doing up there?" Owen heard someone say.

"The chap's gone dotty!" observed another.

Owen wrenched himself free from the crowd, and ran full speed to the gymnasium, opening his claspknife as he ran.

At the end of the long room was a gallery, and from it hung a rope used for climbing exercises. He chopped it loose, flung it into a coil, and was back in less than a minute.

Jarvis was now hanging by his hands from the sill of the burning room. Shaler was no more to be seen.

Up the ladder went Owen like a flash. Great flames came scorching outwards

"Hold on, Jarvis!" he cried, as he reached the topmost rung. "Hold on tight, a minute, and you'll be all right!"

An iron water-pipe ran up the wall beside the window.

It was within easy reach. Owen slipped one end of the rope round it as high up as he could reach, knotted it first, and then, balancing himself on the top rung, made a loop round Jarvis's waist.

"Let go!" he cried, but Jarvis clung desperately to the sill. He was paralysed with fright. "Hold on tight, you chaps below!" called Owen, to those who had hold of the ladder.

He descended a few steps, took a firm hold, and gave the loose end of the rope a tug. Jarvis, with a fearful yell, let go of the sill and fell. But the rope was stout, and so, luckily, was the pipe. He swung a few feet below safe, for the moment at least, from the flames. Next instant Owen had him on the ladder, cut the rope above him, and began to help him down.

They were almost at the bottom when a terrific concussion flung them both violently to the ground. Part of the roof above went soaring into the air, and a rain of bricks and slates came crashing down.

In a panic everyone bolted. But an instant later a number of the boys, ashamed of their cowardice, came running back, and picked up Jarvis and his rescuer.

Owen was comparatively unhurt; but a brick had fallen on Jarvis's head and cut a terrible gash in it.

He was taken to the hospital. Owen went with him to get his burns, of which he had several nasty ones, dressed.

The doctor administered spirits of ammonia to Jarvis as soon as he could swallow, and consciousness began to return.

"My father! Where is my father?" were his first words.

Owen and the doctor looked at one another. Owen touched his head significantly.

"No," whispered the doctor, "I don't think he's wandering. But you must go to bed. Come again and see me in the morning."

As Owen returned to his dormitory he saw that the fire had been got under. Four men were carrying away a litter on which lay something covered with a cloth. He did not need telling what it was.

•    •    •    •    •

For hours that night Owen lay awake, and turned over in his brain the happenings of the past few days. The thought of Tony Gordon was uppermost. The anonymous letter which he had received on the night of the pillow fight had apparently come from someone employed in the powder works. It told him plainly that the Gordons had been seen in the works on the Friday before, and in the forbidden buildings. It suggested that he should warn them.

This letter had worried him desperately. Another trouble —and even a worse one —had been the presence of his disreputable brother Claud, who had actually proposed to him that he, Jack Owen, should use his relationship with Colonel Forbes to steal the secret of the cordite.

When the papers were discovered by Holmes in Tony Gordon's locker, it had seemed to him proof positive that, in some way, Claud had got hold of Tony and used the latter's lack of money to force him to help in his scoundrelly scheme.

But now it was clear that he was mistaken. Claud had certainly been speaking the truth when he said that he had had nothing to do with Tony. Then, if Tony had taken the papers, why had he put them in such a foolish hiding-place? Why had he suspected him, Owen, of the theft? Oh, it was all a hopeless puzzle!

．　　．　　．　　．　　．

In the middle of first school next morning a message came for Owen to go to the hospital. The doctor met him.

"Jarvis is very ill," he said. "Much worse than I imagined. He wants to see you."

Owen went in. Jarvis was lying very still, looking white and frightened. As soon as he saw Owen he began to talk rapidly, and in ten minutes all Owen's doubts and perplexities were cleared away.

It appeared from Jarvis's confession that his name was not Jarvis at all. He was Mr. Shaler's son. His father was a secret service agent of a German powder factory, who had been plotting for years to secure the newest thing in explosives.

Stealing the papers, with the help of a confederate in the works, had been a comparatively easy achievement. But it was necessary, in case the theft was discovered, to have a scapegoat. They chose Owen first, and so hid the papers in his bolster; while Jarvis —or Shaler, junior —obtained a suit exactly like Owen's most characteristic one, and haunted the works wearing it.

Later, however, when he —Jarvis —saw the Gordons actually in the works, the chance was too good to be lost. It was resolved to turn suspicion upon them. With this object in view, a letter containing money had been forged for their benefit, so that it might be supposed they had been bribed; and an anonymous letter sent to Owen, which, it was hoped, would cause trouble between him and Gordon.

The pillow fight and Tony's unconscious appropriation of the documents had done the rest, and it only remained to wait till the end of the term and return to Germany. Had it not been for the fire, all would have gone well. But Mr. Shaler had had some pounds of cordite stowed in his bedroom. The thought of this catching fire had frightened them both so badly that they had lost their heads. The rest Owen knew.

．　　．　　．　　．　　．

That night Jarvis died. The rest may be told in a very few words.

Jarvis's confession, written out and signed before his death, was naturally sufficient to secure the immediate release of Tony and Alec. Their father headed a sort of triumphal procession back to the school, where he and they were received and dined by Dr. Bushell himself.

Tony and Jack Owen found it hard to forgive themselves for their mutual suspicions. But now they are as good, or better, friends than ever. Jack has got his prefectship back. As for Putty Holmes, his prophecy about someone getting the sack came true. He himself was ignominiously expelled, and it was very doubtful whether he had not rendered himself liable to a criminal prosecution into the bargain. Slug and the other youngster of B Dormitory still discuss the point, and wonder whether the punishment would have been "dragging on a hurdle," or "hanging, drawing, and quartering."

THE END.

NOTICE!

The Skipper wishes it to be distinctly understood that his great new character, **YVONNE is EXCLUSIVE** to the 'Union Jack,' and does not appear in any other paper.

NEXT WEEK-1° AS USUAL.

## Charlie Gordon's Schooldays.

Our Serial

### Introduction.

Mr. Collier, a master at Bingley College, makes a compact with a Mr. Skuse, in which he undertakes to remove Charlie Gordon, one of the scholars.

Mr. Skuse is Gordon's guardian, and in the event of Charlie's death before reaching the age of twenty-one, the whole of his considerable fortune reverts to Mr. Skuse.

THE STORY (as recorded in last week's instalment).

In Alfredon Woods. The Second and Third Form boys walk up the pathway leading to the ruined castle. Suddenly the whole party halt as two villainous-looking men cross the path and glance keenly at Gordon, on whose shoulder Collier's hand is resting.

Having reached the ruined castle, Collier sits down and sketches, while the boys play hide-and-seek.

It is Charlie's turn to hide, and he goes into the woods. The others wait patiently for the signal to seek, but it is not given. They search the woods through and through, but fail to find him. At last they come to the conclusion that he has returned to the school.

Nothing has been seen of him at the school, however, and a search-party is organised. In the woods a portion of a bow is found, bearing the initials, "C. G."

The party call at the police-station, and Collier makes a statement.

(Now read on.)

### The Next Day —Vernon Passes Out —Was it a Sign?

The Bingley police, aided by the Sandcombe force, had searched every nook and corner of Alfredon Woods and the surrounding district for many miles. As a last resource they had dragged the river for a considerable distance. And when all this was done they stood and looked at one another.

The reporters of all the local newspapers were there taking notes. Half the village was there, for what had seemed to be at first nothing more serious than a schoolboy escapade was rapidly developing into a tragedy.

Up at the school there was little doing in the way of study. Who could think of books —of Latin, Greek, French, and Euclid —when the Bingley police were dragging the river down by Alfredon Woods?

Dr. Chart himself could not. He was looking worried and harassed when he entered the Third Form-room.

"You can dismiss your class, Mr. Collier," he said. "There is still no news, I am sorry to say, of the missing boy."

The class dismissed without a word. There was no cheering, no exultation. The boys sauntered out into the courtyard, and stood about in groups discussing the question, the burning question, of the day: "Where is Gordon?"

Early in the afternoon the station cab drove into the courtyard, and one or two of the boys caught a glimpse of those who sat inside.

"It's that old chap —what's his name? —Colonel Thingumy," said Lamkin.

He went to shut the gate, that had been opened to admit the cab, and came back in a few moments.

"I say, Vernon, there's a chap wants to speak to you outside — that chap who used to fish down by the river."

"Wants to speak to me —what for?" asked Vernon.

"Don't know; only he looked mysterious, and said, 'I'd like to have a word or two with the young gent who was down at the police-station last night.'"

"Perhaps he means Lee or Cosher," said Vernon; but he sauntered towards the gate.

Mr. Murgatroyd Banks was there, leaning with his back against the wall.

"Can you slip out?" he asked. "I want to have a few words with you."

"Me?"

"Yes. No one must see you. Not Col —not the master. He mustn't know I am here. I'll go down by the bridge, and wait for you there, if you get a chance of slipping out."

"But what do you want to see me for? Is it about —"

"This Gordon business? Yes. Come if you can; it's important."

And Mr. Banks sauntered away.

"What are you doing there by the gate, Vernon? Come in at once!"

It was Collier. Vernon had not noticed him coming up behind. Had he seen Banks?

Apparently not, for Collier never glanced out into the road.

"Shut the gate, and come in at once. Mind, no breaking bounds, young man. I suppose you think you can do anything you like because of this upset?"

"I don't think anything of the sort," said Vernon indignantly.

"No answers. Go back at once!" said Collier.

Evidently he had some suspicion, for he took up his stand by the gate.

It seemed hopeless to think of slipping out and meeting Mr. Banks.

"I wonder what he wants to see me about?" muttered Vernon. "I wonder if he has found out anything —perhaps about Collier?"

He glanced at Collier, who had taken up his position by the gate.

It was quite hopeless to think of getting out. And Vernon turned away, with a sigh; but the next moment his face brightened.

The cab which had brought the two visitors to Bingley College was still standing at the main entrance, and evidently the travellers were not going to return by it just yet.

"'Ere, one of you himps shut the door!" shouted the driver.

"Shut it yourself!" retorted Lamkin.

"Aggrawatin' little beasts, making a man get down from his box!" grumbled the cabman.

"It's all right," said Vernon cheerfully. "I'll shut it!"

He glanced round. Mr. Collier was looking through the bars of the gate into the road beyond.

"Shut it after me! Tell you after!" Vernon whispered to Lamkin, and the next moment had slipped into the cab.

And Lamkin, with a look of mystification on his face, shut the door with a bang.

Vernon lay flat on the floor of the cab as it rumbled over the cobbles. His heart beat a little quicker when the cab came to a stop, and he heard the voice of Collier just outside. Then came the sound of the gate being opened, and the next moment the cab started, and Vernon had passed through the gate under Collier's very nose!

He got up from his uncomfortable position on the floor and seated himself, and drove pleasantly down as far as the bridge; then, opening the door, slipped out, while the cabman drove on, serenely unconscious that he had had a fare.

Mr. Banks was standing on the bridge, with his hands in his pockets.

"I didn't think you'd he able to get away so soon. You are sure no one saw you —not Collier?"

Vernon opened his eyes in surprise.

"You know him?" he asked.

"Look here, youngster, are you the kind that can keep a secret?"

"That depends," said Vernon guardedly

"It is connected with Gordon's disappearance," said Mr. Banks.

"Then you can trust me!"

Banks looked at him for a moment.

"I believe I can!" he muttered. "I dare say you will wonder why I am interesting myself in your chum's disappearance?"

"I don't know. Everybody is interested, I should think."

"Yes; but I have a little more interest in it than most people. You see, I am a detective!"

Vernon stared at the speaker for a moment open-mouthed.

"You a detective? Don't talk rot!" he said at length "You ain't a bit like a detective. You ought to have a long nose and a clean-shaven face, and —and soft felt hat and a cape-coat. Pooh! You can't take me in!"

Banks laughed.

"I am a detective, all the same," he said. "I came down here to find something about that murder up at Sir John's place. I have been after the men all the time I have been here. They are still here; and, unless I am —"

"Much mistaken. Go on!" said Vernon.

"Unless I am much mistaken, they have had a hand in this business also!"

"You mean that they have murdered Gordon!" cried Vernon, aghast.

"I don't know. I hope not. Anyhow, I am sure they have had a hand in it. I believe they are the same two you saw yesterday in the wood."

"I knew it!" cried Vernon. "I knew they were a precious couple of villains! I said so all along, in spite of what Collier said! But what do you know about Collier?"

"A good deal. But never mind. I want to ask you questions, not answer yours."

"All right. Fire away!" said Vernon.

"Not here. I don't want to be seen talking to you. Come this way."

Banks led the way down the Sandcombe Road.

"Now," he said, "I want you to think. When you met those two men in the wood yesterday, was there any reason why they might have noticed Charles Gordon in particular?"

Vernon gasped.

"Good heavens, that's what's been worrying me all day!" he said, in a low voice.

"You mean there was a reason?" said Banks, with a faint smile of satisfaction on his face.

"Yes; but —"

"Well?"

Vernon hesitated.

"It may be all rot," he said at length— "only my idea, you know; but —but —well, it ain't like Collier to be so friendly to any of us, least of all Gordon, and yesterday, when we were walking through the wood, just as those men came up Collier put his hand on Gordon's shoulder, and walked like that for some time."

"Ah!" A flash of triumph came into Banks's eyes. "You mean he walked by his side, with his hand resting on his shoulder like this?"

"That's it."

"You are a sharp boy!" said Banks admiringly.

"It wasn't me, it was Grace who noticed it," said Vernon honestly. "But the moment he spoke about it it gave me the idea that Collier had done it to —to mark Gordon!"

"Then you believe that your master had some hand in this?"

The man and the boy faced each other for a moment in silence.

"I am sure of it!" said Vernon, in a low voice.

"So am I!" said Banks.

"And between us we will get to the truth of it, and fasten the crime on to the shoulders of the guilty ones —eh?" He held out his hand, and Vernon grasped it.

"I'll help you all I can —I'll do all that I can; but —but don't call it a crime!"

"Abduction is a crime," said Banks.

"So is murder!" whispered Vernon, turning pale. "Do you think they —they have murdered him?"

"I cannot tell. The only thing I fear is that they may, if they have not yet, for the men engaged in this are as desperate a set of villains as

194

ever walked. Do you remember that night —"

"When those chaps attacked us, and you fired?"

"Yes. I believe that that was part of this same plot. Do you remember that Gordon was attacked once before, and saved only because Sir John Bulstrode happened to be driving out late? It was all the same plot. They failed twice; this is the third time. They have succeeded!"

Vernon's face went white.

"Don't say that!" he said hoarsely. "You —you don't think they have really murdered him?"

"Honestly, I don't know what to think. But there is one strong piece of evidence in favour of Gordon's being still alive," said Banks.

"What is it?" cried Vernon eagerly.

"Remember that all I tell you now is in strict confidence. If you wish to see your friend again, if you wish to save him, or avenge him, it will depend on your keeping a silent tongue in your head."

"I would sooner cut it out than blab a word!"

"I believe you. Now, listen! Supposing you killed a boy?"

"Me —"

"I put it in this way because I want to impress the point on you. Supposing you killed a boy in Alfredon Woods, what would you do next?"

"I —I don't know."

"Yes, you do. You would try —that is, if you were a hardened villain like these men —you would think of your own safety. The surest way to protect yourself would be to dispose of the body where it would not be found, at any rate, for some time to come."

"Yes."

"But it is not hidden there; you know that. You searched yesterday night. To-day twenty policemen have searched the wood from end to end; but there was no body there. What next? There is the river. You could fling the body into the river: but it is not there either. The river has been dragged for three miles. There is no body there.

Vernon clutched Banks by the arm.

"And you think —"

"That he is still alive. I hope so; but I dare not tell you to hope, too!"

**Mr. Banks Talks —The Fat Fisherman —Mr. Banks Grows**

**Hopeful.**

"Yes," said Banks, "it's certain the boy is either alive or dead, and, as his body has not been found, one can still hope that he is alive."

"But it is easier to hide a dead body than a living one," said Vernon.

"Don't you believe it, my son," said Banks. "Of all the difficult things in the world to get rid of, a dead body —that is to say, a murdered body —is the worst. Don't you remember that old chap Aram something or other found it so. He couldn't get the river to hold it, or the earth to hold it. It wasn't any good, no matter what dodge he got up to, and then he got nabbed. It's a certain thing that a murderer gets nabbed sooner or later."

Banks felt that he must talk to someone. He wanted to take someone into his confidence. Talking, he found, always helped him. When he went over the points of a case, the sound of his own voice often gave him new ideas. It was certain he wasn't going to take the Bingley police into his confidence. He had the most profound contempt for them, as they had for him; and, as there was no one else to listen to him, he decided that Vernon might be trusted, as Vernon was Charlie Gordon's friend.

"Now, if you go and blab to anyone anything that I tell you, it'll be all the worse for your friend Gordon. It'll make my work all the harder."

"I'm not going to blab. I've told you once. If you can't trust me, you'd better not tell me anything!" said Vernon indignantly

"That's right —that's right!" said Banks good-temperedly. "I trust you, sonny. I want you to help me. We'll let those fools" —he jerked his thumb over his shoulder in the direction of Alfredon Woods, where the Bingley police-force were still groping about— "we'll let those fools go on their own way, and then give 'em a shock when we suddenly produce Gordon. I'd give something to see the face of that ass of an inspector when we turn up with Gordon alive or dead —eh?"

"I'd sooner turn up with him alive."

"Certainly, right you are —alive by all means, if he is alive; but if he isn't, of course that's not my fault. Now, look you here. Those two men you saw —depend on it, they are at the bottom of it all."

"I know it! I am sure of it!" said Vernon eagerly.

"So am I —cocksure, ab-so-lutely!" said Banks emphatically.

He slipped his arm through Vernon's, and strolled along the river-bank with him.

"Now, what you've got to look at is this. If those two men have kidnapped or murdered Gordon, what was their object? The boy had not got a stiver on him —not a sou, eh?"

"Not that I know of. I am sure he hadn't."

"Good. Then it was not robbery that tempted 'em. So far so good. They couldn't have imagined that a schoolboy would have any loose goods about him. They may be villains but they ain't fools. The two things don't work together. Besides that, why didn't they attack you and the other chap that hid before Gordon did? Answer me that."

"I can't. I don't understand."

"Then I'll tell you. The reason those two chaps attacked Gordon was because they had been paid by someone else to do so. Now, the question is, who was the person who paid em?"

Vernon thought for a moment.

"Gordon said his guardian hated him, and that if he died Skuse — that's his guardian's son —would come in for all Gordon's money."

"Ah, ha! Excellent!" chuckled. Banks, rubbing his hands. "We are getting warm, my young friend —very warm! This is simply delightful!"

"Glad you think so." said Vernon sourly. "I don't!"

"I mean professionally, of course, sonny. Of course, it s very sad about young Gordon —very sad indeed; but, looking at it from a professional point of view, I should call this a sweet case!"

"Well, go on," said Vernon, pulling his arm away from Banks.

He was not feeling very friendly towards the detective. His callousness disgusted him.

"Well, we have arrived at a certain point. Those two men attacked Gordon and either killed him or kidnapped him, and have carried him off somewhere. Good —very good. This was done at the instigation of another, that other possibly —I may say probably — Skuse the father. You follow my reasoning so far?"

"I think it was my reasoning," said Vernon.

"Yes, yes, exactly, to a certain extent. You are what I may call the labourer, and I the bricklayer. You bring the bricks to me and I set them together and make something out of them. We will work capitally together. Now go on. Is there anyone else you think likely to be mixed up in this? Is there anyone, for instance, who is friendly with the elder Skuse who might act as, say, his agent —his go-between —between him and the assassins? We will call them assassins for the present."

"There —there is someone," Vernon said doubtfully. "At least —" He paused.

"Exactly," said Banks. "At least you think there is someone, and so do I. Now, what does Mr. Collier know of Skuse?"

Vernon started.

"You have guessed it, then?" he said.

"Decidedly. I have guessed it. I have only been leading you on, my dear child. I knew all that you have told me. I knew it all before. I know that Collier and Mr. Skuse are old friends. I know it was owing to the latter's influence that Collier got his position as master at Bingley —eh? And then, of course, there was that peculiar signal we have discussed —eh? Now, why did Collier want to come as a master to this school for?" Banks went on, talking to himself rather than to Vernon. "The man isn't fitted to be a schoolmaster. He can't like the work —oh dear, no! He can't like such a quiet life. He isn't used to it. It wasn't for nothing he came here as a master, and this is the result, you can depend on it. Collier is the man who pulled the strings. It's him that was the go-between. Collier must be watched very carefully. Not a word," he went on, speaking loudly again— "not a word, mind you, to a living soul! Once Collier gets the office, he will clear off. He is too wily a bird to be caught very easily; and if he smells a rat we're done. Collier has got to be watched. You can't watch him out of doors, that's certain. You can leave that to me. But you'll have to watch him indoors."

"I —I don't think I can do that very well," stammered Vernon, turning rather red.

"Eh? What can't you do it for?"

"Well, you see, it's —it's rather a sneaky sort of thing to do —to watch a chap, to pry about, and all that sort of thing, don't you know!"

Banks broke out into a loud laugh.

"Oh, you poor little innocent! Where did you pick up those silly ideas? Come, come! This man Collier has murdered your chum, or he has paid someone else to do it, and now you are too honourable to try and bring the blackguard to justice simply by keeping your eyes and ears open?"

"I didn't think of it in that way," said Vernon. "I suppose it really wouldn't be sneaking to watch him, then?"

"Sneaking? Certainly not! It would be a proper action —just the right thing to do, if you want to either release Gordon or avenge him if he has been murdered."

"All right, then, I'll do it."

"That's right! If you hear or see anything going on that you think I ought to know, just write a line and slip it in that hole in the wall. I'll call up and collect every now and again. Well, I must be off now. I've got some work to do."

The two shook hands, and Banks walked on quickly in the direction of Sandcombe, while Vernon slowly retraced his steps towards the bridge.

"It's a lovely case!" Banks muttered. "Everything in the garden beautiful —couldn't be nicer!" he was evidently delighted with himself; and presently he broke out into a loud laugh at the thought of the Bingley police groping about on their hands and knees in Alfredon Woods, and dragging the river. "Just like 'em —just like these rustics!" muttered Banks gaily. "If anything gets lost —man, woman, or child —and if there's a puddle in the neighbourhood, the first thing they do is to run for drags. Oh, ho, ho! That's it; drag every dirty little paddle in the neighbourhood, and then feel surprised when they don't find anything! Ri-tol-der-ol-der-ol der-ol!"

"You seem 'appy, mister!" said a voice almost at Banks's feet

"Bless my soul, I never saw you!" gasped the detective, looking down.

A fat man was fishing by the river. He was sitting down on the bank, and only the top of his head was visible above the tall grass.

"Been fishing long?" Banks asked.

"What's that got to do with you?" said the stranger grumpily. "That beastly row you've been making'll frighten all the fish into the next parish!"

"Very sorry, I'm sure. I wouldn't have done it if I'd known. I am a fisherman myself. Caught anything?"

"No!"

"Ah, that's bad!"

"What is?" asked the stranger, putting a fresh worm on the hook.

"Why, not catching anything —most disappointing!"

"Why?" asked the fat man.

"Well, if you fish, you fish for fish, and, if you don't catch any fish when you fish, what's the use of fishing?"

"I don't know what you're talking about! I wish you'd go away instead of hollering there!" said the fisherman angrily.

"All right. Only I am interested when I see a man fishing. Been here long?"

"Less'n a month," said the fat man.

"Maybe you were fishing here yesterday?" said Banks.

"Maybe."

"I'd like to know."

"I'd like to know why you don't mind your own business and go away!"

"All right. A soft answer turneth away wrath, uncle."

"Your soft answers are turning away all the fish!" said the fat man.

Banks sat down beside the fat man, and smiled at him pleasantly.

"I wish I hadn't spoken to you. It strikes me you are a barmy lunatic!" said the fat man.

"Never mind that. Tell me —what did you catch yesterday?"

"Nothing."

"How long were you fishing here yesterday?"

"What's that got to do with you? Do you own the river?"

"Yes, it's my river. Nice stream, isn't it? Come, tell me all about it. What time did you pack up last night?"

"I'll pitch you into your river if you don't go away!"

"I'll go away when you answer one or two questions. I'll go and drive all the fish down to you —I will, on my honour. But I don't stir until you tell me what I want to know."

"Well, what is it?" asked the fat man, with a resigned expression on his face.

"Were you fishing here yesterday afternoon?"

"Yes."

"Did you see a boat go by, towards Bingley, about half-past three in the afternoon —a boat with two men in it?"

"Yes."

"Did you notice 'em particularly?"

"No."

"Did you see the same boat return about an hour and a half

later?"

"Yes, I saw the boat come back," said the fat man.

"Did you notice anything peculiar about the boat?"

"Yes. The men seemed in a hurry. They were both rowing like mad."

"Good again; both rowing like mad! Now go on. Did you see anything in the boat?"

"Two men," said the fisherman.

"I know. Anything else?"

"Look here, I'm getting sick of this! Aren't you going away?"

"Only one more question —one more question to pass and then I'm off. Anything in the boat beside the two men?"

The fat man thought for a moment.

"Yes. There was a pile of rubbish —what you call 'em? —old tarpaulin and stuff piled up in the boat."

"Much?"

"Oh, yes, a rare lot! I noticed it all bulging up over the sides."

Banks got up with a sunny smile on his face.

"I'm much obliged to you. Good luck!"

*(Another grand instalment next week.)*

THE PAGE THAT IS <u>LAST</u> BUT NOT <u>LEAST</u>!

### A Word from the Skipper

### NEXT WEEK'S RIPPING YARN;
### "A ROGUE AT LARGE."

Carlac escapes from the prison at Lagos, where, it will be remembered, Sexton Blake landed him after a long and stirring struggle for mastery, next week, my chums. Elsewhere in this splendid issue you will find a reduced print of next week's front cover. I want you to look out for it, and make sure that you get a copy, for "A Rogue at Large" will be a yarn well worth reading.

### A WORD ABOUT THIS FINE DOUBLE NUMBER!

It has doubtless caused a little flutter of excitement among you, my chums, this grand Easter Double Number, and I *know* that it has come as a great surprise to everybody. Is not that so?

But I will at once tell you why I have given this extra treat to lucky "U. J." readers. You will all remember that for some time I repeatedly asked for my chums' opinions, and also asked that every chum would try to get some new chums for me. I promised at the time that I should not forget it, and pledged my word that, sooner or later, I would return the compliment.

Well, I have kept my word! I have given "U. J." chums a double number which will make all other editors of weekly story-papers turn green with envy, and chew at the tops of their pens for a week. But I have only been enabled to do this by the true and loyal support of my chums. For a long time past the "U. J." has made enormous strides in circulation, which far surpasses all my hopes and past dreams, and which has caused quite a flutter in publishing circles.

I can unhesitatingly state that the old "U. J." now stands right at the top of the tree —there is no other story-paper of its kind which can come anywhere near it in circulation figures. But I am not vain enough to take to myself all the credit of this, although, naturally, the excellence of the yarns contributes largely, for I know that without the co-operation of my chums I could never have been in the position to give an Easter Double Number this year.

So therefore, my chums, please let me thank you from the bottom of my heart, and assure you that my appreciation is indeed sincere.

I trust that this issue will convince you of this!

### A REAL SPORTING LETTER.

I gladly publish another fine letter —only one among the hundreds I receive every week —from "Lex," and heartily thank him for it. It is most interesting, and I want all my chums to read it.

*"Kensington, W.*
*"February 19th, 1913.*
*"Dear Sir,—May I add my appreciation of your delightful stories of adventure to that of the other professional men whose letters I have seen in your pages?*

*"The Plummer controversy appears to be a great draw, and I beg you to record my vote in favour of allowing Plummer a long run of success. It would be still a feather in Blake's cap to capture him, say, in the last of a series of twelve stories. I am delighted to see that he is becoming a more lovable character. It is quite right that constant contact with the weaker side of humanity should make a man a little more tender towards his fellow-creatures.*

*"'North Countryman's' admirably sporting letter should convince the most bigoted opponent. Let me enlarge the moral and forgive me my prolixity.*

*"In 1901 —if I remember aright —Yorkshire were the giants of the cricketing world. They simply annihilated every one of their opponents. Speculative interest in the county table ceased quite early*

in the season. The crowds that came to watch them win did so because of the admirable cricket that Yorkshire provided for them, but it could hardly have been termed exciting.

"Now, late in the season it chanced that Yorkshire travelled south to Taunton for the purpose of making a mouthful of Somerset, one of the weakest county sides, before proceeding on their way to the slaughter of bigger game.

"I forget the initial stages of that extraordinary match, but I do know that Somerset in their last innings were set, we'll say, 607 to win —I know it was well over 600. Wisden will no doubt be able to tell you.

"Sammy Woods, Lionel Palairet, and all their merry men treated the matter as a huge joke. They feasted, they jested, and went jocularly to the wicket. I do not know whether they waved their hats above their heads, but that was the spirit in which they went to hit.

"Well, they got that 607. Tradition says that on the Saturday afternoon, after laying about them absolutely recklessly all the morning, they fortified themselves with a lunch that would have incapacitated most men, and then returned to the flogging of the ball until, for the loss of only seven wickets, there was no more to be done. Yorkshire was beaten! Can't you imagine how the cricketing public, after getting over the first paralysis of amazement, proceeded to abuse their luck, as all of us do when we have missed something absolutely delicious and unforeseen? What would they all have done had they had the slightest inkling that there was a chance of anything so interesting as a reversal of form which they had come to look upon as almost mechanical? They would have gone to Taunton from all parts of the country, and paid fancy prices for their seats, and fought outside the gates for admission, and climbed into neighbouring trees.

"Do you remember when Wales beat New Zealand, hitherto regarded as unconquerable? Did you want a copy of the paper in which the result appeared? Badly!

"A wink, sir, is proverbially as good as a nod.

"You have this advantage over the powers that be in cricket. They can never even hint at the possibility of a sensational and unexpected result —or it would savour of something improper. They cannot foresee the good thing for which, did they but know it, the public would be rolling up in their thousands, their pennies in their hands. But you. sir, are in a decidedly enviable position in this *respect. The public and I are awaiting the word to roll up.*

*"Will you not give it?*

*"Yours faithfully,*

*"LEX."*

### My Best Easter Wishes To All!

And now, dear chums, there remains to me the pleasurable duty of extending my very heartiest wishes for a "Happy and Peaceful Eastertide" to all of you. This is a season of joy and happiness, and I trust that you will all enjoy it to the full.

*The Skipper.*

The latest likeness obtainable of George Mar en Plummer, the Man Who Vanished.

### The Man Who Vanished!

*Police entirely Lose Sight of Criminal.*

*Believed to have adopted identity of well-known London Gentleman.*

A most startling case of skilful and audacious roguery has recently startled London.

A cunning rogue, long sought for by the police, was at length run to earth at Richmond.

During a rapid raid upon the place, in which Sexton Blake, the famous detective figured largely, it was believed that the rogue met his death by drowning.

Few regretted the loss of George Marsden Plummer —this was the scoundrel's name —for his undoubted mentality, his daring, his utter unscrupuloushess, and his air of culture, made him a terrible and dangerous social pest.

The knowledge, therefore, that George Marsden Plummer is not dead, as was believed, but very much alive, came as an unexpected and disconcerting bombshell. At any moment we may learn of some fresh toll this master rogue has exacted from society.

REORGANISATION OF THE C.I.D.

Scotland Yard and Sexton Blake are busy on his trail, and it will be an example of the crying need for complete reorganisation of our Criminal Investigation Department if this man is not quickly brought to book.

We have it on excellent authority that George Marsden Plummer is believed to have coolly adopted the identity of a well known member of society. If this is so, it will make the task of the police and Sexton Blake doubly difficult, whilst presenting to the rogue the most terrible and unique opportunities imaginable for the perpetration of his audacious frauds.

A VITAL DANGER.

If this clever scoundrel has stepped into the shoes of some high official, the danger to society is immense. We would draw the attention of our readers to that great, and at the same time, laughable hoax perpetrated some years back in Germany. A madman, posing as a high official sent by the Kaiser, succeeded in getting all the soldiery in a large garrison town to parade before him and do him honour. He was feted, and made much of by the officials in the town, and doubtless could have dipped deeply into their private purses had he had the desire so to do.

If a madman could prove successful to such a degree, with what measure of success is a cool, calculating rogue as we know George Marsden Plummer to be, likely to meet?

London presents to the unscrupulous a greater golden harvest than any other town or city in the world. It is not likely to be long, therefore, before George Marsden Plummer will make some attempt to gather in that harvest. Scotland Yard is obviously awaiting that step with strained nerves. Until Plummer makes a move, they are totally in the dark, and do not know which way to turn to lay hands upon him.

He has completely vanished from their sight, leaving practically no clue as to the identity under which they may expect to find him.

A THRILLING RAID.

We wish Sexton Blake, in whom we must admit, we place even greater faith than in our established force in the difficult and dangerous task he has before him.

It will be readily acknowledged by those well acquainted with the annals of roguery, that George Marsden Plummer, one of the most dangerous and resourceful of his type, has in his almost weird disappearance from the face of the earth, surpassed all his previous remarkable escapes.

At present Sexton Blake himself has confessed that he is totally baffled by the strange turn events have taken, but he has thrust all minor work aside to devote the whole force of his master brain to the solving of the mystery.

The case promises to be one providing unique excitement, and a thrilling series of dramatic happenings may be confidently expected. In the ordinary course of events, it is not unlikely that the general public might be kept completely in the dark until the actual conclusion of the case, but with characteristic enterprise, the Editor of a certain weekly paper, by name "The Dreadnought," has succeeded in making arrangements for the movements in this strange drama to be chronicled, week by week, in his magazine.

Profusely illustrated by one of the most celebrated black-and-white artists of the day, the story of Plummer's escapades and strange doings in another's name, together with Sexton Blake's piecing together of the clues he will undoubtedly obtain, appears in the form of a serial narrative under the appropriate title of

"THE MAN WHO VANISHED."

It is only necessary to add that "The Dreadnought," a splendid magazine containing no less than thirty-six large and well-filled pages, is on sale every Thursday at the moderate price of one penny, being obtainable through any news agent in the United Kingdom and

207

that your Skipper has openly expressed the earnest wish that all those loyal readers who followed the daring exploits of the one and only Sexton Blake in the "Union Jack," will extend their patronage to "The Dreadnought," at least while this narrative of Blake's search after a man who is more a shadow than human in his movements, is running. It should be noted that "THE MAN WHO VANISHED" appears in serial form EXCLUSIVELY in "THE DREADNOUGHT."


### SOME FUTURE ATTRACTIONS.

I have a specially Strong Programme in store for 'Union Jack' chums, and the following are among the early fixtures.

THE SKIPPER.

"SETTLING DAY," OR,
"THE MONEY KING."

A Splendid YVONNE v. SEXTON BLAKE Yarn, introducing a realistic Stock Exchange element, and the masterful way Yvonne handles the market, cornering everything in order to ruin Gorgon Kelly, another of the Jig Saw Mine Swindle Ring. This will be one of the finest story-dramas ever produced in the 'Union Jack.'

"THE WANDERING BARONET."

Another Stirring Story of another strenuous struggle between SEXTON BLAKE and COUNT IVOR CARLAC. It is by the same author who wrote the now famous Xmas Double Number Yarn for the 'Union Jack' (1911), entitled "The Wandering Heir."

DO NOT MISS EITHER OF THESE.

## SOME FUTURE ATTRACTIONS.

I have a specially Strong Programme in store for 'Union Jack' chums, and the following are among the early fixtures.

### THE SKIPPER.

### "SETTLING DAY," OR, "THE MONEY KING."

A Splendid YVONNE v. SEXTON BLAKE Yarn, introducing a realistic Stock Exchange element, and the masterful way Yvonne handles the market, cornering everything in order to ruin Gorgon Kelly, another of the Jig Saw Mine Swindle Ring. This will be one of the finest story-dramas ever produced in the .... 'Union Jack.' ....

### "THE WANDERING BARONET."

Another Stirring Story of another strenuous struggle between SEXTON BLAKE and COUNT IVOR CARLAC. It is by the same author who wrote the now famous Xmas Double Number Yarn for the 'Union Jack' (1911), entitled "The Wandering Heir."

## DO NOT MISS EITHER OF THESE.

**The Astounding Story of an Adventuress**

Amazingly dramatic, remarkably thrilling, and weirdly mysterious, the story of **Judith Hate**, Adventuress, forms one of the most wonderful romances ever chronicled. Begin it at once. The history of "Judith Hate"

Starts THIS week in

**FUN&FICTION**

Another Grand Penny Weekly For You to Read

EVERY TUESDAY,

FUN AND FICTION On our cover this month is Judith Hate, and Judy is quite a girl. Pedants may have shuddered when the editor constantly referred to her as "the wickedest woman in the world" - though it is doubtful whether any pedants were readers of FUN AND FICTION. Judith was the main character -clearly we cannot call such a wicked woman a "heroine" of a serial which ran for many months, and in all the illustrations she was never without that curious spiky headdress which was certainly a symbol of her wickedness.

Fun & Fiction ran from October 1911 till February 1914, a period of just over two years. It is not alone in being a paper which makes one wonder at what type of readers the paper was actually aimed. Officially, it was a boys' paper. Indeed, there were times when the editor claimed that it had the highest circulation of any boys' paper in the world. To substantiate that, there came along the Dreadnought, a companion paper to Fun & Fiction, and run on similar lines. But editors are notorious for talking with tongue in cheek. If, indeed, Fun & Fiction ever enjoyed an enormous circulation it is hard to see why it was wound up, to be replaced with The Firefly, a paper of similar format which soon became a typical comic paper of its time.

Fun & Fiction has a good deal in common with the Champion, which appeared a decade later. Nevertheless, there was never any doubt at which type of readers Champion was aimed. Champion was masculine to the last line.

Recently I have been browsing over volumes of, respectively, Fun & Fiction and the Champion. As an adult, I find Fun & Fiction completely fascinating. I can browse over it time and time again. It never palls. But one helping of Champion was enough. I was interested to con over it once, but to repeat the experience would be tame. Fun & Fiction, I am sure, could never bore.

Neither was a paper which I should ever have bought regularly when I was a boy. Fun & Fiction, of course, had passed on before I was sitting up and taking notice. But Champion was going strong when I was at school, though it never attracted my weekly tuppence.

The astonishing thing about Fun & Fiction now is that it never gives the impression of being old-fashioned. And that is odd, considering its astounding obsession with women, whose clothes date so speedily. In fact, the great and enduring charm of Fun & Fiction is due to its artists, and particularly to J. Louis Smythe who really "made" the paper.

The ingenuity of the writers was startling, ably supported by the art of the illustrators. Lingering deaths and amazing escapes followed one another swiftly on the covers of Fun & Fiction, probably appealing to either the juvenile sense of excitement or the mild sadism which is found in the make-up of most youngsters. In a year or two, cinema serials like "The Exploits of Elaine" were to take up the lingering death story where Fun & Fiction left off. Though why a potential murderer should abandon the swift bullet from a revolver in favour of tying the hero on the railway line or leaving a heroine tied to a rock in readiness for the rising tide has never been explained.

Fun & Fiction bristled with women -all beautiful, some wicked, some good. "Judith Hate" was bad to the core. "The Woman With the Black Heart'" sounded wicked but wasn't. She was so named from having a black heart on her forehead, though the author failed to explain whether the heart was tattooed, a birthmark, or a piece of black sticking-plaster. The serials, "Mother Love," "She Sent Her Mother to Prison," "His Convict Bride," and the like were intended for -well, . . your guess is as good as mine.

Towards the end, Fun & Fiction had been advertising the coming Firefly. "Owing to the success of Fun & Fiction, I have been asked to start a new paper. It will be called Firefly."

A new series, "Branded," a series about convict life, was announced to start in Fun & Fiction. It did -in the last issue of Fun & Fiction, when it was announced that "next week F. & F. will be called The Firefly.~ But Firefly, though it was run on similar lines to Fun & Fiction, had an entirely new programme of stories and pictures. Fun & Fiction was finished. A strange ending for a periodical which had claimed an immense circulation. And, while F. & F. had been a penny paper, Firefly was issued at ½d for 20 pages.

Why did Fun & Fiction fail? Its weekly programme had included melodramatic serials, detective tales, cowboy stories, narratives of mystery, series of articles on stage personalities and even series on famous criminal cases, together with pages of comic pictures attractively presented. The editor, who wrote with more evidence of enthusiasm than good grammar, must have been astounded at what happened.

Maybe the episodes presented in the various series were not well enough written. For the most part, despite their ingenious plots, the tales were crude. Maybe the lurid pictures, fascinating though they were, tended to put off parents who were more particular in those days than they are to-day.

My favourite picture? Perhaps the one of the Woman with the Black Heart leaping from a Thames bridge to fall down one of the funnels of a passing steam yacht. The episode was passed over in a few lines in the story itself. Quite absurd? Maybe. But no more absurd than many of the spy tales seen now on TV and in the cinemas.

chrome-extension://efaidnbmnnnibpcajpcglclefindmkaj/http://www.friardale.co.uk/Collectors%20Digest/1966-05-CollectorsDigest-v20-n233.pdf

The only library listing copies of this magazine is the British Library! /drf

A Long, Complete Story of Thrilling Adventure, introducing Jack. Sam and Pete —the Three Famous Comrades.

**SEXTON BLAKE ON THE STAGE.**
No Nottingham Chum should Miss the Great Detective
Next Week At The GRAND THEATRE, NOTTINGHAM.
For Six Nights ONLY!